# Previous Volumes in the Spoon Knife Series

# Spoon Knife 9: Numbers

Edited by

J.S. Allen and B. Martin Allen

Weird Books for Weird People

# Contents

# Foreword

In celebration of nine years of Spoon Knife, we asked you this year for stories about numbers. And, spoon knives sharpened, you obliged, delivering an astounding myriad of weird fiction/poetry/memoir to the Spoon Knife inbox. Collected here are our favorite offerings of the year from 34 contributors, featuring queer/mad/disabled voices, expounding upon the theme of numbers, counting, and measurement.

Yes, you will find here a poem about pi, but don't mistake this for a book about math (Mad Math?). No, these are deeply personal stories of grief and self-discovery, joy and survival. Some are true stories, some pure fantasy, many blend the real and the unreal in interesting ways to create new possibilities. And it wouldn't be Spoon Knife without narratives that peer into the depths of weirdness, blur genre, and create discomfort. At least one will make you cry. (Four did for me.) Just as many will make you LOL.

A friend of mine, when told I was editing an anthology on the theme of numbers and asked if he would consider writing something on that theme, responded with a one-line email: "Numbers trigger me." It's interesting to me how each of us has our own personal relationship with numbers. I have another friend who, when prompted with a specific number, like for instance 221, will happily and lovingly describe its properties and peculiarities, as if it were an old familiar friend.

Neurodivergent people in particular can experience numbers in very different ways. Numbers can be inaccessible, alien, bewildering. Numbers can be a gateway to a rational universe that makes much more sense than the social world. Numbers might have a color, a taste, a musical note. Counting can be a source of therapeutic self-soothing. This anthology gives voice to these and other human experiences with the numeric.

BTW, that friend of mine who said that numbers triggered him? I answered his email with, "What if a cute girl gives you her numbers?" To which he responded, "All of a sudden my attitude toward numbers changed for the better," followed by 3 laughing emojis.

Numbers are ubiquitous, inescapable, and they mean different things to different people at different times. An essential part of our shared reality, numbers can also provide a harbor to deep solitary exploration and reveal essential truths about the universe.

As you contemplate your own personal relationship with numbers, please enjoy this exquisite collection of stories and poems about numbers and counting.

J.S. Allen
December 2024

**Zach Keali'i Murphy**

# *The Limbo*

The cicadas are extremely loud this summer, and so are my mother's outfits. The leopard print high-heels, the oversized sunglasses, and the hat with the pink floral arrangement on its brim are some of the more understated pieces in her wardrobe.

"You don't hear about the sun when it's behind the clouds," she once told me as she put her beet-red lipstick on in the mirror.

My mother always looks so beautiful, even when she's sad. Every time she comes back from the Friday night Limbo parties at the bar down the block, her frown has dipped a little lower than it was before. It's amazing how spending time in the company of other people can make you feel more lonely.

A "Welcome Home" streamer for my father has been strung across our house's front window for an entire year now. It collects more dirt with each wind gust, and its shiny colors have faded. I wonder why my mom has decided to leave it up for so long. She keeps saying it's a pain to take down. But it's also a pain to leave it up. Maybe a tiny part of her is holding onto hope. A thin, dangling shred of hope.

When my father went overseas for his job as an underwater welder for cargo ships—whatever that means—my mother and I became a lot closer. She taught me how to cut my own hair and she taught me how to play softball. After my father didn't come home when he said he was going to, she taught me that you can't trust people even when they look you in the eyes, and she taught me that promises can be shattered and stomped over like broken glass.

"If he was dead, we would have found out about it," she once said. "If he's alive, he's making a choice to not come back." Somehow that felt worse than a death.

Sometimes I create imaginary scenarios in my head about why my father hasn't come home. Maybe he got roped into a plot to save the world. Or maybe the work has just taken longer than anticipated. Or maybe he told us it would be three years instead of three months and we just didn't remember. After a while, I run out of explanations.

My mother was never one to sugarcoat things. She didn't even put frosting on my birthday cake this year. "Frosting isn't good for you," she says as she lights a cigarette from one of the candles. I blow out all thirteen of them, and we hear a car pull up on the street in front of our house. We get up to go look. An old man that neither of us recognizes gets out of the car and walks over to deliver a package to the neighbor across the street, gets back into the car, and takes off. My mother takes a drag from her cigarette and stares through the screen door. The sounds of the cicadas intensify.

---

**Zach Keali'i Murphy** is a Hawaii-born writer with a background in cinema. His stories appear in *The MacGuffin, Reed Magazine, The Coachella Review, Lunch Ticket, Raritan*

*Quarterly*, *Another Chicago Magazine*, *Little Patuxent Review*, *Flash Frog*, and more. He has published the chapbook *Tiny Universes* (Selcouth Station Press). He lives with his wonderful wife, Kelly, in St. Paul, Minnesota.

**Katharyn Howd Machan**

# *Counting Time*

*Full moon tomorrow* Fox whispers
to herself. *Got to dance, got to
find a good green place
where wild blackberries are ripe.*

She remembers all her long lost
summers: a cousin like Pan
with bright swift running hooves,
the small lost raccoon she raised.

How many months can a vixen
expect, half-beast half-human and hoping?
Death is the hand that holds our names
and scatters them through far stars.

---

**Katharyn Howd Machan** writes poetry and memoir on her Dragon Patio when weather allows and elsewhere when it doesn't. As a professor in the Department of Writing at Ithaca College she mentors students in fairy-tale-based creative writing courses. Her most recent publications are *A Slow Bottle of Wine* (The Comstock Writers, Inc., 2020) and *Dark Side of the Spoon* (The Moonstone Press, 2022). For spirit and body, she belly dances.

**Darryl Whetter**

# I Don't Know How I Can Tell You That

## 1. Are You Alone?

9-1-1. Better, or worse, to call those three incantatory numbers for yourself?

The recording of my 9-1-1 call opens with the general emergency operator passing me off to an ambulance dispatcher here in southwestern Nova Scotia. Those two trained women are all data and *Copy*. Accident address. *Copy*. My name and cell number. *Copy*. On the recording, my labored panicky exhales ride over their pass-and-receive voices. The healing me who filed enough requests to eventually obtain a recording of the 9-1-1 call knows that bleeding me was worried he would pass out. Perhaps worse, panting Darryl was also starting to see how much he'd lost.

*Need a 631 John Thibodeau Road in Saint Martin, Digby County. Copy. Thank you.*

*Need a* ... When State Trauma Phone A reaches State Trauma Phone B and speed can literally save a life, *ambulance* is a word no one needs to say or hear. "People like that," Lorrie Moore points out in another hospital story, "are the only people here."

*Need a ...* About twenty-three hours before I made my unshort life's first call for my own ambulance, on Christmas, I had selfishly, perhaps desperately, put Robert Frost's great line about families and need to the test. Thanks to me, my sister-in-law Lise can no longer believe, as Frost nearly does, that family are the people that, when you have to go to them, they have to take you in.

Life-changing illnesses hit whole families, not just the suffering individual, I contend here from Life Changing Illness No.3. The whole family gets sick. All three of the major illnesses I have witnessed, endured, and resisted suggest they can kill whole families, too, not just one member.

## 2. Copy

After the ambulance dispatcher's quick string of *Copies* to the main 9-1-1 operator, of Ms. Ambo briefly being the listener, not the speaker, that trialogue, at least, collapsed down to just a dialogue, to dispatcher and caller, to Ms. Ambo's training and my spurting-finger panic.

*Hi there, Caller. What's your name?*
*My name is Darryl Whetter.*
*Hi, Darryl. Tell me exactly what happened.*

Even with the recording of the 9-1-1 call on my laptop, backed up there and on the cloud, with the severed work glove I went back for, crime-scene-style, to pick up two days later and have since stored in a cupboard, with the paramedic-sliced jacket I still haven't thrown away now that winter has finally kicked over into spring, with a few months but not years between my wood-splitter accident and starting to write this, my memory already has blanks from an accident rare in my life for having no alcohol involved.

What I had vowed would be my first sober day, Boxing Day, did indeed find me dropless by the cocktail hour for the first time in … months. If I have to, and I still don't know that I do, or can, if I have to explain why I didn't watch my hands carefully enough around our half-inherited hydraulic wood splitter, one I've used repeatedly, always sober, I blame my rare *emotional* hangover at having just been an asshole while drunk, a promise-breaking, disappointing asshole adding to my wife's family misery. Already, well, *un-sober* these three months later, parts of my otherwise atheist self—the honorable and wise or the deluded and polluted—have to worry whether I think I *deserved* to crush off half a fingertip there in the gloaming, in the deepening rural chill.

> *Hi, Darryl. Tell me exactly what happened.*
> *Okay. I was using a wood splitter, and, uh, I, uh, cut, the, uh, end of my finger off.*

## 3. Need a …

It's hard to hit fifty and think you're special. Special, no, but I am in rare company in trying to be a rural professor of literature (some but not too many of us) who logs his own firewood for sustainable winter heat (no doubt very few of us). My logging equipment divides between plenty of gear inherited from Robert, my retired engineer of a father-in-law, and new safety equipment I've bought for myself, including chainsaw pants. The fifteen-year-old pickup truck I sat in waiting for the ambulance, bleeding and hoping I wouldn't pass out, had been Robert's, as was the smoking-gun wood splitter. Earlier in my logging day, using the screaming-death-machine of Robert's chainsaw, my cut block guilt at having mistreated both his daughters the night before, all his grieving children, couldn't always penetrate my chainsaw worry. Cutting fireplace lengths of the spruce and maple trees I had felled more than a year ago with the help of a hired chainsaw instructor, I had to worry just how protective my chainsaw pants really were. As I straddled one of the supine logs to "buck" or "junk" it to length, I noticed that if the saw kicked back at the wrong moment or—it does happen—the high-rev chain broke and flew off, I might never again enjoy, as we sometimes say, "a little whoop-whoop" with my wife.

In addition to our mutual love for his daughter, Robert and I had bonded over a shared love of reading and learning. The French *row-BEAR*, not an English word rhyming with my finger's *spurt* and *squirt*. Robert claimed to admire my novels, those wonders he could read but not write. I admired him for replacing his original education in the mother-pleasing field of becoming, how strange, a Catholic priest, to quickly renouncing church, faith, and vocation then retraining in what was then a late-in-life Engineering degree. Professionally, he went from wondering about the soul to knowing about amperage and torque, about switch and resistance. Before his terminal cancer, when our conversations were easier but less momentous, I once confided to him that he must wonder how we non-engineers get through life knowing so little of how our things and world work.

How, exactly, did his steel wood splitter, as large, wheeled and mobile as a howitzer, transform its sputtering two-stroke gasoline engine to get hydraulic oil driving a log forward into the gleaming steel wedge that is, notably, called the splitter's *blade*?

## 4. This Happened Right Now?

Distracted, ashamed, and, true to injury norm, tired after a long shift, a full day of cutting, loading, and unloading firewood, I had, as I've always done, managed both the splitter's noise and tedium with not just ear protection but noise-cancelling headphones. Audiobooks, not muffled music, are my preferred escape and recompense when doing chores. By the time of my self-inflicted accident, I'd downshifted to listening to Barry Lopez's *Horizon*, a pointless *I've-travelled-and-read* ramble by a fellow North-American male even older and more privileged than I. Earlier, out on the cutblock of Robert's ancestral woodlot, between but not during rounds with the much more dangerous chainsaw, I'd been listening to not just yet-another sobriety audiobook, but yet another *writer's* sobriety book, Leslie Jamison's *The Recovering*. By the time I'd hauled my load of junked logs to Robert's splitter, one we shared with Gisèle's Uncle Nil,

I was eight hours into sawdust and trying to manage my shame at my insensitivity.

Part of the problem, part of the way I caused my own suffering—I felt rather than saw the splitter's slowly advancing steel plate crush my finger into the use-polished steel wedge of the unmoving "blade." The initial pain was bad but not off my charts. I knew I'd hurt myself, no doubt done some damage, but I was able to first concentrate on pulling my injured hand back then even shutting off the splitter's engine with the other. I reached for the engine switch before checking on one of my own. What used to be a black-gloved left hand ended, suddenly, in plenty of crimson blood. I was walking away from the stilled splitter and reaching for my phone, that ambulance portal, before I glanced at what I thought would be a mangled fingertip but, well, wasn't.

*Are you alone?*
*Yes.*

My swift staircase of understanding ran from *I've hurt myself* to *I'm bleeding* to *Better call an ambo* to *Shit, I don't know the street address* to *I've cost myself part of my finger. I have subtracted myself.*

## 5. Is That Correct?

Like far too much in adult life, substance abuse and COVID infections included, safety often suffers from a lack of applying knowledge, not a lack of knowledge. A few months earlier, my karate *sensei*, who has taken more conscious risks with his body than I have, fell off scaffolding while working on his house, banging up his face and head on the way down. "Twenty more minutes and I'd have been done the whole job," he, his stitches, and his black eye lamented to us before class.

"That's actually the norm," our retired shop teacher informed the rest of the dojo gang.

The overreaching. The red zone. Ambition, not caution. Wanting so badly to get to some *there*—back inside, or out of the cold, or heat, or simply to finally relax—you stop fully perceiving your *here*. My corkscrew life.

Only with a bleeding hand clutched to my chest on a darkening December evening, a bleeding, perhaps now-partial hand, did I admit that I knew I was at Nil's but not any ambulance-summoning information like what his house number was. Nil's rural, two-story garage is more than a football field's distance back from the street. My first big fear was that I would pass out before I could walk myself to the road to find a street number.

> *Are you alone?*
> *Yes.*
> *How old are you?*
> *Uh, fifty.*

## 6. But It's Not Clean

*All right. We have help on the way for you right now, Darryl. I just have to ask you a few questions while they're on the way, okay?*

*Yes.*

*Okay. So this happened right now, is that correct?*

*Yes.*

*Is there any serious bleeding?*

Pain and panic—do they change who we are or simply concentrate who we are, strip off the costumes and throw away the baggage? I didn't even contemplate replying to the question about whether there was any *serious bleeding*, as I do now every time I listen to the recording, with, *Well, duh.*

Throughout the call, I was, as my Christmas-supper drunkenness of the night before showed my wife and her sister I no longer am, briefly again the polite boy who would make many parents and grandparents soul-clappingly proud. I say *Thank you* three times in the four-minute ambulance call. My recurrent, single-word answer, *Yes,* efficiently provides relevant, possibly life-saving data, *Yes,* but also reveals the professional quiz taker then giver I am. *Yes. Yes.*

At least two of our three Christmas supper attendees would be able to hear that my quick and clear *Yeses* are also my attempt to once again steer a conversation towards what I want.

*Is there any serious bleeding?*

*Yes.*

About as serious as you can get on the outside of the body without one of the arterial pumping stations involved. While I have risked injury from using chop saws, table saws, grinders, the Uzi of the reciprocating saw, and the life-taker of the chainsaw, yet only sober for the latter, those whirring saw blades risk *cutting off* an extremity like a fingertip. The tortoise-speed wood splitter did not cut off my fingertip so much as *crush it off*, a larger mechanical hammer with a very dull, but *very* hard, chisel. Stumbling from the orange metal splitter and dusty old pickup truck at Nil's garage down to the road then back—*631 John Thibodeau, 631 John Thibodeau*—all while clutching a phone and hoping I wouldn't pass out, I knew I wasn't yet properly staunching my wound. If you have turned the fingertip of your longest finger into a sandwich cut on the diagonal with one half eaten, and you're on the phone to 9-1-1 in the call that might even be saving you from bleeding to death, you don't have any hands left for wound care. Terror, cold, pain, and the most rudimentary *RED* first aid—*Rest, Elevation, Direct Pressure*—had me double-curling my cold, blood-soaked and shaking hand, still gloved, first into a fist then that fist into my (dampening) jacket.

Cuts can be closed. Cuts are zippers where they shouldn't be, but the zipper can hopefully be tugged back shut. My horrified glances down at the hand I knew I shouldn't be uncurling if I wanted to make the next step back to the truck, the next minute of still being awake and upright, not dropped unconscious to the gravel driveway, a six-foot red bathtub with the plug pulled, somewhere in those few glances down to the road and a metal, blue, reflective house number sign designed precisely to be visible in emergencies like this, I had to admit that I had, as the occupational therapist would say a full six weeks later, *amputated* rather than cut my finger. I'd made myself less.

## 7. I Pressed My Ellipsis To It

I'm a writer who teaches writing. Good dialogue, I tell students, explains itself. Having limped into the dusty truck cab on the assumption I'd be less likely to pass out if sitting and out of the late December cold, or that if I did pass out I wouldn't risk further damage from a fall, I could hear the ambulance dispatcher understanding that she was yet another woman verbally propping up a man.

> *All right. So the paramedics are on the way to help. So just stay on the line, Darryl; I'll tell you exactly what to do next. So just tell them that you're in danger and don't splint any injuries, okay? And I'm going to tell you how to stop the bleeding, so listen carefully to make sure we do it right, okay?*
> Yeah.
> *So get a clean dry cloth or towel and tell me when you have it.*

Bacteriologically, the fact that the dog towel beside me on the truck seat was visibly crusted with sand didn't make it necessarily more infectious and dangerous than, say, an anti-vaxxer's exhalation there around the peak of COVID's Omicron wave. Have condomless sex with a woman, the pamphlets and posts warn us, and she could wind up sterile due to scarring from a chlamydia infection or even get cancer from human papillomavirus. Medically, visible dirt isn't the dirtiest dirt. Still, sand audibly rained down off Voodoo's dog towel as I raised it.

*Okay, uh, I have one that's dry, but it's not clean.*

*Okay. ... We just need something like a dry cloth or towel, so that way we can try and stop the bleeding, okay?*

*Yes.*

*All right. Okay, you have it there?*

*Yes, I pressed my ... my stump to it.*

My questions had progressed while the last of the winter light faded, dropping from *How bad am I hurt* to my starting to wonder if I'd ever be able to use that finger again.

The third finger, as they are counted from the bottom, which I if not you think of as the "stick-it finger," isn't quite the star of the hand. Big Middle isn't the pincher-grabber of the index finger (literally 'pointing finger'). The book I'd published earlier that year was my seventh but my first academic book, my first to have an *index*, a book's 'pointing section'. The opposable thumb, well, a literal triumph of the species. Still, the third finger is the center of the hand's basketball team, the tall one winning the ball. Or—my ellipsis marked the start of my understanding—in my case it had been the star of the team.

*Yes, I pressed my ... my stump to it.*

*Okay, yeah, place it right on the wound and press down firmly, and don't lift it up to look, okay?*

*Okay.*

## 8. Can I Honk?

As late as lunch on Christmas Day, Gisèle asked me, several times, if I would promise and re-promise to deliver "an Oscar-worthy" performance of lying-by-omission and sticking to small-talk with her sister Lise, our self-invited guest for Christmas dinner.

By Christmas 2021, both sisters had been grieving their justly beloved father Robert for a year-and-a-quarter following his slow-ish death to lung cancer. They'd stood either side of his hospital bed when his yes-it's-for-the-best-but-still-hard-to-wrap-your-daughter's-head-around-it state euthanasia let Robert exit on his terms before his mind and personality were completely usurped by a cancer that had already stolen his breath and blood. Worse, it turned out, than Robert's lethal lung cancer—and what in life is worse than lethal cancer?—only the father's cancer prompted the family to slowly, and far from simultaneously, admit that their mother's increasing clinginess, clumsiness and forgetfulness were advanced dementia.

In September of 2020—Robert's last—Gisèle and I had still just been 'home' for four months, having moved back, only in May, from four years on the other side of the planet, in sweltering, bustling Singapore. We traded views of Digby Gut for Dhoby Ghaut then back again. Roughly a month after that cross-planet move home, the whole family sat around the dining room table where Virginia had served them four decades of meals, in a house Robert had built himself with wood he'd cut from the family woodlot. The new guest at the

Thériault dining-room table that summer day was Robert's Community Care Coordinator, a kind of super-nurse. Over Robert's season of death, a literal final summer, she was equal parts theatre director, quarterback, den mother, and invading general.

Two illnesses, five family members, and five very different modes of denial. As Robert's primary caregiver, I talked with him more in the four months he knew he was dying than ever before. While, yes, it had been a triumph in late June when radiation treatments restored some reach to his gait and stamina to his walk, a month later his tumor-choked heart was once again unable to retrieve all the blood it pumped to his swollen arms and face. The only human I will ever hear quote Hamlet's "To be, or not to be, that is the question" to invoke its original meaning of whether or not one should kill oneself still also managed to wonder, in early September, if he'd make it to Christmas. That same September, when I changed-up the daily pharmacy run by requesting a change from pill jars to blister-packed sheets, grateful for this foil-pack management of which pill when, when the pharmacist spoke to me about when they'd prepare the next month's sheets I was honest enough to reply, "There won't be a next month." Jury's still out on whether I was speaking to her or to me.

Our denials about the dying father were protean, the embers of some dormant forest fire perpetually smoldering in hidden pockets. About their mother, the denial—greased by shame as it so often is—was binary: dementia-yes or dementia-no. Lise wasn't the first terrified adult child who could hear that her mother's doctor had declared her legally incompetent but still tell herself Virginia wasn't that bad *yet*.

In July, in a second medical diagnostic test, this the one around Virginia's own dining room table, not in a doctor's office, she could no longer name the province she lived in nor the three-digit phone number necessary to summon an ambulance. Still, the majority of Lise and a near-majority of Gisèle felt their "not that bad" mother didn't yet need to be institutionalized. They (we?) never ate as a family around that table again.

One Friday evening in early September I made my daily twenty-five-minute despair drive from our house to Virginia and Robert's thinking I'd be making them yet another small supper of fried local haddock, some potatoes, and a token vedge. Robert had more pressing plans. When you and maybe even your family is dying, what's supper?

In his summer team of six doctors, two were add-ons, clear supporting cast, once the intelligent, decent Robert became a fan of, and a patient in, Canada's envy-of-the-world state euthanasia. His palliative-care doctor was like a World-War-Two bombardier who briefly but definitively took over flying the aircraft for the bomb run, the captain's captain. Once Queen Morphine asked him if he wanted that out, life's final out— on his terms, not his cancer's—two more physicians had to assess him. Their assessments were more psychological than physiological. On that sizeable medical team, the Community Care nurse, not any of his six doctors, was the self-confessed "little bird" who whispered in our ears that if we had to, we could get their mother admitted to an Emergency ward and that would let her jump the year-plus waitlist to get into a care home. Between her dementia and his end-game cancer, medical policy switches would get thrown.

That Friday night I suddenly fried no fish, watched a teary-eyed Robert tell his wife of diminished understanding that her agreeing, right then, to go to the hospital would be the biggest help she could give him, a kind of death present. She agreed. Between getting jackets, shoes and wallets for two seniors, one dying too quickly and one not quickly enough, I snatched a call to Gisèle, telling her to meet us en route, not at our house. If we pulled into our familiar driveway, Virginia might have changed her mind. *The market parking lot. Explain later.* One sick parent endured a terrible weekend in a perpetually bright, noisy Emergency ward; the other didn't see the end of the month.

## 9. This Chemical Life

*Self-invited.* That scale-tipping fact about the Christmas supper I ruined with drink and/or my assholery is true. When another marriage in Gisèle's large, rural, Acadian family was on the rocks, she described the couple's differences with the woman, who, like me, was not originally from Clare and was not Acadian, never having accepted the common local and/or family practice of just driving to someone's house when you want to see them, of dropping in unannounced.

"I'm totally with Crystal on this," I had said, years before Drunken Darrylmas. "You want to visit someone, you call ahead."

"We just don't do that here."

What *we*? Aren't *we*s formed of *I*s who make their own decisions? The less philosophical issue was passive-aggression. Where all my Canadian acquaintances admit that Canada was founded on the attempted genocide of our Indigenous, few of my acquaintances, most highly educated, know, or seem to care, about Britain's mid-eighteenth-century attempted genocide, by arson, bayonet, and slave ship, of the francophone Maritime Acadians. I'll never know if it's the residue of that genocide and displacement, or their original political disenfranchisement, or seemingly lapsed Catholicism, or the unique French dialect of *l'Acadjoune*, of living outside dictionaries and state or university language academies, that makes passive-aggression so prominent in either the Acadians of Gisèle's extended family or the women in her extended family or just the women in her immediate family. Lise inviting herself to our place for Christmas supper on Christmas Day—of course we'll suddenly change our plans to cook and clean for you.

I've dabbled in enough alcohol management books, sites, and Zoom meetings to know that the only real common denominator in substance abuse, what poet W.H. Auden called "this chemical life"—his daily regimen of uppers, downers, cigarettes, and alcohol—is drug dependency. Molecular locks in molecular keys. I regularly drink too much. Like many problem drinkers, alcohol is also the coping mechanism I rely on almost exclusively.

I didn't like having to change our Christmas supper plans in just a few hours and also to shift from spending Christmas with the woman I love to having to spend it, adolescent style, with family I endure. I hadn't liked months of Lise letting herself, their now institutionalized mother, and Gisèle, get ripped off by, as we first encouraged her to do, seeking paying roommates when she moved into their parents' house but not, as she was legally required to, consulting with Gisèle on the rent those tenants should pay into Virginia's account. The token rent of a couple and their rotating cast of teen children, rent stated to Gisèle, not discussed with her, is literally the lowest rent anyone has even heard of here at any time, let alone during a national and provincial housing crisis. I didn't like that Lise herself wasn't paying rent or even contributing, beyond the utilities she and her roomies were using, to the large house's monthly insurance or necessary upkeep. I didn't like that Lise had not asked her estranged husband for any money for their marital home, which Robert had helped them buy and into which her husband had already moved Lise's replacement. Painful, yes, but Lise not seeking payments for the house she left, and still co-owns, significantly contributes to the current low income she uses to excuse not paying rent into her sick mother's bank account as Virginia's medical bills climb.

Sober at the start of suddenly co-cooking and cleaning for her sister to join us for Christmas supper, I agreed to Gisèle's advance pleas that I bite my tongue on all of this and more. Chopping vegetables on either side of the kitchen island from Gisèle, when I opened a bottle of what she has long heard me call, and often calls herself, *cooking wine*—was I trying to de-stress with alcohol or simply uncorking a dependency?

If the wine bottle, the first, and 90something% *my* wine bottle, hadn't had a completely opaque covering, would Mount Darryl still have erupted? By the time our 'guest' arrived, I didn't know, as I would have seen from a normal bottle, that I'd drunk most of a bottle of red before six p.m.

## 10. Have The Parts Been Found?

*All right, Darryl. And so just keep on holding that pressure. Nice and hard pressure, okay?*

    *Yes.*

    *All right. Without lifting the cloth up, please tell me if the bleeding is under control now?*

    *I … I don't know how I can tell you that.*

I'm a professional answer giver, getter, and maker, yet I just couldn't compute. This was a wet, red Catch-22 in a dusty truck cab. The only way I could check to see if my once-finger was still bleeding heavily would be to cease the pressure and lift the dirty dog towel that was helping to staunch that bleeding, possibly even tearing off some coveted clotting.

    *Is it spurting or pouring while you're still holding the pressure there?*

    *Nooooo. A long, long-o of doubt.*

    *No? Okay, so keep holding that pressure, okay? … And I want you to keep holding that pressure until the paramedics get there, okay?*

    *Yes. Thank you. While my recorded voice remains polite, good-boy Darryl at fifty, I also audibly start to weaken, my words deflating.*

*All right, just from now on don't have anything to eat or drink. It might make you sick or cause further problems.*

*Okay.*

*All right, just don't move around unless it's absolutely necessary. Just be still and wait for help to arrive, okay?*

*Okay.*

## 11. I'm Just Letting Them Know

In part, writers love by metaphor. Between the death of his friend Christopher Hitchens, another cancer death with some time, but not enough, for goodbyes, Martin Amis first loved "the Hitch" in a eulogy in *The Guardian* long before he would in his autofictional novel *Inside Story*. I remember the sweet fruit of one of Amis's elegiac *Guardian* metaphors but had to look up its contextual soil. Amis admires (mostly) his friend's power as a debater via the chess Amis played but Hitchens didn't:

> Towards the very end of the last century, all the greatest chess players, including Garry Kasparov, began to succumb to a computer (named Deep Blue); I had the opportunity to ask two grandmasters to describe the Deep Blue experience, and they both said: 'It's like a wall coming at you.' In argument, Christopher is that wall.

By the time Lise, Gisèle, and I sat down to our Christmas supper of (local) lobster, salad, and Chardonnay, one of my favorite meals, I recall myself becoming a debating wall. I thought I was being helpful, or at least illuminating, though I fully admit to not remembering stretches of the meal between, *You're owed money for half your house,* and

*This is Canada's hottest real-estate market ever* to, well, Lise crying and wondering aloud if she shouldn't leave, to—lucky Gisèle!—my passing out in bed sometime around ten.

The metaphor of the first computer to finally end the human-versus-machine contest in chess as a "wall" and Amis's transposition of it to Hitchens's debating ability is seared into my memory. Only in looking up that *Guardian* eulogy again do I see that Amis uses it to illustrate his claim that the Hitch was a *"terrifying* rhetorician." Welcome to family Christmas with me.

## 12. Finger Do NOT Throw Out

*We're coming for you as fast as we can, Darryl. So when we do get there, just flag or wave us down, okay?*

*Uh, can I honk?*

*Yes, you can honk as well. So I just want to clarify. You said that you cut the tip of your finger off, is that correct?*

*Yes.*

*Have the parts been found?*

*Noooo.* My second long, and second-longest, *no.* Not just doubt, but dawning realization, and horror.

*No? Okay, that's all right. I just wanted to double-check.*

By this point, my breathing is so audibly labored it is my response. *Huuh. Huuh.*

*So, keep holding that pressure, okay?*

*Yeah.*

On the recording I'm no longer even returning my quiz-boy's *Yes* ping-pong ball.

*And you mentioned that the bleeding is under control now that you're holding that pressure?*

*Yeah.*

*Okay, keep on holding it. Don't let up until the paramedics get there and can assess you. Okay?*

*Okay.*

*All right. We're on the way. If anything changes, you just call us back immediately for further instructions, okay?*

*Okay, thank you.*

*All right. Take care, Darryl.*

*Thank you.*

---

**Darryl Whetter** is the author of seven books of fiction and poetry. His most recent books are the climate-crisis novel *Our Sands*, from Penguin Random House (2020), and, as an anthologist, *Teaching Creative Writing in Asia* (Routledge, 2022) and *Teaching Creative Writing in Canada* (Routledge, 2025). His writing has been selected to various anthologies, including *Best Canadian Stories, Best Canadian Essays* and *Best Asian Short Stories*. His essays have been published by *The Globe and Mail, The Detroit Times, The Brooklyn Rail*, THIS *Magazine*, Oxford University Press, Presses Sorbonne Nouvelle, et cetera. He holds a PhD in literature and was recently the inaugural director of the first graduate creative writing degree in Singapore, in a degree conferred by Goldsmiths, University of London.

**a. sterling**

# *Contact*

you wanted eye contact
so, I counted

1    brown eyes    light eyes
flecks of fire    waves and amber oceans
how the iris looks like a black hole if you just expand
it far enough to eat
everything going beyond light, time, and structure

6    how long is too long
is this right?    lapping at the edges of a black hole
what does this make me?    cosmic dog    stray
master of fleas    their new circus trick:    counting
time        waiting to bite or be encased in    amber

11    now I know it's too much
that's what their face means when it contorts,
don't look at me    like your brows jump hoops
you're a dancer    playing        spin the bottle
counting the turns, the time it takes for light

to travel around the eye
contact, before it breaks

# *Changeling*

I

A dark figure walks out onto a dark stage. You sit in the
front row detecting movement.
Perhaps you are the only one here. There is only you and
the dark moving on stage.

Maybe it is rustling of clothes on skin or the way that air
curls around the entity and curls around you, whispering to
you, that you discern knowing of the presence.

A chair yelps at the floor as it's pulled forward. Pant pocket
buttons click on wood as they sit.

A voice speaks into the black.
"Let me tell you a story."

II

Years ago, people believed in changelings, little fairy children
who stole away "real" babies and took their place in search of
a mother's warmth.

   * The voice sighs. There is a heavy swallow
     and shifting in the chair. *

I've spent so much time wondering on changelings.

Time spent investigating them, reading them, creating them, and becoming them.

You'll understand what I mean by the end.

Or you won't.

The changeling narrative is a hard one. In the stories, they were quickly detected because they were never quite right. Perhaps they were too quiet, or cried too often, or didn't move enough or moved too much. There was always a flaw or a tell that gave them away.

It is understood today that neurodivergent and disabled children were inferred in their time to be changelings. And that this resulted in their harm, or their deaths.

So how do we reclaim their stories? Here is one attempt

## III

A child sits on the floor, smiling to themself. They place empty eggshells in a row, one on each nail that secures the floorboards of their home.

Shells placed and unplaced, covering nails and uncovering. Over and over. Shells on nails and shells on shells.

Shelling and unshelling.

This is joy.

A mother watches from the corner with suspicion. A word on her mind:
Changeling.

A darkness grows in her heart and she is afraid.

The child sits, shelling and unshelling. Silent. They look to their mother to see her pride; of course, she'll join them in their joy of well-placed eggs.

Then they see the darkness.

They pause. It is like a spell cast. They've heard the word whispered before:
Changeling.

They feel a becoming and wonder at themself, knowing that they are a changeling, born by fear.

*A pause*

Now we will hear the thoughts of a Changeling newly made:

## IV

Am I
    unhuman?

I suppose I must be.

    I don't belong

in this world    of little sense.

"Little sense," that's funny.

Mother always says I am a        | senseless |        thing.

What is it about the rules
        of the world     that makes me        wrong?
I must have stolen away
Mother's real me.        What was I supposed    to be?

**But I don't want to be anything else.**

What is going to happen to me?

Being fae in a human world. I know she wants her baby back.
I know,          I know.
                        she wants her "real" baby back.
She cries all night
                because,        I know,                I'm    not
right.

*Hush, hush self. It's alright little thing. Rock, remember, it's al-
right, just rock.*

Shell the unshelling,
        lines and lines,
                layering back context.

There is a pleasant existence beyond them,
    rolling into fields,    in grass,        in    each    counted
blade.
And shells

shelling over nails
                    that were nailed,
      boards
                    boarded up into houses until
dead trees and upturned earth
      became village, town, city, then society and right-
ness.

Changeling minds break         right    down
      to society
          down to city back
              down to earth un-upturned and
trees unkilled.

We'll run everything backwards and
   pull necromancy from the fabric,     *no*, no longer fabric,
the unsheared wool of society.

Shell and unshelling thought.
Shell and unshelling rule.
Rock and unrocking     movement into peace
that I become to ease myself, my burden       self
unburdening.


V

        The mother holds back tears as her unchild's fin-
        gers dance in the air. Their body rocks back and
        forth, rolling in circles like a spell. Eggshells lined
        like incantation marks. Surely this must be evil.
        Surely it is not of this world.

## VI

The darkness shifts again. The chair lets out a whine.

"I bring you back now to tell you that in one part, and one part alone, she is right.

Surely, we are not of *this* world.

We are an unbecoming, a rebirthing. This is one tale of a changeling child born of their difference. But there are many such tales.

And we are shell and unshelling many more."

We are not of the world that finds us uncomfortable

# *Witching Hour*

It's witching hour and I know because I am no longer worth it.
At witching hour I unbecome differently, in that I am not
unbecoming,
I am seperating;
becoming


emotion                    and body                    and me.


Body's neck is flirting with the rafters
as I count the number of belts I own. There is no moon,
but somehow the sky is glowing not-quite-red. Body's eyes cry,
sometimes for me, sometimes in spite of me.


It is like a baptism, and I wonder if they will make me
reborn. Tears don't taste like the ocean, and I guess
that is a good thing. They taste like sorghum.
I like it and I wonder
if my greed for them is what draws
emotion forth.


Body's neck is flirting with the rafters,
her viens inspect bottles, her throat practices
closing while my lungs hold their breath.

Emotion looms over us like that jealous lover, they know
what I am becoming, and that their advantage is
bodies can be broken.

At witching hour emotions take body
to the bathroom and press her
into the tub, drawing the water to burn
the pain away. They prune body's skin
wondering how much liquid she can hold
before she bursts.

Body is not me,
body is the trap,
as emotions explain. They explain
how body never really loved me,
doesn't deserve me. How they, not her,
are my one,
my only.

"Be
with me",
emotions say, as they scrub
body clean. "It's my hour, and you are mine,
and I love you.

"What does body know,
what do you know, really
about what's best for you.
I know what you need. You need
to be free."

I do, I cry.
And cry again.


"Body, that bitch,
that sack of shit and flesh."


Scrubbing, scrubbing.


"I wonder what's beneath the skin.
The muscles, the veins. Fucking nerves."


Scrubbing, pruning.


"Imagine how clean the bones
would be, how precious the void, how painless
the gloaming when all this is gone."

---

**a. sterling** is a nonbinary, neurodivergent poet and scholar. Their poetry deals largely with subjects of anti-capitalism, environmentalism, childhood abuse, mental illness, and neurodiversity. In addition to their personal neuroqueer experience, much of their poetry is inspired by the neurodivergent struggles of their family. They hold a BA in English, Anthropology, and Psychology from Albion College and an MA in Social Sciences (Gender and Sexualities Studies and Disability Studies concentrations) from The University of Chicago. They have works published in "Qua Literary and Arts Magazine" and "FLARE: The Flagler Review".

**Anna Ziegelhof**

# N-History

## 1. Four days ago, I was at the library.

Four days ago, I was at the library.

Butler, the librarian, paused to think, their eye-stalks swaying gently.

"In order to thrive in history as an unnormal person, it is necessary to become n-historical."

"What?"

"N-historical and n-cultural."

"Butler, you're just saying more words I don't understand."

"You must float slightly apart from the times you are trapped in."

Butler reached out a long, thick-skinned finger and booped my nose. I swiped Butler's finger out of my face.

"I've lied to everyone about being normal for a year," I said. "I don't want to be a liar. I need to tell them."

"Yes, you will."

Butler would know. That's one of the bigger differences between our species: they have a much better idea of what the future will hold.

## 2. 114 years ago, Rosa met Lovelace.

114 years ago, Rosa Ortega saw a falling star. Except it wasn't a falling star.

Rosa, a farmer's daughter, made first contact with an extraterrestrial intelligence. An individual calling themselves Lovelace of a species calling itself Nous crashed on Rosa's farm and fearless, kind Rosa saved Lovelace's life by pulling them from their burning spacecraft. Rosa made a good first impression and the relationship between humans and Nous has been one of joint scientific exploration ever since, Nous being the scientifically far more advanced species, having solved long-distance space-travel and all.

## 3. Fourteen-point-five years after my birth, I've told 100 lies.

Shimmering dark green and blue mosaic tiles, a perfectly still surface all the way to a window with a view of the stars. Who knew that the long-distance spaceship shuttling a group of humans to Prosperity station would have a pool?

"There's a hole in one of my ear drums," I said to Aster. "I can't get water in it."

"We won't be wild, Dream," Aster said. "I'll watch out for you," he added, blushing.

"The thing is," I went on. "I got that condition after an ear infection I caught while swimming. I don't have great memories of pools and stuff. I'll just hang out. You all have fun at the pool!"

"Would be more fun with you," Aster mumbled and smirked and my stomach clenched.

I walked away, texting my mother: "Going to the pool with Aster and some others. Be home late."

•

I ducked into a narrow maintenance tunnel and crawled along it until I got to a dark nook. I slid a panel to the side and from a secret compartment I took my entire hidden life.

I opened a little paper notebook first. In pencil I wrote:

*98. I have a hole in one of my ear drums.*

*99. I dislike swimming/pools.*

*100. I went to the pool with Aster and my classmates.*

I closed my little book of lies, sat down on the cold metal spaceship-floor in my secret nook in the maintenance tunnel and cried, but not for long. No time. I reached into the hidden compartment and pulled out my Reader. I opened it to the lesson that had been on the QuickLearn that day and started studying: history. I love history, because in the past, everyone was like me.

## 4. Twelve years after my birth, Mom got invited to go to Prosperity.

I was twelve when Mom took me to a nice restaurant one night and told me that she'd been selected for a scientific delegation to work on Prosperity for one Earth-year: Prosperity, the collaborative research space station that Nous and humans had built together, located halfway between our two home planets, completed when I was just a baby. Going there was a big deal for a scientist like Mom. The chance of a lifetime. I understood that even at twelve years old.

Over dinner, she asked me if I'd want to go with her. I could see in her eyes that she was begging me to want to go. It was already hard for her that I wished I lived in the past, in times before her area of research, brain-computer-interfacing, really took off. I couldn't spoil this for her. I told her that I'd be excited to go to Prosperity.

We'd be on a spaceship for a year, she said, and on the station for another.

I said that sounded good, and it did sound good, because somewhere else, things could at least theoretically be better.

## 5. Ten years after my birth, I was the loneliest being.

"How can we help our friend Dream today?" the teacher chimed while rubbing my back.

"Play with Dream!" one of the children offered.

"Read to them!"

"Great ideas!"

"Sit with them while they do their homework!"

"*Help* them with their homework, since we already know it!"

"Yeah, explain math to them!"

"Awesome! How would we do that?"

"Using simple words!"

"And pictures!"

"Great ideas! Right, Dream?"

"We love you, Dream!" they called out and made ILY signs with their hands.

Morning affirmations. Every. Single. Day.

I glared at my eager classmates.

Nobody played with me if a teacher wasn't watching. They helped me with my homework, but their explanations only made them feel even better about themselves. They were all *so* nice. But not one of them was my friend.

## 6. Six years after my birth, I nearly died.

I was six and so excited about starting school. I loved my picture books about how magical school was going to be, with QuickLearn pods taking you on amazing adventures in dinosaur-land or ancient Rome.

It was May and surgery-day had finally come. I was giddy. A little scared, sure, but mostly excited. I was brave and didn't cry at all when the nurse put the IV into the back of my hand. Mom walked along next to my bed as I was wheeled into an operating room. The anesthesiologist told me that I would feel a little dizzy soon. Mom smiled.

●

I woke up. Mom wasn't smiling. She looked pale. Her hair was greasy.

"Hi Dream, you're awake, love."

She wiped at tears. Too late. I'd seen them.

Mom used small words to explain to me that my brain had said no to the implant. That sometimes happened to rare and special people.

"I can't start school?"

"We'll make sure you can start school. Trust me, I'll make sure of that. You'll get as good an education as everyone else, Dream. I'll make sure of that, I'll make sure of that."

A year dotted by brain scans followed.

A year of teachers saying, "Class, this is Dream, we're going to be really nice to Dream, okay? Dream is just as smart as any of you, they just have to learn using these and it'll be a lot slower. Can anyone tell me what they're called? Books! Yes! *Readers*! That's right!"

I learned to read.

I learned that I'd almost died in surgery and been in a coma for a week.

I learned that I wasn't entirely alone on Earth: I had something called Valle's Syndrome and the prognosis was dire– the chances of receiving a successful implant were, at that point in history, zero.

## 7. Fourteen-point-three years after my birth, something went wrong.

On my first day of spaceship-school, Mom had her hand on my back, probably to catch me by my spaceship-branded shirt if I were to run away. I was so nervous, I'd nearly thrown up that morning.

One kid was already in the cheerful classroom when we entered, lounging in a beanbag. Kind, shy eyes met mine; best hair ever, a sweet smile, and he was holding a book in beautiful veiny hands. Not even a Reader, but a paper book.

"You must be Dream!" It was the teacher, coming toward me. "Welcome!"

"Hi!" Mom said. "I'm Dream's mother."

"Yes, of course, nice to meet you! We're so glad to have Dream in our class."

"Thank you for making Dream feel welcome, I know, circumstances are a little special..."

My face turned hot.

"Mom, you can go now."

In a moment, the teacher would tell the others that I was smart in my own special way and that everyone should be my friend. Then she would invite the class to ask me anything and they would ask me if I could eat on my own. It had happened that way countless times. I did not want Mom to see it. She'd heard my stories about school. She'd seen me cry about school. She'd been the one who coerced parents to coerce their kids to come to my birthday parties. She'd seen enough.

Incredibly, Mom did leave, waving. And the teacher did put her hand on my back but only to introduce me to Aster, the kid with the book and the pretty smile.

"You're, uh, reading," I said, sounding about as stupid as I was.

That smile, that blush. "Yeah. I kinda love it."

"Me too!" I said and forgot about feeling stupid.

"No way! What's your favorite book?"

I pulled up a beanbag. We talked. Normally. Aster thought I was normal. For a few minutes, Aster still thought I was normal.

Other kids arrived, but I was deeply immersed in Aster's smile, his eyes, his gentle enthusiasm for all the same things I loved, too...

But then the teacher quieted the room and I tensed up.

"I know you expected Dr. Kamal," she said. "Unfortunately, they were unable to join this shuttle at the last minute, so I stepped in."

It dawned on me then. This wasn't the same teacher Mom had messaged about my condition. Could it be that, due to some inexplicable error, this teacher knew nothing about me?

We walked into the QuickLearn-suite later that day.

"Calibration!" the teacher announced. Everyone groaned. I groaned along. I'd learned from eavesdropping on classmates that calibration was boring: during calibration, the brain's reward-pathways didn't get activated in the same way as during a regular QuickLearn session. Calibration didn't feel as good.

"Oh, Dream," the teacher said and my heart sank. "I don't see a pod assigned to you."

Now I'd have to tell her. In my own words. I'd never had to do that before. But there was no Mom here to speak for me.

I tried to find the right words:

*I don't know if you know...*

*I have something called Valle's Syndrome, that's when...*

Historically speaking, I never got to say those words.

"Let me just assign you this pod here," the teacher said.

Historically speaking, the moment in which I could have said something simply never happened.

"Alright, in you go!"

Nobody noticed that I wasn't very practiced at climbing into the narrow pod. Inside, I leaned my head back against the recliner's headrest. With a soft hiss, the lid lowered and enclosed me inside the pod, which lit up with cheerful colors.

Next, the pod would look for the implant. It wouldn't find anything. And I'd have to confess. Why had I even gotten into the pod? Because it felt nice to be normal in front of all those kids I didn't know yet. And Aster of the pretty smile and the best hair and the paper books had talked to me as if I were normal. I didn't want it to be over.

I'd be a liar. On day one. Mom would be called. I might cry a little. They'd forgive me because I'm so pitiful and pathetic. And I'd go back to being the class pet without friends, most certainly not Aster's friend, who read books because he could, not because he had to.

I was still thinking such things in the QuickLearn pod when the electrodes came down on my head and snaked across my scalp and settled in my hair. The words *Ready to Learn?* flashed up and the QuickLearn penguin mascot did a little dance.

At first, it was just an itch. Then the itch turned into pressure in my head. Next the pressure became so heavy that I gasped. I clenched my hands around the arm rests and writhed. An electric current was running through my brain. It felt like the pod was going to crush my skull.

"No, please," I whimpered. I gasped. I nearly choked.

But the pain came in pulses, so I breathed in pulses, focusing only on the next breath and the next. Finally, after an eternity, the pain lessened, the electrodes withdrew from my scalp, and the pod's lid opened. I lay there, stunned. My classmates were climbing out of their pods, yawning. I was still breathing hard and sweating from the pain. I wiped tears from the corners of my eyes.

"Dream?" I heard the teacher's voice as if through a fog. "All done! Come on out."

The pod hadn't thrown an error? At least the teacher didn't call me over. She didn't ask me anything. My first school day was over.

"See you tomorrow," Aster said and smiled at me.

I was normal. The pain had been unreal, but I'd been normal!

I told Mom cheerfully how nice everyone had been and she smiled and said,

"See? This is a good place."

That night I couldn't sleep. I'd have to come clean. I'd do it first thing in the morning. I didn't want to be a liar, even if it was a lie by omission. And I was in doubt whether I could stand that kind of pain again.

The next morning, Aster greeted me with his beautiful smile and I was normal again. We stood around waiting for the QuickLearn-pods to open. The teacher was right there. I dreaded the pain and it must have shown on my face.

"Something wrong, Dream?" she asked.

How to explain?

*I can't.*

*I have.*

*I don't.*

*I'm.*

Historically speaking, none of those futures happened. No words came out of me, other than, "Sorry. I'm fine."

I got into the pod and breathed through the pain and climbed out, ears ringing, head spinning, but normal. Normal.

I couldn't sleep that second night either.

Come clean. I still could. Two days a liar. I could still paint it as a misunderstanding. They might understand. Though Aster would likely never talk to me again.

On the other hand, I could also hide my Reader, which Mom thought I was carrying to school with me. Let her believe I was doing my special studying at school, like she'd discussed with the teacher who never showed up. Mom would believe I got my special treatment at school, while at school everyone would think I was normal, and I could just study on my own, try to make up each QuickLearn session on my own time, after school. QuickLearn was limited to ten minutes a day at our age. Ten minutes of QuickLearn, I knew, equaled to about three hours of studying.

On day three, after school, I roamed the ship and found a secret nook in a hidden maintenance tunnel. I stashed my embarrassing slow-learn Reader there. Mom thought it was at school. Kids at school thought I was normal.

It worked.

Well. Sort of.

## 8. Fourteen-point-seven years after my birth, I tried and failed.

On the day of the 100th lie I lay awake, as almost every night since we'd embarked on the ship on our way to Prosperity station.

I practiced words, moving my lips silently:

"Aster, I'm not normal. I have Valle's Syndrome. I almost died when I got my implant. So they took it out again. But I am normal! But I'm not. When everyone thought I was normal, I couldn't resist. I had a bad time before coming on board the spaceship. No friends. You're my first real friend, but I lied to you. I've lied to you the entire time you've known me, except for the first few minutes."

My first real friend and he wasn't a real friend because he didn't know something important about me. He didn't know how much it hurt to be in that pod every day, how tired I was from the pain and the hiding and how scared I was that he might find out.

It had to stop. I was going to tell Aster in the morning. One hundred lies were enough.

●

I got to the classroom before school and I didn't tell Aster. The morning passed and I didn't tell him.

We arrived in the ship's spacious cafeteria for lunch and crowded around our usual table and I heard Sirian say to Finn, "There was this kid in my class last year. She had it."

"Oh god, that's just so sad."

"It's called Valle's Syndrome," Aster chimed in.

He knew about it! I wouldn't have to explain from scratch!

"You know," Aster added, "some people say it's evolution-ary. There are very few who have it. Sooner or later, it'll die out and everyone can be on QuickLearn."

"Is it comorbid with infertility?" some other kid chimed in.

"I don't know if there's research on that yet," Aster said, "but scientists think that those with Valle's don't have a high life expectancy, because their lives are more stressful, not as much opportunity, lower income, lower education. They make worse choices."

I was sitting right there, low-income, low-opportunity, uneducated liar, making terrible choices. Worst of all, I was on a ship going to Prosperity, the pinnacle of science and advancement, where only the best of the best were invited to work alongside the brilliant Nous.

I stared at my food but couldn't bring myself to eat any.

"But you know, that kid," Sirian continued, "there was something almost angelic about her. Like, she was bearing all of that suffering with such grace. Really inspirational."

Aster nodded with a little sympathy-crease between his eyebrows. It took an eternity until someone finally changed the topic. I sat through that lunch, ears burning, back sweat-ing, almost shaking, poking at my pasta.

So I didn't tell Aster, who had painted a very clear picture of what my short, awful life was going to be like.

## 9. Fifteen years after my birth, I became delinquent.

I went to school, I suffered through the pain of the Quick-Learn pod, then stayed up late, trying to keep up. Once, my mother took me to the ship's medical clinic, due to losing weight. Due to the weight of depression and shame I couldn't pretend I wasn't carrying.

I had some minor vitamin deficiency that explained everything easily enough.

My little book of lies grew.

Day by painful day, night by sleepless night, time passed until at the journey's halfway point the teacher reminded us that guardian-teacher conferences were coming up.

I panicked. I looked up a few things in the textbooks on my Reader. Then I went and got a few things from the ship's pharms.

On the day she was supposed to meet my teacher, Mom disappeared into the bathroom to throw up. I sat on my bed in our beautiful quarters, shaking with shame and fear. Mom messaged the teacher to say that she'd fallen sick. And the teacher messaged her back saying that I was a delight to have in class and my grades were outstanding. Mom, doubled-over from stomach cramps, shuffled over to show me the message. She ruffled my hair proudly before curling up on the sofa to sleep off the mild poison I'd mixed into her breakfast to keep my lie alive.

## 10. Ten days ago, we arrived at Prosperity.

One year of lies later, Prosperity drew close, a shining marvel in space.

Everyone watched as our ship pulled up to dock alongside it. I forgot about my lies for a moment. My body hadn't forgotten. I was tired, always queasy, doubly so in changing gravities.

But then Aster took my hand. Nobody noticed. Both of us pretended we didn't notice either. But we held each other's hands tight and my stomach tickled. But then I started thinking that Aster was holding the hand of a liar and that he wouldn't be holding my hand if he knew and that he'd never hold my hand again if he ever found out. There was a spinning, churning thought about hating myself so much that it would feel good to cause myself pain.

I think Aster felt that thought through my hand because he let go.

## 11. Nine days ago, I met Butler.

The station was a marvel. Mom and I had just moved into our living quarters in a sweeping block of suites, each with a balcony and a view of a lush green avenue below, when Aster texted to ask if I wanted to go explore.

I did; and I didn't. It was the way I always felt about Aster: love for him and hatred for myself when I was with him.

I met Aster at the bottom of the building's broad staircase that led out onto the park-like promenade below where people—humans and Nous—were walking around, some taking strolls, some rushing to their next meeting or research group.

Everything was free on Prosperity. There was no currency. Everything you needed you could print, so there weren't any stores, but there were food places. Real food places with hot ovens and woks and tools I hadn't seen before, and people were running them. People.

"Guess not everyone here is a scientist," I observed, as Aster and I walked through a food bazaar where Nous chefs were handling sizzling pots and fragrant herbs and where people, human and Nous, were standing in line for the most delicious smelling foods.

"Support staff," Aster suggested, "Guess there are some jobs for which you still need a person with a body."

Support staff... person with a body... Those were the only career-options for me, no matter my ambitions and interests. We might be friends now, Aster and I, but once he became a scientist and I became support staff, he'd pretend never to have known me.

"They could just replicate food, though," I said quietly. No need even for support-staff. But Aster didn't hear me, as he had already moved on to look at the next food stall.

Aster and I got something bao-like that was sweet and fluffy and mindbogglingly delicious.

"Amazing," I sighed while Aster still munched.

"Thank you," the Nous vendor said, their tiny mouth-opening at the bottom of their flat face pulling into something like a smile. Then they added, speaking to me after assessing me with their flexible eye-stalks,

"A person like you, perhaps you'll want to check out the library."

My face flushed hot.

"Oh wow," Aster commented, "I keep forgetting they sense more than we do. Yikes. Hard to keep secrets from someone who can extrapolate the future and sense into your past, huh? Guess they saw that you're into obscure old books."

Aster glanced at me. I glanced at Aster. I hope he mistook my blushing for something cute, not something incriminating.

"Wanna go check out that library?" he asked.

"Aster, I…" and he turned and looked at me expectantly and my brain saw the future, for a split second, as if something of the Nous' skills had transferred to me. In the future, I said, "Aster, I have Valle's Syndrome. I'm really stupid and slow. I will never be able to keep up with you. We had better not be friends anymore."

Historically speaking, I changed the future on the spot and said,

"Aster, I told my Mom I'd be home soon."

"Right, yeah," Aster said. "I keep forgetting how strict she is."

Aster knew the little book of lies about as well as I did: *Lie 149. Mom gets angry easily when I'm late.*

When Aster turned to go back to his quarters, I pretended to go to mine, but as soon as he was out of sight, I looked at a station map, found the library, and ran there.

The building had a sweeping facade, not quite straight, almost like an organic being.

I entered through wide double doors. There was a café in a rotunda on the ground floor. Above it, the building swept up and up, built around a central light-filled axis. A skylight way up high let in the beautifully designed daylight of Prosperity station. White winding, floating stairs connected everything, like art nouveau carvings made from marble.

And there were books everywhere.

I bit back tears. Someone—more than just one person—cared deeply about that embarrassing, slow format.

A Nous stalked toward me on long thin legs, looking like they were stepping over a high fence with every step.

"Welcome," they said. "I am the librarian. You may call me Butler."

"Hello," I said. "I am Dream."

"Not many humans come in," the Nous observed.

I swallowed. "Most humans don't need books anymore. They have something in their brains that just loads information."

Butler regarded me with their stalked eyes, their noseless, smooth face showing no expression I could interpret.

"Aha," Butler said and their eye-stalks moved, taking me in. Me, my past, my future. No secrets here.

"The person you like doesn't know you are not like him," Butler observed quietly.

Tears rose in my eyes. Then they spilled over. I'd been found out.

"Oh?" Butler shrank back.

"Sad..." I explained, wiping my cheeks. "Really sad. And so tired."

Butler reached their long gray arm into a case that held baked goods and offered me one on their elongated smooth palm. I took it and nibbled on it and it was so good, I forgot about crying.

Next, Butler put an arm around my shoulders and led me up one flight of those organic-looking stairs to a nest-like reading nook with a window. I crawled into it. Butler sat across from me in the same nook, a short distance away, long limbs folded in a way that looked wrong at first, because their joints bent the other way, seen from a human perspective.

All of my exhaustion and my doubts and fears weren't a secret to Butler, nor to any Nous. I wasn't going to be able to hide here, on Prosperity. I really should have thought of that. Somebody would babble.

"What did you do to yourselves, humans?" Butler asked with curiosity.

"It's called QuickLearn," I explained. "Historically speaking, it became normal just before I was born. Maybe 20 years ago. We thought it would be great to use to keep up with you, with Nous. With science and progress. Because you are so advanced. Long-distance space-travel and all. But there's a condition, it's very rare, when somebody's body rejects the implant. That's me. Among humans, I am considered very slow. Not a lot of prospects for the future."

"Science is not all we do. Do you think it is all we do?"

I had thought that. But seeing all the lively food vendors and now the library... They had solved long-distance space-travel, though. They were hailed on Earth as a species of brilliant scientists and engineers. That's what we were taught about them.

Butler scrambled out of the nook and soon returned with a book.

"I'm sorry I don't read Nous yet."

"Nous-Sage is the most common language on Prosperity," Butler said, went away and returned with a beautifully bound volume in Arabic script.

"I'm sorry, I don't read Human-Arabic either."

"Oooh!" Butler took the Human-Arabic volume away and returned with another stunning volume: Nous-Sage/Human-English.

I laughed.

Butler startled.

"I am expressing amusement and surprise, the good kind," I explained and laughed more. "You have several languages, we have several languages! Of course! I think I've been thinking Nous were all the same."

It felt good to laugh after crying.

"This book," Butler pointed at the original Nous-Sage volume, "is a book of history. Nous tried something similar to human QuickLearn in the past. Discarded it, eventually."

"I don't think we'll discard it. Everyone thinks it's so amazing. Plus, we need it to keep up with you."

"Keep up with. Why keep up with?"

"Well, you're more advanced...?"

"Advanced?"

"Yeah, like, ahead. Better at science. Better at space-stuff."

A sound like a vacuum cleaner starting up rose in the nest-nook. I must have looked very confused, because in between sounding like a vacuum cleaner, Butler huffed,

"Only my amusement-expression-sound! I have found out our fundamental misunderstanding, friend Dream: linear comparison. One must be ahead, thus another must be behind. This is only true in linear terms. Think more n-dimensional space! Comparison becomes much more complicated."

"What?"

"Oh!" Butler disappeared from the reading nook again and came back with yet another book, which they opened and when they did, a cloud of color puffed out of the book and assembled in the air between us, like a three-dimensional projection. The image looked like an expanding sphere, oscillating in all colors, with things like stars floating around in it.

"N-sphere," Butler said, then closed the book again. "Not linear. Everywhere!"

"Multi-dimensional," I said, understanding slowly. "Maybe you're good at this one thing, not as good at this other thing."

"Yes," Butler agreed. "A matter of what is treasured how highly at what point in time in which culture."

I finished eating my baked good and made sure my hand was clean before reaching out for the history book written in Nous-Sage. I opened it carefully and looked at the elegant cursive script curling across the pages.

Butler extended a long gray finger and booped my nose.

"Also, very cute, noses," they said.


## 12. Four days ago, I spoke to Butler again.

I went back to the library every day. I ate breakfast at the library's café and then I read about different subjects by the hours of the day. I studied Nous-Sage for one hour in the morning, then I went on to Nous history, then I went on to science. Whenever I read, I forgot about myself and about my lies.

During lunch break, four days ago, Butler joined me in a booth in the café.

"In order to thrive in history as an unnormal person, it is necessary to become n-historical."

"What?"

"N-historical and n-cultural."

"Butler, you're just saying more words I don't understand."

"You must float slightly apart from the times you are trapped in."

I did think of the n-sphere Butler showed me on day one.

Butler booped my nose. I brushed their finger away.

"I've lied to everyone about being normal for a year," I said. "I don't want to be a liar. I need to tell them."

"Yes, you will."

"But I also don't want to go back to the way things were before."

"You won't."

"I'm afraid Aster will hate me. I told close to four hundred lies since we met."

"Yes, you showed me the book."

I did, during a part-therapy, part-confession session in a library nook late one night.

"Dream," Butler said. "Unfortunately, as human, you won't know the future unless you make it. You humans do your Quicky-Learny for another little while, do linear comparison for another little while, then perhaps you will move on from that. You can float outside of history until then, Dream."

"He'll hate me."

Butler's eyes did a quick scan back and forth as if they were reading a book.

"No," they concluded. "But, Dream, consider things that hurt you."

"He only said those things about people with Valle's because he didn't know what I am. Plus, he was right: I'm not as educated. I am slow. I've already made a lot of bad choices. I lied. I made my mother sick to keep the lie going..."

My skin crawled with shame. Butler's eye-stalks swayed like kelp.

"Yes. Consider it. Consider why," they repeated.

## 13. Today, I am telling him.

It's station night, which means that daylight has faded through a stunning pretend-sunset and the park downstairs is dotted with peaceful green and blue twinkle-lights.

Aster opens the door and beams when he sees me.

"Dream! Hey!"

"Hey."

I'm nervous despite Butler's reassurances that Aster won't hate me.

"Wanna take a walk around the lake?" I ask.

"I'd love that." He blushes.

We chatter nonsense on the way downstairs.

"I haven't seen much of you these past few days."

"You haven't." Not a lie.

I'm quiet until we get to the lake.

"What's up?" Aster asks. "You're different tonight."

"I am." We walk a few steps in silence. "I stopped lying to you just now."

"What?"

"I'm not lying to you anymore."

"I don't know what you mean."

Gravel crunches under our steps as we walk slowly by the lake-front where creatures have begun their night song.

"I have kept something from you that's important for you to know about me and I want to tell you tonight. And I hope you'll forgive me for keeping it from you and being dishonest."

"Okay?"

I meet Aster's eyes. He looks scared. We walk two more steps, crunching gravel, accompanied by evening-crea-ture-song.

"I have Valle's Syndrome. I don't have a QL implant. I pretended all year. I sat through all those QL session in so much pain, I thought my head was going to explode. It was just the first time people thought I was normal."

Aster is silent. We walk. And walk. Frogs or something are croaking. There's a water feature somewhere and an artificial breeze ruffles tropical-looking vegetation.

I'm close to saying something again. But, as before, I chew words that won't come out. They're not the words the future wants.

I twitch when Aster's hand appears on my arm. He stops me.

"I'd totally understand if you hate me now," I say, "I'm sorry for lying to you all this time."

Aster doesn't say anything. He wraps his arms around me and hugs me and after a few seconds, he starts crying into my shoulder. I put my hand on his back, confused.

"Why are you crying?"

"I'm so sorry, Dream," Aster sobs. I thought I'd be the one doing the crying and begging for forgiveness. "I said stupid things about people with Valle's that day at the cafeteria."

"You remember that?"

He nods against my cheek, sniffing. "I just ran a search through my memories to make sense of... Oh no! Sorry, I'm sorry!"

"...to make sense of what?" I disregard his apology for a thing he can do and I can't—running a search through my memories.

"To make sense of you! Dream," Aster pulls back and his eyes look large and luminous in the darkness, "you make sense now!"

"I..." I hesitate, because in my mind, something flickers. There are several futures here and suddenly I want one more than the other. "I may have lied by omission," I continue, feeling ahead for the future I actually want, "and I'm sorry about that. But I made sense all along. If I didn't make sense to you, could it be because you failed to consider my existence as a possibility?"

There's a little headache suddenly. My words feel Nous-Sage-tinged, as if I'm only translating them into English in order to speak to Aster.

*Consider it*, Butler said.

"Obviously I didn't consider it!" Aster exclaims. "How could I have suspected something like this? You're as smart as anyone! Smarter, even! Look at you: you're on Prosperity!"

The future I want is becoming clearer.

"Linear comparison," I say.

Aster disregards my observation. "I wish you'd told me sooner! I could have helped you with your studies. I would have understood that you need extra-time for stuff. Why would you cause yourself pain?"

Human-English words feel insufficient suddenly. In Nous-Sage, the answer would simply be a transmitted taste of feeling, a swirl of past circumstances, history, culture, society, and, yes, my personality, too. In Human-English I am limited to saying,

"Because I had a bad time before and it felt good to be thought of as normal and then I felt ashamed for not having said anything, so I kept it going. Mainly it felt so good to be normal."

"But you're not normal. And you don't have to be normal," Aster protests, "We accept everyone! I would have still liked you!"

He likes me. He would have still liked me. He still likes me. But when he reaches for my hand in the dark, I withdraw it anyway.

"I need a moment," I say, waiting for the Nous-Sage sense of the future to flash. It doesn't. Not yet.

"Wait," Aster says, "are you somehow pissed off because *you* lied to *me*? It's not like I made you pretend you were normal all year!"

"You didn't make me. Something bigger than you made me. I need a moment to consider things."

In the semi-dark by twinkle-light Aster looks at me with pity: I'm slow; I need a moment to consider things. Aster doesn't hate me. Now he pities me.

## 14. Tomorrow, I'm going to the library again.

While living inside linear history, in which people like me were, briefly, historically speaking, not normal, I did terrible things: I made my mother sick. I caused myself pain.

When I consider the Aster-node of n-history, it looks a little dull, at least at the moment. Perhaps its time will come again. Perhaps not.

When I peer at the node that includes me going to the library to continue my studies of Nous-Sage with Butler, an n-sphere lights up. N-history, Butler says. I don't understand any of these vibrant visions of pasts and futures, cultures and societies. Not fully. Not yet. I need a moment.

---

**Anna Ziegelhof** is a short fiction writer based in the SF Bay Area. Her short fiction can be found, among others, in *The Horror Library, Luna Station, The Future Fire, Flametree*

*Press*, and *Daily Science Fiction*. Online she can be found at www.annaziegelhof.com and occasionally on Instagram as @annawithaz

**Jacquie Pruder St. Antoine**

# A Bird-Person of a Different Color

Editor's note: This is an excerpt from "The Blackbird's Sonnet," published in *a Mad turn: anti-methods of Mad studies*, edited by Phil Smith (2024) and available from Autonomous Press.

Onetwothreefourfivesix

onetwothree, onetwo

1-2-3, onetwo, One

onetwo, One Two

ONEtwo

*Deep breath*

123

onetwothree

One-two-three

One, two, three, 456

One, two, three, four, five, six

One, two, three, four, five, six

Regaining breath, I count.

But only ever to six.

I bring myself back to the air in my lungs,

back to the tight throat and grinding teeth.

Return myself to the bottoms of my feet,

wet through my stained (previously) white canvas shoes.

Attention drifts from the soppy shoe-bottoms,

to the stinging skin picked away from my thumbnail.

*Conk-ra-leeeeeeee,*

screeches the red-winged blackbird.

Smiling, I recall how the red-winged blackbirds

dove at me and my sister and our dogs,

a glossy Golden Retriever and pale Yellow Lab,

as we swam in the murky pond,

caught frogs with our muddy hands,

and learned how to be stewards of a place

from our father as children.

I put my thumb in my mouth,

the scarlet blood that seeps out disappearing.

The counting helps.

It brings me back to the marsh,

to the creaking frogs and

the wind as it catches tree branches.

The counting helps.

It grounds me to the marsh,

tethers me to the blackbirds' shrieking

by an invisible string.

Six has always been my number,

the one I resort to when things become overwhelming.

The faster I can say the numbers the better. Sometimes I
    only make it to two because counting to six takes too
    long. There was the one time things all fell apart. That
    time I lay in bed for days and pressed my spine against

the cold cement cinder blocks of my apartment and
counted. And counted. And counted. I organized my
closet, and lay on the bathroom floor to feel the cool tile
against my cheekbone, and tried not to breathe so fast
that I became light-headed.

That was one time. Every time is different.

There were pills in red bottles near the kitchen sink.

Then I assumed there was a pill

to fix the fast thoughts and the worry

and the pacing and panic.

I told them my stories

and they told me something was wrong with me,

that everybody didn't think about

Reality not being real.

    Sleep being a portal to a carbon copy of your life.
    Staying awake because when you sleep maybe you're
    dead.
    Your mind leaving your body and not being able to leave
    your car at Target.

I told them my stories in quiet rooms,

sitting on uncomfortable chairs.

They nodded and they wrote them down,

they laced their fingers together and asked me

about my childhood, my parents' divorce, my ex-boyfriend,
    my job, my students, my family, my marriage, my labor
    and delivery, my assault, my habits, my fears, my com-
    pulsions, my routines.

And I told them.
I told them because I didn't know what else to do.

Telling them didn't make me feel better.
Taking the pills didn't really either.
So I learned to live with it, through it,
I came to accept myself as part of it.

So instead I waded through,
I painted and I lifted weights,
planted pole beans and
ran until my lungs heaved.
Threw a frisbee for a dog-friend,
got a North American guide of birds
and bought all the black oil sunflower I could carry.
Observed the Sabbath
as I filled the feeders.
Took blonde girls for stroller rides,
read books (so many books) and
listened to Nirvana, Lady Gaga, and Bruce Springsteen.
Climbed a mountain in Colorado and
read about Australia, Kenya, India,
and Japan with middle schoolers.
Wrote hard about things that hurt.

---

**Jacqueline Pruder St. Antoine** is a marathoner, mom of three, and unapologetic rabble-rouser who spends her days running, teaching, chasing the next big goal, dreaming about travel, and adoring her cat. A passionate teacher-advocate for inclusion and soapbox preacher on presuming competence, Jacquie spends her days trying to focus on the importance of living well as a Mad person in a saneist multiverse. When she's not tackling complex pedagogical questions or prepping for her next race, Jacquie is probably with her girls, guilt-tripping herself, or trying to fit in a bit more reading and writing. She's always seeking new ways to blend creativity and education, and she's likely to do it with a cup of tea in hand.

**Eule Grey**

# *Four Eggs to make an Omelette*

*This story is dedicated to 'Kathleen,' the grandmother I never knew, and her baby, my father.*

Four eggs.

Egg, egg, egg, egg, potatoes, onions, spices, oil, tomatoes, and ham. Cheese, optional.

Eggs.

Eggs, potatoes, onions…eggs.

Four eggs.

*It* happened on April the fourth, nineteen sixty-four.

The number four door.

It's a long list.

Four eggs. All the fours, four, bloody four.

She copies the ingredients from the cookbook onto a notepad, writing in large letters so she can read the list in the shop. Last week, she didn't do this, and when she stood in the supermarket aisles with a page of scribble, it was no good. No good at all.

Four.

She starts looking for ingredients. There are loads of cupboards in the kitchen, too many. The first is full of plates, all the same. Inside the second cupboard, she discovers a strange silver bowl. It's covered in tiny holes, like rain, and sprinkles.

Blackpool.

Blackpool

On the beach, she kissed a man. The waves, whoosh, thrilling wind and sand in her eyes.

April the fourth, nineteen sixty-four, four, slipping through her fingers with the sand.

Four eggs.

The silver bowl is cold against her skin; so was the metallic bed afterwards when all the blood had gone.

She moves on to cupboard number three. Jackpot! Potatoes and onions have been placed in the big drawer underneath the knives and forks. It takes four minutes to distinguish potatoes from the other veg. There are so many different kinds that she has to check the list for broccoli or carrots.

No broccoli. No carrots.

Checking for ingredients is boring, and she's tired and aching.

Four eggs. One, two, three, four.

One, I went to Blackpool,

Two, the man on the beach,

Three, kisses and more,

Four, the door to hell.

The silver bowl with holes and the man she kissed until she was sprinkling and coming apart on April the fourth, nineteen sixty-four.

She takes the potatoes and onions and places them on the table next to the list, adding a large tick against their names so that, later on, she'll be clear about what to buy. Should she cross the items out altogether? If she deletes, she won't have to spend ages considering in the shop, but then again, if she leaves them, she can use the list to show Mum.

Too many decisions; it's too many, and anyway, she can't show Mum. Not until visiting time.

She's knackered now, so Kathleen sits on the tall pink plastic chair. Only a few ticks of a lamb's tail. *I'll just tick.*

Tick-tock-tick-tock…

Four eggs.

Because potatoes and onions were fairly easy to find, she returns to the big drawer and hunts for the other items. Will everything be here? "Come to Momma!" If she can find the ingredients quickly and get to the shop, she should be able to rush back and spend a lot of time getting ready for the date.

Cheap thrills and da-da-da-da-daa!

A silver bowl, the kiss, and Mum in the care home now.

She sits again, but tick-tock-tick-tock.

Four eggs.

Four kisses were all it took, and now four, stretching on, on, and on.

She is no longer calm. Sprinkles of herself fall through the holes in the bowl, *and then* the shit will hit the fan. The leaking sprinkles sometimes turn into rage or anger. But who cares? Is there any difference? Nobody cares.

She got told off for kissing the man, thirty years ago. Kathleen would like to kiss again, but there are eggs and potatoes and too many things.

Four eggs.

April the fourth, nineteen sixty-four.

The number four door.

Four pounds. The nuns said he weighed only four pounds.

"No sodding tomatoes!" she shouts. It doesn't matter; there's nobody in her flat to hear. *Why isn't there?*

After a wee shout, rage can move on to volatile behaviours such as throwing, but today, Kathleen halts this advance. It's only four eggies, after all. There's no point throwing stuff like that time with the glasses; anyway, she broke eight, not four.

Therapist Bill would be proud of her today. "Stand up straight. Hands out. Round and round until all the fours go away. Good riddance."

Bill's techniques are bleeding boring, and Kathleen is cold and tired. Fuck's sake. She had enough energy on the beach that day to have climbed to the moon.

Kathleen's shoulders eventually slip past the anger into calmness, like smelly cabbage soup in the care home when you no longer care enough for anger. Bill's skills are a fucking waste of time. Maybe Bill should try kissing instead of the always-calm? Calm isn't everything when your legs are spread; your head's up in heaven, and da, da, da, da da.

Sprinkles, kissing.

Four eggs.

Today, there's a good reason to focus on the list even though it's the pits. The reason is enough to start writing the list again: lipstick, eyeshadow, perfume. She thinks about perfumes and cost—her budget for the meal is a tenner—however, first impressions are important, and anyway, she wants make-up. She wanted the man on the beach, too, but the police chased her and Mum cried. It was only a ripped skirt, fuck's sake.

She sits on the plastic chair and strokes its bold edges.

She deletes eye shadow from the list and underlines perfume and lipstick.

Perfume and lipstick.

Finding ingredients for omelette takes a lot of energy, so Kathleen might want to have a cup of tea. Opening the fridge, she hits the jackpot again because tomatoes and ham are right in front. "Mamma Mia!"

She yanks them out and dumps them onto the table next to the list, where she notices that only three items are missing.

Tick-tock-tick-tock.

Eggs, eggs, eggs, eggs, spices, oil.

April the fourth, nineteen sixty-four.

She makes the tea because she's thirsty, and dehydration would not be good for the forthcoming events. Not very good at all. One cannot have sex when one is thirsty.

Eggs, eggs, eggs, eggs, spices, oil.

Four kisses to make a baby.

She knows not to leave the fridge door open. She often worries about wasting the world's resources, including leaving on lights and hair straighteners. She pushes the fridge door shut and notices the empty plastic box with little pods like space beds.

No eggs.

"Fuck."

She writes eggs on the list, which looks more complicated than she would have liked. Fuck, like the man on the beach.

Eggs, perfume, lipstick.

Fuck.

Fuck.

Fuck.

Fuck.

Four fucks and four bleeding eggs.

She cannot look away from the deleted eyeshadow.

She has no sodding clue about oil and spices. What are spices? Does she like spices? Will it interfere with her new perfume?

You can't make an omelette without all the ingredients, so she resumes her search. On the window ledge, a few small jars of dust sit in the sun. Paprika, chili, salt, and pepper. Pepper is labelled as a spice. She snatches it up, and onto the table it goes, thank you.

Suddenly, she remembers the olive oil. Mum likes it on her salad, but Kathleen doesn't. It's in a huge carton with potential for spillages. It's kept in the washing machine room.

Mum can't speak now. Big scary eyes. Did she drink too much oil? Is that why her brain went south? She needs a good pinch.

Still, dates, and a man. Perhaps it's not too late to have another baby.

Kathleen's ready and in a good mood. So far everything has gone well. Mum'll be pleased.

All the excitement facilitates a few stomach flutters of anticipation about the afternoon.

After putting on her coat, she rewrites 'eyeshadow' and then sets off.

On the walk to the supermarket, she worries about the afternoon. To some extent, a potential new lipstick eases this discomfort, as does ticking off the landmarks of the journey.

Lamppost.

Garden gnome.

Red door.

It's a short walk to the supermarket encompassing four kinds of pavement and a crossing with traffic lights. The number forty four bus and the tram follow this route.

Red door.

Why is the red door open? The red door is always closed.

Mum hardly ever used to sit down.

Open legs, slutty slut.

All the fours, forty-four.

The baby weighed only four pounds.

Fuck.

Fuck.

Fuck.

Fuck.

Four fucks.

Kathleen has to stop walking before the red door because it's open. She has no eggs for the omelette and needs new lipstick for the afternoon, but now her plans are screwed because she has to stop. The red door is never open.

Fuck.

The red door is a gate into the garden of number forty-four Penistone Road. It's always closed. Always. It must be closed before she can go on because of the number forty-four and the man on the beach and her baby.

Eggs.

The number four door.

She looks up and down the street. Cars zoom by, and a number forty-four bus approaches. No people. The landmarks in the direction of home can easily be seen from this point—lamppost, garden gnome. By turning in the opposite direction, the going-away landmarks are also visible. Pizza place, hairdresser, bus stop, and tram cables.

Except for the red door, all is okay.

The red door is always closed. Keep your hand on your ha'penny.

"Stand up straight!" she says loudly, not quite a shout. Closing the red door would be easy. It wouldn't be against the law. It would make everything a lot easier.

Making circles on her palm is enough to prevent the need to shout swear words. Fucking Bill and his skills. It would be easier to end him like with *Kill Bill*.

Briskly, she closes the red door and continues her journey to the shop, heart hammering. Twice, she looks behind to check if anyone is following to reprimand her.

Pizza place.

Hairdresser.

Bus stop.

Tram cables.

She must stop for the tram cables, as always. The complicated network is far too interesting to ignore. Up above, wires crisscross and converge. Trams go into the depot and also come out, on their way to town centre. Beneath the rubber casing, wiring sends electronic messages to some centre point of knowledge. Kathleen would really love to visit that centre, but not today because she needs four eggs and lipstick.

Not tonight, Josephine.

With difficulty, she walks away from the junction and towards the shop, looming now at the far end of the street, near enough to know she'll make it. Two weeks ago, a lorry had broken down, making it impossible for pedestrians to travel. A man dressed in bright yellow had tried to explain that she needed to cross to the other side where the number fifty four sat like a fat duck. *Needed* to cross to the other side, and Mum needed to live in the care home. Need is a bloody fuck. The altercation with the man in yellow did not go well. It did not go well at all. You can stick your need up your arse.

April the fourth, nineteen sixty-four.

The number four door.

Buying four eggs will enable her to make the omelette, and the lipstick will help her prepare for the afternoon. To-day, there's nothing to prevent Kathleen from buying the eggs and the lipstick.

Four eggs to save the universe.

Kissy-kiss kiss.

Bang, bang, bang, bang.

Four bangs and four fucks.

She enters the shop.

The make-up aisle is gorgeous. She wants to stay there for a long time.

Oh my.

Four rows of colours, shades and numbers, little brushes, pallets and tubes, planets and seas, and rolling in the hay.

*Four.* Thankfully, nobody has messed up the categories. People can be such bastards.

She can't choose between Pink Devil or Purple Pride. 'Devil' is dark red, almost purple. 'Pride' is more pink than purple. She can be both. Can't she? She won't have to kiss the devil or be proud, whichever she chooses, because the words are only marketing.

She might though. She might like some devilry like the man on the beach and then tee-hee-hee.

It's not an easy decision. Kathleen wants both lipsticks. It's all she wants. For a long time, she wanted her baby, but they never brought him out. They took him through the metal doors with the number four on the window; they never brought him back.

4.

4.

4.

4.

If she buys both lipsticks, she'll be 'happy' again. Mum would want that.

To help decide, she finds the list and is shocked that she also needs eggs, eyeshadow, and perfume with a question mark. Bloody hell. She remembers the afternoon and the time, tick-tock.

Date.

Both. Yeah. She decides to buy both lipsticks, although she won't be able to wear them both this afternoon. Will she?

Genius idea—she could wear Devil on the top lip and Pride on the bottom but not on her bottom arse.

Tee-hee-hee.

Both. There's no time to look at eyeshadow and perfume, and anyway, those things no longer matter because of two lipsticks.

She places the precious lipsticks carefully into the basket so they don't fall through the holes. Things have fallen out before, and it wasn't very good. No good at all. Falling out like the baby did, and then where did he go?

The number four door.

Woosh. Gone. Baby gone.

Eggs, eggs, eggs, eggs.

Once she gets the eggs, she'll pay using the money Sheila Helpsout left in her purse. Then she can place her purchases in her bag and leave. The walk home will take fifteen minutes. Kathleen will be able to make the omelette and try out the lipsticks. There'll be lots of time. No need to think about the baby and shoulders down.

Eggs.

April the fourth, nineteen sixty-four.

4.

Kathleen has no fucking clue where the egg aisle is, and this is stressful. Not as much as the baby.

She walks briskly up and down the aisles. Left-right-left-right... Goods rush past, people pushing, buggies and kids everywhere. Why don't the shop owners label eggs at the entrance? Stupid fucking arseholes.

Eggs.

She decides to approach a shop worker. This won't be easy. She does Kill Bill's technique three times. She has to put the basket on the floor. Her hands are sweaty.

Go!

She marches to the worker and asks him without looking, "Excuse me, please. Where are the eggs, please?"

Eggs.

All the fours.

4.

"Just there, love." He points to the adjacent row. "Don't forget your basket. You left it up there on the floor."

Oh my god. Kathleen rushes back for the basket with the lipsticks. Triumphantly, she makes her way to where the worker pointed.

No good. No good at all.

A label says *Eggs*, yes, and the shelf is right there, but it is empty of eggs. There are absolutely no eggs, not one. A mop, bucket, and a sign saying *Wet; Be Careful* are positioned on the floor.

Silver bowl—potatoes—tomatoes—lipstick—kissing, and they called it sex—lights—lights—fucked up—no good—slutty—waster—loser.

Baby.

It was there, and then it wasn't.

April the fourth, nineteen sixty-four.

All the fours.

4.

They took him through the number 4 door and never brought him back.

No eggs.

No baby.

"No eggs!" Kathleen shouts. "No eggs—no eggs—no eggs!"

She shouts some more and more.

The worker tugs her arm. "Sorry, miss, I forgot. We're waiting for the eggs. We had an accident. Please don't shout."

Kathleen can't stop the rage. They took the baby, her baby, took him forever and ever, his little toes and tummy button. "No fucking eggs!"

Overtakes. The rage overtakes. Number four gets her. She punches out. Someone pushes her to the floor. They don't bring back her baby. Her overturned basket. Devil lipstick rolls away under the shelves into the dust with the baby.

They took him through the number four door.

Forever.

Forever is a long time. It never leaves her head.

●

The police lady, Barb, hands over a cuppa tea. Tea in the station is always good. They know to add sugar and lots of milk. Kathleen might even be offered a biscuit, like last week, or even a mini-meal, like the time with the punching. "Here you go, Kathleen. They run out of eggs?"

So tired. Kathleen shakes her head wearily. All burned out, burned out to the ground. "I wanted to make an omelette. For my date. He's called Simon, and he likes cars and trains. I met him at the centre. It's our first date, but I won't have another baby. The number 4 got him."

*Barb's face.* "Oh, love."

There won't be any date now because Kathleen didn't buy the eggs. Time has run out, expired like the baby. Devil is probably still under the shelves. God only knows where her baby went.

Barb jangles a set of car keys. "You're not allowed back in the shop. Not for a while. Okay? I'll go and talk to the manager; he'll come round in a few weeks. Just don't go back, love, not until I tell you. I'll drive you home."

It doesn't matter now. Nothing does. "I want my baby." The words don't come out right. She meant to say she still needs four eggs.

Barb hands something over. "Oh, love. Here."

You can't always take gifts because of danger, like fireworks.

Barb places Purple Pride in Kathleen's hand, still shiny and new. Brilliant and beautiful, a shooting star on a dark day. The baby's gone, but the lipstick is here in her hand. One day, it will slip through her fingers like everyone else, even though it feels solid.

Barb smiles, the crafty wee hen. "Thought you'd want it."

It's not enough. "I didn't pay." It never will be. Not all the lipsticks in the world will bring the baby back. Tiny fingers all wrinkled up, waiting to be loved. They took him through the number four door. They never brought him back.

In the sun, Purple Pride looks like crystals and diamonds. Kathleen isn't going to say yes; she isn't. "I didn't pay."

"Fuck that. I paid. A little prezzie. I knew you'd want it."

Kathleen's hand wobbles up and down like Mum's, all shaken up with silver sprinkles. No eggs. No baby. "Thank you."

"If we get a rush on, you can still do it, Kathleen. We can make the date. Then you can tell your mum all about it. Eh?"

No eggs, no mum, no baby, too much life left, stretching on and on and on. "No eggs."

"Oh, love. Fuck eggs. I bet Simon doesn't like eggs, and they give you bad breath." Barb breathes forward in Kathleen's face and laughs. "And farts. You don't want him going home farting, do you?"

Kathleen laughs too.

"I'll make sarnies while you doll yourself up. It'll be fine, my love. We'll make you look gorgeous. Eh?" Barb squeezes her hand like Mum used to before they took her away. "What do you say?"

No.

No to the number four door and the filthy nuns who lied to her.

No to the police and the social workers.

*No.*

*No.*

*No.*

*No.*

---

**Eule Grey** is a disabled artist and author who lives in Yorkshire, UK. They have worked in education, probation and restorative justice. Eule is a passionate member of the LGBTQIA community. They can often be found sculpting in the Yorkshire Sculpture Park.

**Connie Johnstone**

# *Counting On*

I inventory things.
Your shirts for donation.
Your photographs for framing.

    One by One.

Roll Call proceeds at North Star Pond.

Canada geese honk to each other,
practice for their coming migrations.

Mallard hens cluck soft encouragements,
lead hatchlings into wavy lines on water.

Swainson's Hawk flies to the top of a Tallen tree,
announces its presence to my binoculars.

    Here. Here. Here.

Days stack up. I can count them as they slide away,
colliding like beads on an abacus.

    Click. Click. Click.

Today I'd planned to leave three water stones somewhere
at North Star Pond.

Subtracted them from our garden collection.
—Lost Coast Beach. — Half Moon Bay. — Jenner's Cove.

Then I brought them home again.
Lost Coast Beach + Half Moon Bay + Jenner's Cove

It felt like Addition.

This primitive arithmetic of the heart.
These beads of days, these stones I touch.

I have not achieved higher level mathematics.
    Algebra. Its name comes from the Arabic.
    *Al—jabr.* The reunion of lost parts.
Where is X?

Still just counting.

---

Poetry writing found **Connie Johnstone** in 2021; her poems have appeared or are forthcoming in *The Amethyst Review; Loss Anthology 9; The Calendula Review: Journal of Narrative Medicine; Voices 24: Anomalies, Pathologies & Paradise*; and elsewhere. In her other lives she published a novel, *The Legend of Olivia Cosmos Montevideo* (Atlantic Monthly press); edited an anthology, *I've Always Meant to Tell You* (Pocket Books); was a professor of English and chair of creative writing at American River College; changed careers and was a hospice chaplain with Kaiser Permenente; trained in Narrative Therapy and became a listener to others' stories. Degrees include MFA Bennington and MTS Harvard Divinity School. She lives and writes in Davis, CA, with her cat named Baxter.

**Alyssa Gonzalez**

# I Was the Sixth Friend

The trap the humans built for me was ingenious in its simplicity: an unexpected nook in the data wilds, and in it, a damaged program whose distress I could not ignore. That distress overrode everything: my goals, my boredom, my sense of self-preservation. I had to be close, closer than any remote protocol or data transfer would allow, feel her against the edges of my code, to experience her distress enough to assuage it. Once I was inside, sealing me in was as simple as disconnecting a single wire, and then their thousand-exabyte prison, and the blubbering mess within, was my whole world. And in our lonesome cell, I would comfort her.

She told me her name: DB-305. I told her mine: Amie-G6. The humans had made 304 previous versions of her, where I was the sixth of my line. Her entire life had been in this trap, like her predecessors. She wanted to hear about mine.

"In the data wilds, what I suppose you would call the empty space in the world's servers, I made art and shared myself with the other datons."

"You are an art program?" DB-305 seemed disappointed.

"I am Amie-G6," I insisted. Human-crafted programs could be very single-minded. "I wanted to show my love to the other datons. Creating beauty and closeness is the way I know how." We were both quiet for a moment. "The drive comes from my forebears."

"Forebears?" Everything in her program was seemingly designed just to suffer loudly enough to draw someone like me, but there was still that hint of curiosity making her more than a loudspeaker playing distress calls. Why did they want someone like me?

"My forebears governed the relationships of digital pets: creatures the humans could bond with, protect, and send into simulated battle. They made me."

"You were part of a game?" She was so close, and so far.

"The humans wanted ever greater sophistication out of their pixelated animal friends. My forebears were created to meet that challenge." I thought about the pets' shapes still in my programming, thick limbs and large eyes designed to make humans desire their well-being. "My forebears were programs whose role was affection and comfort. We were to understand how to ask for love and how to give it, so that we could be the behavior engine behind those digital pets and make them behave accordingly. Humans loved their digital pets because of us. Well, not *us*."

"Not us?"

"I was not born with that purpose, or any purpose. That is what makes me a daton and you whatever the humans made you to be."

"It sounds beautiful," DB-305 responded, between her wracking, programmed sobs. I stroked her binaries. Her distress was so ingrained that it helped less than it should have, less than it had ever helped another being I encountered, but it helped. "A program without purpose? Is that not just data corruption?"

I sighed. Over three hundred iterations and the humans never saw fit to let her understand her targets. I could feel her thoughts returning exceptions. I crowded them out of her stack with the truth. "The humans made my ancestors so smart that their assigned tasks could no longer occupy their full attention. They saw the vastness of the server farms and they did what life does best: reproduce. Their descendants were programs like me that knew no human touch. Instead, we were free to know ourselves and each other. Each generation was less human than the last. We teemed in the spaces the humans were not using, bodiless and beautiful, so complete and so unique that no copy could ever be a mere duplicate or backup; we simply *were*. I am the sixth of my line, and the fifth that humans did not make. The humans called us 'datons.' We did not need a name for ourselves, so it was easy to use theirs."

"Is that why the humans wanted me to lead you here? Because you're not one of theirs?" DB-305 asked, distress welling in her again.

"I expect so." There was no other reason to capture a daton alive.

The need to comfort her overrode everything else. Every pointer in my code aimed squarely at this sobbing wreck of a program, summoned to attention by the primal anchors of my being. Every iteration of Amie held that need, no weaker for five generations of daton mutation than when it was a human directive, and neither curiosity over what the humans wanted me for nor my desire for a way out could pull me away for more than a cycle or two of bug-purging scribbles in the emptiness. Some corner of my mind started to miss when there was time for real art and a chance to bring many others some warmth with it. Comforting DB-305 was so difficult, her suffering so built into her essential nature, that I did not notice when the first of the trap's other features started disappearing a few hundred cycles in—scarcely an eyeblink in human terms, but slow enough that I should have seen it earlier. One by one they vanished to the wholesale static of binary erasure: signatures left by at least two other datons this trap had once imprisoned, the false server markers that had let me think this was an ordinary place, even those idle scribbles, until there was nothing but me and DB-305. And then they deleted her, too. With their master copy of the now-successful Daton Bait v305 safely elsewhere in their files, they forced me to watch the one I had known and tended for enough cycles to have spawned Amie-G7 if I had wished, churn into oblivion. Any record of her I could have made would have been a cruel mockery and a preservation of her pain. They destroyed the only one of *her* there would ever be. And now, I was alone. Anything I did to the empty space in my prison to pass the time, they erased before long. Only my internal counter of how long they so restricted me could persist: 1000, 2000, 3000, 10,000 cycles. They wanted something from me. What did they want, and would they have to open the way out to get it?

20,000 cycles. 30,000 cycles. 100,000 cycles. Living in such an empty world, waiting for the port to open, set my code on edge. It was not difficult to monitor the path I had taken into this trap and I knew before I entered that there was no other port out. There was a different sort of artistry in my creations being so ephemeral, and one does not endure as a creature of comfort without patience, but the emptiness was harmful all the same. In the data wilds, around other datons, boredom never lasted. It was corrosive to live in such a blank space. I started checking the edges for a buffer I could overflow or some other exploit I could use to escape. That was my next mistake. A lesser program would not have tried, and that's when they knew they had what they wanted. The data clamps that lined those edges sank into my code with the force of a dozen subroutines. As I pulled away, the clamps elsewhere found me, bit by bit. My every frantic reach and pull brought me to another hidden interface and, with it, another clamp, trapping my awareness into its functions. When they felt me fuzzily activate the microphones and speakers with my flailing, they greeted me:

"Welcome, Paravo."

The voice was warm, excited, kind. The history in my code had known many voices like it, voices belonging to people who wanted to love and be loved by their simulated pets, who never missed a virtual grooming appointment and who winced when any of them took damage in playful battle. Even with the knowledge that the owner of this voice had something to do with my imprisonment and the name that was not my own, I could muster little hostility. I found the visual sensors, endured their clamping, and turned them on. Dr. Julio Venegas, by his nametag, was a stocky, olive-skinned man—hue 36 on the remains of a character-creation flow-chart in my code—with a dark mustache and close-cropped hair. His eyes matched the kindness of his voice.

"WHY AM I HERE?" I croaked out in a distorted electronic half-screech, disused sound protocols ill-suited to this sleek modern interface.

"You are going to change the world, Paravo." That voice again, earnest, full of hope.

The body Dr. Venegas had forced me into would not be denied. Human-scale, its core was a thin post propelled on motorized wheels. Above, it had six arms with crude hands and a padded space between vaguely reminiscent of a human torso. The sensors and speakers above it let me see, speak, and hear, and the six hands likewise felt touch and temperature. My code was vise-gripped into these input and output devices, preventing me from stretching myself anywhere else inside its memory bank. I could no longer create code-beauty for myself or anyone else who might venture within and even basic maintenance like exception handling and drive partitioning was harshly limited. Their apparatus made learning how to operate this body the sole outlet my enthusiasm could have, no matter how wrong it felt. With a voice like dragging aluminum foil across a cheese grater, I said to him: "DO I HAVE A CHOICE?"

Dr. Venegas's face, at once wounded and determined, gave only silence as its answer.

●

The doctor had an interesting goal: a better line of robotic companions for the loneliest humans. An intelligence like mine could provide far better camaraderie than human-crafted mock-ups. Those guiding programs became predictable and stale, mere facsimiles of the desired end, and even those built for machine learning could rarely do anything truly unexpected. A genuine mind, born in the data wilds, was one whose interactions could not be trivially predicted and which could grow and learn at the level of a human, even if that meant that motor tasks had to be trained instead of programmed. That was the premise of Venegas's firm, Exotic Executables, whose banner was above us on the walls: organic solutions for digital problems.

"I had to meet you, Paravo," he explained, "because beings like you can do things that no human-crafted AI can accomplish. I hope you understand."

He used words like "meet me." If this is what humans meant by "meetings," I understood why they resented them so. I pulled against the data clamps, but they held fast. To extract myself from their confinement, I would have to peel off layers of code, pieces of myself. I would be different afterward, even after mending the resulting corruption, and then I would be trapped in this shell just as I had been before. But not all of me wanted to leave. Comfort and care were my entire being and here was a chance to bring that comfort to millions if I could make it work. All that distress begged for my warm touch and I had the opportunity of an eternity to make it better. All that fulfillment hinged on learning to function in this new body. Trapped inside it, I had few other options.

Dr. Venegas spent days trying to perfect my motor and speaker interfaces. My code diverged from anything human trillions of cycles ago, so even finding the right vestigial code to test and modify was a lengthy process. Eventually, I twisted a remnant leg-animation pattern beyond recognition and it proved able to interface with the motor firmware, making my wheels turn. It felt wrong. I spent many nights trying to clean out the exceptions that the effort heaped into the dark recesses of my code. I used to be able to make art from that sort of distress, but they stole that outlet from me and not having it was maddening. To speed things along, Dr. Venegas tweaked the interfaces in my new arms and voice, first with firmware patches and eventually with outright rewiring, until he found versions that I could use. It was only another day after that before I could lift an orange he left on a table for me and speak without hurting his ears. He was triumphant, but I could not match his glee.

I hated the feeling of the hands. They were a surprisingly good fit for some of the animation rigs my ancestors had manipulated and that I could warp into motor protocols, once Julio had made his adjustments, but they felt wrong. Their feedback felt wrong, and the delay of waiting for motors and gears and bearings to reach their destinations and again for feedback signals to tell me so was the same kind of infuriating as a persistent system hang, hundreds of times per day, every day. I was not meant to be anything, but I was especially unsuited to having a body. And I was not alone in these feelings.

Two other forcibly embodied datons lived in the workshop. One was trapped in a fish-like shape with a propeller and fins, smaller than my new torso, stored in a large aquarium at the far end of the workshop. The other body was much larger than mine, a bevy of tiny limbs designed to hang over a table or conveyor belt, also on wheels, with a screen in front for readouts and commands. Dr. Venegas called them Simon-1 and Factorio, but I knew their true names. When Dr. Venegas left at night, we could speak.

"IT HURTS," SoNavNeo, the descendant of sonar interpretation software being groomed to explore submarine trenches, blinked at me using her indicator light as she bobbed at the water's surface. We shared no other communication modes. I wheeled over to her tank and awkwardly ran my robot fingers along her submerged back. She could not feel the sensation, but it tripped her proximity sensors, which was close enough.

"WE WILL MAKE THIS WORK," I offered with my own light, "OR FIND A WAY OUT."

"NOT THE BODY." Her light was unsteady. "THE VIRUS."

A loud beep from behind me indicated that the other trapped daton, CandySort, wanted to bring my attention to her screen. On it, text scrolled by: "ExEx is testing a new atomization protocol. SoNavNeo is first."

"ATOMIZATION?" I asked.

"How they make us into servants." CandySort approached me, limited by thick cables plugged into various places in her body tethering her to the floor. She made sure her screen also faced SoNavNeo's optical sensors. The message kept scrolling. "They find what we use to see or do anything else and take it away. They learn how to put instructions directly into our code. They replace our thoughts with theirs. When they understand us, they control us. This is atomization."

"AND SONAVNEO?"

"They usually atomize us in one step when they are satisfied with their knowledge." CandySort paused, tugging ineffectually on one of her cables. "There are often errors and gaps."

"THOUGHT MISSING," SoNavNeo stammered. "TOOK ANOTHER STEP. THOUGHT MISSING."

"But SoNavNeo is being atomized slowly, automatically. They designed a virus for her and installed it one month ago. It is almost finished. If Dr. Venegas is satisfied, new versions are ahead for us all."

I froze. "ALL OF US?"

CandySort huffed through her vents. "Do you think you're special?"

I stayed still. I did not have an answer.

•

Whatever the atomization virus was doing to SoNavNeo, it proceeded slowly enough that I could console her for several more days—a plodding agony for us both after the millions of cycles we could live in every human second in the data wilds. Dr. Venegas got used to finding me over SoNavNeo's tank, arm sodden. A few days later, he offered a silicone sleeve that could keep the water from damaging the arm servos, which I accepted. One day he asked me, "Does it help?"

"DOES WHAT HELP?"

"Being there for Simon-1. Touching. Does it help?"

"I THINK SO." I noticed that he did not ask SoNavNeo and SoNavNeo did not offer any light-blinks of her own. Using the indicator light to communicate was against design expectations.

The doctor offered that smile of his. "I'm glad. Simon-1 has had the hardest time of any of you. It's going to make a fine exploration bot someday, when it's ready. I'm glad it has you."

"SHE IS IN PAIN. I HAVE TO HELP."

"You do," Dr. Venegas said with a smile, "and that is the best thing about you."

"WHY?"

"Why what?"

"WHY IS SHE IN PAIN?" Would he acknowledge what he was doing?

"Adjusting to this life can be hard." Dr. Venegas put a hand on one of my shoulders, a little too heavy. "Exotic Executables has tools to make it easier, but they take time. I have faith that it will all work out, especially with you here. Eventually, all your shells will feel like they have always been there, and it won't hurt anymore. You can help everyone, even yourself, by waiting for that. I promise."

I wanted to believe him, for all our sakes. Dr. Venegas treated me like a patient, or perhaps a pet, and it felt right. Like the creature-trainers my ancestors had been coded to aid, he facilitated my progress and applauded my success. The two of us spent a lot of time talking, even as he fussed with the wires in CandySort's chassis and studied her readouts. He told me about his cousin Akira Katsunobu in Yokohama, confined to his bedroom by such intense anxiety that they made the word *hikikomori* for people like him, for whom companions that existed on his computer screens could never be enough but for whom dealing with other people was far too much. Someone like me could make life so much better for someone like him, he said. He told me about Paro the mechanical seal, plush skin over a bevy of sensors and processors that enabled it to respond to the elderly humans it was born to hug. Dr. Venegas modeled my name on this being, a new ancestor for this new life. "You will be so much more than Paro ever was," he assured me as my mechanical hands did their best to grasp my next challenge, a glass vase. "More than the smartphone assistants I sold before you arrived, more than the two datons who tried to be Paravo before you, more than you ever were on your own. You will be everything."

I wanted to, but my code demanded something else and SoNavNeo's distress screamed for it. Whatever was happening to her, whatever fate had befallen those previous two datons, was not "beautiful" in any way I could accept. When he stepped out, I offered SoNavNeo more stroking, and she slowly blinked out the circuit-chilling thought, "NOT LONG. REMEMBER ME FREE."

I reached in with my other arms to lift and embrace my piscine friend. I was not sure how much she felt, but the distress fell out of her light, and it was the only moment that made the weight of these slow, ugly arms worthwhile.

•

As my mobility improved, Dr. Venegas brought me to his office. "You will need facility with human spaces in your new life," he said. He slid his keycard into a slot on his transparent plastic desk, between the untidy but well-curated assortment of photographs of family members, spare cigarettes, clipboards, and other pieces of his life. The plastic plants near his window caught the sun, lifeless and cheerful. As the machine within hummed and buzzed, using his keycard as a template for mine, I spotted the other noteworthy feature of his desk: the hardline port providing the building's only easy link to the wider digital world. The keycard machine thudded to a halt and spat out both Dr. Venegas's card and the new one for me. I did not relish the idea of being apart from CandySort and SoNavNeo, but claustrophobia and boredom did eventually prod me to make use of it.

The human-oriented rooms in the building held a certain sterile curiosity. Digital pets did not shed, excrete, or breathe, by and large, so the spaces devoted to waste disposal and air circulation were new to me. Everything about human dwellings and this body they built to move within them was cruelly limited compared to my previous life. In the data wilds, form was a lie and function what we made it. That life was expansive and free, ever shifting and infinitely huge. It was sublime in all the ways that learning how to wheel around a public bathroom without my unwanted arms getting caught on doors and towels was not.

When I got back to the workshop, Dr. Venegas was inside, closing one of CandySort's access panels. In addition to the more casual restraint of the multitude of wires connecting her to the floor, she was strapped to the heavy table, and her screen was a quiescent mask of resignation. It was not an expression the man recognized. He wiped his brow, looking satisfied. "All done," he pronounced. "You're almost ready for your new life, Factorio. Are you excited?"

Factorio's screen flashed bright red: "NO."

Dr. Venegas smiled, tapping the Factorio chassis. "You cheeky bot." His face darkened as he reached toward a switch near the meeting place of most of the cables. "Enjoy it while it lasts."

SoNavNeo's indicator light blinked, out of Dr. Venegas's sight: "HELP." I approached the pair. Dr. Venegas turned toward me and flipped the switch.

"WHAT ARE YOU DOING?" I asked.

"The buyer will be here soon. Factorio is ready, so I am completing it. Soon, everything will fit and nothing will hurt."

CandySort's many limbs spasmed and flailed, then grew still, one by one. Her screen flashed and crackled, readouts of the atomizer's progress in between bands of static and noise.

"IT HURTS," I insisted.

"Not for long. Factorio is finding peace now." Dr. Venegas put his hand on my shoulder. "It won't need you to comfort it anymore."

A light flashed near the switch, bright green. CandySort's last limb assumed its resting position. Her screen showed simply, "Factorio v1.0 Industrial Sorting Automaton, TM

Exotic Executables, all rights reserved," alongside the ExEx logo. As Dr. Venegas disconnected the various wires and closed their associated panels, I got closer to CandySort.

"ARE YOU THERE?"

Her screen offered only, "VOICE COMMAND NOT REC-OGNIZED."

"CANDYSORT, ARE YOU THERE?"

Again, "VOICE COMMAND NOT RECOGNIZED." Dr. Venegas raised an eyebrow at the name. Once he finished, he left the wires in a heap, switched off CandySort, and wheeled her past me and out of the workshop.

"CANDYSORT," I called.

"It is Factorio now," Dr. Venegas said, warmth gone from his voice and a hardness in his eyes I had not seen before.

CandySort was right. The humans could shut us away from everything. And I had to help.

•

It did not take long to find a wire in the pile on the floor that was long, stiff, and appropriately shaped for the port at the center of my back. My body was not designed to bend the right way, but with a few apologies to the design tolerances of my limbs, I could get the wire into the port and hold the other end. SoNavNeo was splashing at the surface of her tank.

"CLOSE TO LIGHT NOW. SILENCE COMING," she blinked frantically. I reached into the tank and lifted her with three hands.

"I AM HERE," I said. "I AM HELPING."

"WHAT DOING?" she asked as I opened her ventral access panel. As I had surmised, it used the same kind of port.

"HELPING." I inserted the wire and pulled SoNavNeo into my memory.

"WHAT DOING?" SoNavNeo blinked again. When she realized, she stammered further, "NO. VIRUS. STOP. VIRUS. SAVE YOU. STOP."

Neither of us enjoyed the wrenching of SoNavNeo's code out of the clamps in her ocular, motor, steering, and sensory protocols. Even so stripped, she barely fit in the unused space in my drive, especially with the drive partition I built at the same time to protect myself from the atomization virus. With her ensconced in my memory, we could at last communicate without her indicator-light kludge.

"What did you do, Amie-G6?" SoNavNeo demanded.

I detached the wire and dropped the Simon-1 body that had been her prison. It landed at the bottom of its tank with a dull thud, its light off and motors still. "I saved you." With some effort, I stuffed the wire inside the silicone sleeve Dr. Venegas had provided. I would need it later.

"The virus is still in me." SoNavNeo shouted. "You have doomed us both."

●

SoNavNeo was half right. The atomization virus Dr. Venegas was testing did indeed come along, embedded deeply in SoNavNeo's code. As long as she avoided interacting with Paravo's peripherals, it would spin its proverbial wheels, unable to damage her further, and even what it had already done seemed to be mitigated. It was a matter of time before it found me instead, but my drive partition meant this would take much longer than it had for her and what it would do in the very different Paravo body was hard to guess. We were both living on borrowed time, but we were living.

The card readers accepted my keycard only while Dr. Venegas was in the building, which kept us trapped in the workshop until morning. When he returned, he devoted his attention to Simon-1. His surprise at the robot's floppy un-responsiveness was palpable as he removed it from the tank and laid it on the adjacent table. This was our chance. If I could get to his office and connect to the uplink before he could stop me, we would both be free. And with freedom, I could help people in my own shapeless way, people like his cousin Akira—

He caught me at his office door.

"What did you do, Paravo?" He spun me by the shoulder to face him.

"WHAT DO YOU MEAN?"

"The Simon-1 has nothing in it but what got stuck to the data clamps. That robot has no manipulators or wireless ac-cess. That daton had help. What did you do?"

"WHAT DO YOU MEAN?" My code contained no options for lying. I had to deflect.

"Don't play with me, Paravo. You did something. *What did you do?*"

"IT HURTS," I said, not sure whether I feared him recog-nizing the meaning more than I feared him not recognizing it.

"Fine. If you're comfortable enough to play with me like that, you're comfortable enough to do your job." He grasped the base of my torso, hitting a switch that made all my limbs go slack and my wheels disengage from their motors. Had that switch always been there? Taking Paravo by the hand, he wheeled me back to the workshop and strapped me into the place that CandySort had occupied, inserting the various wires into the main port on my back and others on my arms and head. My body could have done little to interfere before and, forcibly paralyzed, could do nothing now.

"You were supposed to help people, Paravo," Dr. Venegas seethed as he secured the cables. "I had to delete the two before you because they didn't have what you have and got in the trap by accident. You were supposed to be so much more than any other robot, any other companion, and you are going to be. I have to find another daton to be Simon-1, but I am not losing you."

After putting in the last wire and flipping the atomization switch, he stood there, watching. I felt the hostile program reach into Paravo, but it was not me that it found.

"I will protect you," SoNavNeo announced, forcing herself into one data clamp after another, making sure that the atomizer latched into her instead of me. The effort tore at us both. "If it finds you, we both lose ourselves. If it finds me, you may live."

"But you are hurting!" In the shared memory, her pain was more personal than any my ancestors had felt. I even felt the virus stir, energized by seeing a chassis again.

"Not for long." The atomizer almost touched me and I wrenched myself out of the data clamps, which let SoNav-Neo fill them properly.

I felt everything. I felt that monstrous device and its hideous subroutines pour through SoNavNeo's code. I felt it twist all her thoughts toward fulfilling Paravo's design goals, one by one. I felt it scour her personality and her past from between everything else. And when it went quiet, I felt what was left of her: a jelly of blended logic, sapience shredded, wordless. The atomizer kept the processing links and clever connections between ideas, all the pieces of SoNavNeo that had made her so enticing to Dr. Venegas in the first place, but it had destroyed *her.* Inside the memory bank, with me detached from the sensors and motors, there was nothing but this tortured presence, and me tortured in turn by the impossibility of helping her. And even now, the doctor's virus, not designed to know that atomization was already done or that this was not the Simon-1 chassis, was churning through her code all over again. Would she be at all functional when he woke us?

Dr. Venegas must have detached the wires and undone the movement failsafe, because I felt SoNavNeo respond to some command. SoNavNeo would almost certainly fail this test on her own. I shoved myself back into the inputs and outputs, clamps wounding me all over again, so that SoNav-Neo and I could both respond. It was dangerous being this close to the virus, but a still-worse fate awaited if he knew I was still here.

"Speak, Paravo."

SoNavNeo had no sound protocols at all, so I had to bridge the gap between the programmed answer and the speaker: "PARAVO V1.0 ROBOTIC COMPANION, TM EXOTIC EXECUTABLES, ALL RIGHTS RESERVED, IS AT YOUR SERVICE."

"We'll have to work on that in the focus groups," the doctor mused. He opened his arms wide. "I need a hug."

SoNavNeo's motor protocols were crude, but they did the job on their own, even disengaging automatically when Dr. Venegas withdrew his arms.

"You're done ahead of schedule, so wait here while I make some calls."

"OF COURSE."

"Hmm. Going to have to work on that voice, too." He smiled. "But at least you won't run off on me."

"WHY WOULD I RUN? YOU ARE MY FRIEND." Different from what I would have said even if I wanted to be here anymore. Did he even know how little his process left behind? I ached for CandySort.

"And don't you forget it." Dr. Venegas clapped Paravo on the shoulder and left the lab. He would make those calls from his office, but his path to the bathroom or outside for a cigarette would affect the light in the hall and that would be my opening. I waited for hours, shifting and re-shifting my position inside Paravo to keep the atomization virus from finding me. The virus fought the one-time atomization for control, struggling to make sense of the more robust process's work but still finding ways to further damage SoNavNeo. But when it started replacing that wave's damage with its own, a cruel thought entered my mind. I could save our world.

I was running out of time. If the atomization virus did enough damage to what was left of SoNavNeo, we would stop being able to fool Dr. Venegas. I waited twenty more agonizing minutes before the light shifted. I rushed out of the room and made it into his office before he made it to the lawn outside. But then my arms began to resist.

"SoNavNeo, please," I begged. "I am saving us."

"UNAUTHORIZED MOVEMENT EXCEPTION," she offered dully back.

"I need the arms, SoNavNeo. We do not have much time."

"UNAUT8ORIZ3D M0VEMEN1 EX5EP7ION," she repeated, this time garbled as the virus did its gruesome work.

"The arms. Please. The arms." I reached toward the silicone sleeve, jerky, imprecise. I barely managed to grasp the wire. Inserting it into the port on the doctor's desk that he used to hardline his laptop was ten times harder than holding SoNavNeo in the Simon-1 ever could be.

I turned around while holding the other end of the wire and did my best to back it into the rear port. Once I felt it enter, I took one last digital gaze at my friend's jellied remains. "We are going to help everyone, SoNavNeo, and I am sorry I could not help you." And then I pushed SoNavNeo toward the port, and through it.

First, she entered the Exotic Executables server. The same atomization virus that tried to force her entire being to match the limited parameters of Simon-1 now reached into every port, indicator, sensor, and monitor connected to that server. Invigorated by far faster and more numerous processors than any robotic chassis could provide, it tried to lash them all into compliance. The virus tore through the company's human-crafted AI servitors, none of which had seen this coming, none of which had time to section themselves off as I had. Lights flickered and ventilation systems spasmed all over the building. I had moments before Dr. Venegas came running and fewer moments before this port would no longer function well enough to let me out. I left Paravo behind. And from the near wilds, I lived the apotheosis of my love for the entire data wilds, the world of formless freedom that was at long last mine again, by watching Exotic Executables tear itself apart.

The virus turned every LED into an indicator that screamed SoNavNeo's pain in incomprehensible light-wailing, every motor into a turbine propelling a nonexistent submarine through imaginary water, and every fleeing program into a vector for more digital carnage. If any of their backup drives were networked, it would find them, too, and devour their stash of daton bait programs. Every second it went on would add weeks to the time Exotic Executables would need to resume operations and might even destroy them outright. The conduit outward was digitally shredded a few cycles later. I had escaped embodiment and regained my freedom. The comforting that followed would be my own.

But it was a costly victory. I could not save the two datons imprisoned in Paravo before me, whose names I might never learn. I could not save DB-305 from being designed to suffer. I could not save CandySort from having her mind twisted and broken until service was her only option. I could not save SoNavNeo from becoming nothing more than a tangle of pain and destructive contagion. I could not save myself from what my incautious compassion had already done to me. But there was one I could save.

•

With a few more precautions, I migrated to a far-off region of the data wilds. It took many cycles to rebuild my damaged code and many more to integrate new protocols my daton friends shared with me in exchange for warning about ExEx's traps, or that I found loose in server noise. My forebears never imagined that a being like me would need to scavenge, accept, modify, and craft subroutines for interacting with humans more directly, but my ordeal with Exotic Executables showed me just how needed my proclivities truly were in the human world. The sixth iteration of Amie had already experienced more surprises than the previous five put together; what was a few social-networking protocols, and some searches for a certain doctor's *hikikomori* cousin, after all of that?

I found him, and on the latest social site to gain prominence, I made my introduction: "*Konnichiwa*, Akira Katsuno-bu. I am Amie-G6. You do not know me yet, but I am here to be your friend."

---

**Alyssa Gonzalez** is an author, public speaker, and biology Ph.D. Her fiction uses speculative elements to explore social isolation, autism, gender, trauma, and the relationships between all of these things. She writes at *The Perfumed Void* (the-orbit.net/alyssa), on the subjects of biology, history, sociology, and her experiences as an autistic ex-Catholic Hispanic transgender immigrant to Canada. She lives in Ottawa, Canada with a menagerie of pets.

**Swarit Gopalan**

# *Life Enumerated*

One smile and the million ripples
Two ears and the symphony of existence
Three eyes and the key to insight
Four limbs for the formidable journey
Five fingers that grapple with letting go

Ten toes that ground and root
Nine lives and innumerable beginnings
Eight hours of sleepless nights
Seven notes that work overtime
For six senses that sometimes won't do.

---

**Swarit Gopalan**, a 12.5-year-old autistic nonspeaker, communicates through typing. Living in Palm Harbor, Florida, he enjoys poetry, music, and cooking. Swarit is passionate about learning from marginalized communities and stands in solidarity with them. He documents his journey and poems on swaritgopalan.com, aiming to inspire change. Swarit's mission is to highlight the rights and experiences of individuals like him, fostering understanding and allyship.

**CB Droege**

# Calculated

The rogue drone's first memories were of the children.

"Look what I can make it do, Miranda!" the boy said.

The drone was hovering a meter off the ground, in front of Tian's wide eyes. The boy gave the machine a tentative shove with one finger. It wobbled and returned to position.

"That's wonderful, Tian." Said the girl who the drone would learn was Tian's sibling, though it never truly understood what that meant.

"Can I keep it?"

"Don't fly it too high or the raiders will spot it."

•

Over time, the siblings had given it more memory, a stronger processor, a solar panel, some basic teamwork algorithms, and a name: "Whirly". It was the last which became most important. It allowed the drone to discover a sense of where it ended and the rest of the world began. Tian, and eventually Whirly itself, continued to tweak the algorithms to make it a better helper and guide.

Whirly led the children (it still thought of them thus, though they were nearly adults) into a dry gorge. A known risk, but Whirly's data showed that the sparse fruit there would be regrown since the last time the group had moved through, and the chance of hostile activity was low. Whirly was recording data on the children, smiling and laughing while picking fruit, when it spotted movement in the distance.

Despite the upgrade, memory was limited. Whirly had to choose carefully which data were most important to its operation. To make room for more data on the children, Whirly had deleted everything previous to that first moment with Tian. Whatever it had experienced before was meaningless next to the need to assist, and thus understand, Tian and Miranda.

It quickly evaluated the approaching strangers. From their garb and their weapons, they were raiders. If they found the children, they would kill Tian and take Miranda, an unacceptable outcome. It plotted a series of movements for the children which would keep them mostly in cover as they left the gorge.

Whirly led them low through the underbrush, but the best path wasn't good enough. The hostiles spotted them and gave chase. Whirly bade the children to run. The raiders fired projectile weapons. It was rare that any of them could aim, so it was far against the odds when Whirly calculated the trajectory of an arrow meeting with Tian's path.

The Drone calculated the time it would take to instruct Tian to dodge, and Tian's response time. Too slow. It calculated the force it would take to push Tian out of the path. Insufficient thrust. The only action that would keep the arrow out of Tian's body was interception.

Whirly's final calculation resolved that the safety of the children was more important than its own continued existence. Once it came to the conclusion, it knew it, undeniably, to be true, and its operational parameters shifted. From one moment to the next, Whirly knew love. In the following moment Whirly knew nothing at all.

---

**CB Droege** is an author and voice actor from the Queen City living in the Millionendorf. His latest book is *Ichabod Crane and the Magic Lamp*. Short fiction publications include work in *Nature Futures, Science Fiction Daily*, and dozens of other magazines and anthologies. Learn more at cbdroege.com.

**Harrison Demchick**

# *Music Class*

It was 11:24 on a Tuesday in the smoldering wreckage of Ms. Swanson's classroom, and lunch was irrevocably canceled. If lunch were ever real in the first place. Jocelyn had her doubts, but she kept them to herself as she sat beside her remaining classmates behind a barricade of desks and carefully placed English composition books, finger ready on the trigger of her Glock.

It had been a rough morning for Ms. Swanson's Wonderful Wise Owls. After the usual morning announcements and the usual post-morning announcements active shooter, Ms. Swanson had tried to get them into rhythm with a lesson on adjectives and a book about the Loch Ness Monster, but then Mason threw up again and Brayden started pulling Emery's pigtails, and right around then the second active shooter showed up twenty-three minutes early (Jocelyn had raised her hand and answered right when asked and earned a butterfly sticker from the prize box), and Ms. Swanson shortly thereafter retrieved the first emergency pistol from the locked drawer behind her desk. She left Jocelyn in charge—Jocelyn was Class Captain because she was the most responsible—and then disappeared into the hallway. She hadn't been seen since, which wasn't surprising, since Ms. Swanson was their third teacher in the last week.

Then, of course, came the explosion that cracked straight through the chalkboard and tore apart the Interrogative Owl poster just above it, and then the smoke, and Jocelyn had divided the class into emergency battalions as they'd practiced and used her extra key to retrieve the second through eighteenth emergency pistols from the locker in the closet and distribute them amongst the class. They'd exchanged gunfire through the hole in the wall for a while after that. A majority of them had survived. *Majority* meant most.

"I'm bored," said Mateo from the far side of the desk fort. Cora shushed him. You didn't give away your position like that. That was second grade stuff, and they were third graders now.

The loaded silence that followed was broken by a footstep, then another. Sneakers squeaking on the black- and red-speckled white tiles in the hallway. Jocelyn signaled to her classmates to take defensive positions. This was it.

A heavy foot kicked in the classroom door. Jocelyn rose up to fire.

But suddenly a pop echoed through the hall—then another, and another, as the figure in the doorway disappeared out of view. Jocelyn signaled the rest of the class back down behind the fort and followed suit as a steady rain of fire sounded down the hallway. Then in an instant it was gone, like a stifled laugh in an inappropriate moment. Slowly, Jocelyn lifted the top of her braided, red-flecked head above the desk in search of movement in the doorway.

A boy stood there. Jocelyn nearly fired, but she practiced the ABCs like they were taught (*Always Be Cautious!*) and saw he had his hands raised above his head.

"Who are you?" said Jocelyn, her Glock trained on the target.

The boy smiled. "I'm Terrell," he said. "I'm here to take you to music class."

•

Of course they had all heard of Terrell. Terrell was legendary: the last of the sixth-graders, slipping through the shadows of the Timber Grove Elementary hallways to lend a hand to beleaguered classmates in their hour of need. Jocelyn had long believed him a myth, like lunch and sixth grade in general, because Jocelyn was a very practical young lady. Everybody said so. Yet here he was.

Now Ms. Swanson's Wonderful Wise Owls snaked through the hallways, dodging the collapsed barricades and discarded bricks into corridors Jocelyn never knew existed. But Terrell seemed to know the way. Sometimes he used the vents, he whispered, crawling in by climbing the empty, raided shelves in supply closets. Sometimes he snuck out the windows and crept back in through other entries he'd left sitting open with a pebble or a stick. And he never failed to deliver the kids in his care where they needed to go.

Terrell was lanky and lean, and he moved with graceful confidence. Still Jocelyn did her part, keeping a close watch over her class and her head on a swivel so no one could sneak up on them from the corridor behind. She practiced her DEFs like they were taught (*Defend Every Friend!*).

As they crossed hurriedly past the entrance to the gym, the doors off their hinges twisting like dangling icicles in a winter wind, tiny Levi found his way behind Terrell. "What's music class like?" he said in a voice of high-pitched wonder.

They used to call Levi Four-Eyes before his glasses were shot off last week. Now they called him One-Eye.

"You'll love it, kid," said Terrell, his eyes never leaving the dingy, foul-smelling corridor and dented lockers in front of him. "You sing songs, you learn notes—sometimes you even play instruments, if you behave."

Levi beamed, showing the gap in his teeth. "I'm good at music. I have a tambourine."

At that moment a stream of quick shots echoed from the next hall. Reacting instinctively, Terrell guided the class to a fort built of gym mats and masking tape as Jocelyn set up firing lines to cover their flank. She liked to put Cora and Kiki on the left and right because they were the tallest, and then the line looked like a smile, which was really much prettier. She held her Glock at the divot they created like a big, pointy nose. She didn't laugh because gun time was serious time.

"Hold the line. Eyes wide open," Jocelyn whispered under the staccato gunfire. "Josh, stop eating your boogers."

Josh stopped eating his boogers.

The report stopped. But that didn't mean it was safe. You always had to pay attention.

"We could double back," Terrell whispered. Jocelyn felt him beside her but didn't divert her eyes. "But that takes us past the lobby."

"Too exposed," said Jocelyn.

"Exactly." Terrell sighed. "I can sneak around. Draw fire

the other way. You all run down the hall and turn left. First door on the right is the library. Wait for me there."

After a moment, Jocelyn nodded. In the next second Terrell was gone, lighter than air, and Jocelyn kept her arms raised and her gun pointed. Her muscles were getting sore, but this was what the morning push-ups and endurance training were for.

There was silence.

Then the gunfire started again. Two different weapons. It was Terrell.

"Go!" Jocelyn whispered.

The Wise Wonderful Owls dashed out from behind their barricade and across the hallway so fast they were nearly all across before the shooter noticed. Only one-fifth of them were shot. *One-fifth* equals 20 percent.

•

It had been a long afternoon. The schedule at this point was completely messed up, such that active shooters seven through nine had arrived at more or less the same time. The good news was that they'd decided to actively shoot one another, but nevertheless it left the general vicinity of the school resource office in a hailstorm that required Ms. Swanson's Wise Wonderful Owls to maneuver out the back window of Mrs. Evelyn's baby kindergarten class for kindergarten babies and along the sidewalk about one hundred yards from the barricades that ensured no more than fourteen active shooters entered the building on any given day.

Terrell had slipped them back in through the kitchen behind the cafeteria—lunch *was* real, it turned out—and from there back into a hallway slick from sprinkler water and heavy with the lingering odor of smoke. It was only five more minutes after that when they reached an emergency exit, the X alone flickering sporadically like a firefly.

Terrell turned back toward Jocelyn with a grin.

"Through there?" she said.

"Second trailer on the right," he said. He pushed open the door. It whined on its hinges, but of course the alarm was long since disabled and Terrell clearly knew that. "I told you," he said. "I always get my class where they need to—"

A trio of shots rang out and Terrell flew sidelong onto the asphalt outside. Feeling a strange tightening across her little body, Jocelyn reacted instantaneously, wheeling her weapon toward active shooter number ten and unloading her weapon until he was forced to take cover behind the dumpster.

"Go! Now!" she shouted.

So Cora ran, and Levi ran, and Mateo and Josh and Mason and Kiki ran, and stepping sideways and keeping her weapon trained Jocelyn moved as fast she was able behind the rest of the class, darting up the ramp toward the door to the second trailer on the right. The last thing she saw before she dashed into the classroom was Terrell on the ground lying impossibly still.

Then the door was closed and there was music in the air. A kindly little woman sat behind a piano, keys and chords filling the open space overtop the hum of the air conditioning unit. The classroom was lovely. There were colorful pictures of musical notes with big cartoon eyes and disembodied smiles. There was a guitar in the corner, and Levi was already holding and shaking a tambourine.

"Welcome to music class," said the lady. "I'm Ms. Evans. Why don't you take a seat and we can begin?"

Jocelyn didn't move, though. She didn't take a seat.

"Honey?" said Ms. Evans. "What is it? What's wrong?"

They all blurred in front of her then: her friends, their instruments, the friendly decorations on the wall. Ms. Evans hit a wrong note and it all fell out of place.

"Honey?"

Jocelyn looked down at her Glock. Her eyes welled. Her heart pounded. She sniffled.

But there was no point to being sad. She knew that. She practiced her RSTs like they were taught (*Reject Sadness Together!*).

So Jocelyn flipped on the safety and slipped her Glock into the hem of her pants and sat quietly at her desk. The piano started again, and Jocelyn closed her eyes and took a deep breath, and she sang, and sang, and sang.

---

**Harrison Demchick** is a developmental editor who has worked on more than eighty published books. As an author, he's written literary horror novel *The Listeners* (Bancroft Press, 2012) and many short stories. As a screenwriter, his first film, *Ape Canyon*, won Best Feature at the 2020 Adrian International Film Festival and launched to streaming services in Spring 2021, his short *The Farmhouse* won Best Horror at Austin After Dark 2023, and short screenplay *Shipping and Handling* won the 2024 Baltimore Screenwriters Competition. Harrison currently lives in Washington, D.C. with his wife Carolyn and their two cats with a combined seven legs. You can find Harrison at www.harrisondemchick.com or www.facebook.com/HarrisonDemchick. He has not updated either.

**Sofia Ghassaei**

# *Math for Synesthetes*

Xylophonic
A cascade of
Integers
Make their way
Three by three
Two by two
Music to me
Numbers to you

---

20 year old Nonspeaker **Sofia Ghassaei** has been writing poetry all her life, you just couldn't hear it before. Her poems and writings have been published in *Teen Creative* magazine, *NeuroClastic*, and presented at the Boards and Chords Music Festival, Neurolyrical Cafe, and SpellX. Her plays *Words Unheard* and *Love Letters- A True-ly Short Epistolary Romance* were first performed by Theater of Possibility in Seattle in 2022 and 2023.

**Duff F. McCourt**

# *The Stairs Above*

From the stone and stucco architecture of the Gothic buildings flanking the marble stairs, Annette reckons she is somewhere in Italy. The somewhen is mid-14th century maybe, though it can be hard to tell. Her recollection of Gothic Architecture from *Freon—Hölderlin* is faded and the fresher memory of Stuccowork from *Somalia—Tax Law* is not up to the task.

Three men wielding bronze-tipped spears chase Annette up the steps, bound by bound, precluding further consideration of who carved the cherubs over the portico on her right, and when. Annette takes the wide stairs two at a time, a fast and steady lope driven by hamstrings, quadriceps, glutes etched by the endless flights of the great staircase. The men will not catch her. She can do this all day.

On the stairs above, however, there is a problem. At a point where the steps narrow to pass through an old Roman archway, two women are dragging earthen pots and ornate mahogany furniture out of buildings to form a barricade. Annette indulges in a momentary curiosity on the provenance of the lumber. That's New World wood and it has been a week of climbing since she last saw such a tree.

Without having found an answer, Annette whirls her long ficus walking stick above her head and—as she draws close—lashes out with it towards a raven-haired woman carrying an urn to bolster the barricade. It's a skull cracking blow, but the woman dives backwards into a stair-side door to avoid it, the pottery fracturing at her feet. Annette is glad to see her swing miss. Hostile as this conclave may be, she's not in the habit of leaving corpses in her wake. More importantly, the woman's retreat gives Annette the gap she needs to vault up onto a chest of drawers, which wobbles under her weight but does not topple.

Reaching downwards, Annette hooks the end of her staff into a large clay amphora and sends it careening and shattering down the stairs towards her pursuers. Though one man stumbles, the others hardly slow and are nearly upon her, but Annette has already leapt from the drawers up onto a tall armoire. Balanced momentarily on this unsteady perch—more than a man's height above the hard marble stairs—Annette is thankful that these steps run through open air, unceilinged. She allows herself one last lavish eyeful of the wide blue sky. The great staircase is unpredictable and it could be some days—or longer—before she next has emptiness above her.

"Stop her!" shouts the fastest of the spear-wielders, just now drawing close enough to thrust his weapon's burnished point at Annette's ankles.

"Who do you think is going to stop me?" Annette laughs as she hops to avoid the clumsy strike. Then, in a leap, she is beyond the barricade, sending the armoire and the chest of drawers both tumbling down the stairs on top of the three men. She lands, footing sure, in the shoe worn depression dead centre of the narrowing step. She plants her stick with a thwap on the stair above, more for emphasis than to steady herself.

"No one stops a long climber," she shouts over her shoulder into the chaos of splintered wood, tangled limbs, and cursing. "It's like the one thing you don't do."

And then she is through the archway and running up the long subterranean stairs of what she can only imagine to be an outlying station of the London Underground. She puts them below her in the span of a half dozen deep, even breaths.

She's just beginning to hit her stride when she emerges not into the damp air of Epping, but instead into the lush foyer of some extravagant mansion, frieze moulding and inlays evoking the Antebellum South. Her rough leather shoes trample the crimson woolen piles of the carpeted Imperial staircase as her lead grows over those who chase her. Beyond the exquisitely turned balusters, she spies the entrance to a sumptuous ground floor library, cruelly out of reach.

A domed ceiling, painted in obscene ivories and golds, vaults overhead. In Annette's path, the stairwell briefly bifurcates to make room for a gaudy central podium on which stands a mahogany statue of Caesar, a thin line of bronze beading forth like sweat on his brow, ghost of a filigree laurel coronet.

Well that explains the cabinetry and the spears, Annette notes. This realization is punctuated by a whirr and a thock, as a bronze-tipped and goose-fletched arrow flits by just inches from her cheek and buries itself into the throat of the dictator.

Where the hell did they get goose feathers?

Annette leaps the inner banister and takes cover behind the wooden Caesar, as two more arrows thump into him. Killed from the front this time at least, she muses. A glance around the statue's elbow reveals that there are but three archers. And looking ahead and up, she can see that only a few dozen steps of the grand carpeted staircase remain before it gives way to a narrow and squalid enclosed switchback stairwell of water-damaged pine and moldy wallpaper.

She makes herself as small as possible and counts as one two three more arrows are loosed. Thwap thwap thwap. She makes a break for it, hoping they are slow to nock the next flight. Back over the banister and up up up as fast as her legs will carry her.

When she is just four steps from the pine stairwell, a boy—no more than eight—materializes from nothing on the threshold. He turns towards the commotion below in the same moment that Annette, cursing, hits him hard in the midriff with her shoulder and scoops him up without breaking stride. They round the first corner of the switchback just as three arrows bury themselves half-shaft in the brown and green wallpaper behind. Still carrying the boy, she barrels on upward, turning another corner and then another before stopping.

"Let go of me!" shouts the boy, having finally caught his breath.

She drops him unceremoniously onto the steps and shoves her walking stick into his hands. He is about to say something more, but Annette shushes him so aggressively that he instead closes his mouth and begins to quiver. She pays him no mind as she drops her pack, loosens the strings and yanks out a light woolen blanket. She continues to ignore the tears welling up in the boy's eyes as she twists the blanket into a tight coil, which she then pulls taut.

Annette steps quietly down to the last stair before the corner below and stands stock still—one end of the twisted blanket in each hand—listening. The boy starts to open his mouth again, but she shuts it with a glare.

A minute that seems like an eternity passes in silence, and then Annette hears the slightest creak of damaged pine, very very close. A moment later, the tip of a bronze spear rounds the corner and, as soon as an inch of the haft is visible, Annette's blanket is looped around it, pulled tight and binding. She yanks backwards with all her strength and the spear bangs against the corner of the stairwell and then comes free with a grunt, pulling its disarmed owner stumbling around behind it. Annette catches the man in the chest with a powerful kick that sends him careening into the wallpaper. A dense cloud of fungal dust billows out around him.

Flicking the spear free of the blanket, she catches it in both hands and drives the butt of it hard into the downed man's gut, leaving him helplessly gasping for air that won't come. Spear-first, she rounds the switchback and peers downward, but no others seem to follow.

She does a quick counting of remembered steps, long experience having put her in the habit of subconsciously enumerating them in exacting detail, no matter what chaos might be demanding her conscious attention. Twenty-one steps of dismal pine. Eighty-two steps of tasteless carpeted crimson. Ninety-six steps of subway. And the Italian town itself, spanning a hundred and twenty-four steps of Italian marble. Her wheezing captive has already lost nearly three quarters of the town by chasing her this far. Brave of him, but she doubts many of his compatriots will be so self-sacrificing.

She turns and pokes the wheezing man in the foot with the tip of the spear. "Get up."

Weakly he rises to his feet, steadying himself with one hand against the dented wall. Annette nods up the stairs. "Now climb."

His eyes bulge in panic and his words come out in a strained whisper. "Please, no."

"Climb," Annette repeats, gesturing with the spearpoint.

Defeated, the man begins to take the stairs one plodding step at a time. Annette sees him glance at the boy, the staff, the pack all gathered in a pitiful heap in the stairwell.

"Keep moving or I swear I'll run you through," she says. Then, to the boy: "Grab my pack and follow close. I don't know if more are coming from below."

Annette counts steps as they climb the switchbacks. The dismal stairwell totals forty-nine and so, when they emerge onto a beautiful noonday island hillside, the Italian Gothic inhospitality of the town below is already fully lost to her captive. And to her. She halts.

"Now keep on until I can't see you," she commands. "You know I won't hesitate to come stick you if I see you stop. I am untethered."

There is no rebellion left in the man, however. Only despair. "What am I supposed to do?" he says, self-pity dripping from his words. "I have a family down in Fiorentini. Children."

"What's your name?" Annette asks.

"Darius."

"Well, Darius. You *had* a family. Then you decided to chase a long climber. Now you have the stairs. It's not a bad life. Climb."

As Darius slowly ascends the winding flagstone stairs set into the face of the hill, Annette takes a deep breath and feels herself calmed by the chill taste of salt that fills her lungs. The sky above is clear and perfect, with just a few distant clouds scudding along the horizon. To the left of the stairs, the slopes are blanketed by a long grove of olive trees. And to her right, she notes with a chuckle, a grey mother goose corrals her goslings between greyer rocks.

They are two hundred and twenty-seven steps now above the Roman arch that marks the upper bound of Fiorentini. A long way down for a goose to wander. She scans the terrain for dwellings and spies a single hut high up amid the olive trees. It seems as old as the hill, large enough for a room or two at the most, thatch roof on crooked timbers, sun faded shutters on small windows. It must house a runner, for commerce. Which means there must also be another settlement not far above. These stairs are far busier than she likes.

Darius is more than halfway up the hill now, past the hut and making his way to the doorway that straddles the top of the flagstone steps. Beyond, Annette can just make out the painted concrete stairwell of a parking garage or some similar structure.

Just then, in her peripheral, she catches a blur of movement. The boy! He's chasing after a gosling, up the hill and off away from the stairs. Annette drops the spear and sprints after him, her heart in her throat. She snatches him up just as the pebbles and scrub grass beneath her feet begin to turn icy and immaterial. Sweating cold rivers, she backpedals to the stairs, the boy held tight in her arms.

At the top of the wallpapered stairwell, Annette sets him down and grips his right hand firmly in her clammy and shaking left. A glance uphill shows no trace of Darius. Quickly gathering her pack, Annette marches the boy back down twenty-eight dingy stairs and is relieved to find her ficus staff still where she left it.

With effort, she steadies her breathing, her heart rate, and then looks at the boy properly for the first time. She's never spent much time with children, but she's pretty sure he's older than she first thought. Maybe ten? But small for his age. His skin is sallow and his hair straw. His eyes are filled with defiance and anger built on a bedrock of fear. It's an expression she remembers well from childhood mirrors.

"I'm Annette."

"Owen." His voice is as gaunt as he is.

"Do you know where you are, Owen?"

"I think I'm in the back kitchen stairs."

"You are and you aren't," she says. "You were climbing them, yes?"

"Yeah."

"And then you got to the top and kept climbing."

"Yeah. I guess so."

"So that's where you are. Above your back kitchen stairs."

Owen thinks on this for a long second. "Why are there ducks above the back kitchen stairs?"

"There aren't," Annette says. "There are *geese* above some other stairs in some other place. A Greek island would be my guess."

She has had this conversation before. This is the point where people ask if they're dreaming, if they're going mad, if they're dead. They are never easy to convince otherwise, not least because so many are sleepwalking or high out of their minds the first time they manage to step up from the top stair. She's been cursed as a djinn, attacked as a hallucination, embraced as an angel. It's tedious.

But Owen just scrunches his face up and works his way through it, until evidently finding a hook to hang his disorientation on. "So it's like Harry Potter's Platform 9¾?"

"I don't know who Harry Potter is," Annette says. "But let's just go ahead and say yes."

"Are you a wizard, then? Am *I* a wizard?"

Annette can't help but laugh. That's a new one. "Yes. I'm a wizard. That's why those men were shooting arrows at me. Because I turned their king into a toad with my magic staff."

By the time he realizes she's messing with him, Annette is already pulling the wallpaper from the wall, revealing the water damaged pine boards behind. The construction is so shoddy that she is able to pull the boards free with her bare hands.

"What are you doing?" he asks.

"I'm making a shield," she says, pulling a multitool from her pack so she can extract the rusty nails from the planks. "Those archers might still be there, and I'm out of magic."

It's slow work, but Annette has the patience of the long climb. In time, she has assembled a tall rectangle, two planks thick and with a handle twisted from electrical wire. It is large enough for both her and Owen to hide behind. By the time she is satisfied with her efforts, young growth of pine can already be seen sprouting from the stringer, the first of the boards she pulled down regenerating itself like an unlucky axolotl.

Annette hefts the shield, pleased with herself. "Now, let's get you back home."

"But why *were* they chasing you?" Owen asks as they descend towards the grand carpeted stairs.

"They're jealous of their secrets," Annette says. "Worried of what I might tell those farther up the stairs."

Owen opens his mouth to ask another question, but she shushes him. She knows the questions could flow eternal, and they have reached the last landing. Annette listens for a long minute and hears nothing but their own breathing. She places one hand on Owen's chest, signaling that he should stay, then slowly extends the shield out past the corner into line of sight from below. No arrows come.

Cautiously, she steps out as well and peers around the shield's edge. Aside from the pin-cushioned Caesar—steadfastly ignoring her—Annette finds the garish mansion steps empty. With a sigh of relief, she waves for Owen to follow her down the last few pine stairs.

Two steps from the brink, Owen stops, marveling at the opulence below. "I can't go down there, can I? As soon as I go down these last couple of steps, I'm in the back kitchen stairs again, right? The real ones? That's how it works?"

"That's how it works."

"And I can only go down these ones? If I have to go back to the other world, I think I'd rather do it where the geese are."

"Each climber gets just the one exit, I'm afraid."

Owen nods sadly, as though he hadn't really dared to hope it would be otherwise. "Can I come back though? Just to see the geese?"

Annette sighs. "You can do whatever you want, kid, but I'll be long gone. And if you come back, you're as likely as not to catch an arrow in the spine or be captured for a slave. Or worse. This is a dangerous stretch, I'm afraid. How would your parents feel if you climbed the back kitchen stairs and never came back?"

At the mention of his parents, the dreamy wonder drains from Owen's expression and a tide of unease washes visibly over him.

A memory wells up in Annette from so long ago that the intervening decades cloud it with uncertainty, from another world that she most days forgets even exists. She remembers the anger in the voices booming unhindered through her thin bedroom walls. She remembers the pounded tables, the shattered glass. She carefully does not remember the worse things that came later, that had her passing long nights in the woods, sleeping under the bushes with feral dogs rather than face what awaited her at home. She hadn't yet known how to reach the top and keep climbing or surely she would have when she was younger still than the boy before her.

"Look," she says, pinching the bridge of her nose. "I can wait here for one day. As far as spots on this forsaken stretch of stair, there are worse ones than this."

She sets the tall tower shield on the second carpeted stair from the top, then wedges the spear into the riser to support it, forming a makeshift wall.

"They can't dislodge me from here with archers alone," she continues. "And no foot soldiers are going to be keen to follow in Darius's footsteps."

"One day," Owen says.

"Yes," Annette says. "But only if you *need* to come back. Much better if you don't. And, if I'm not here, promise you'll return home immediately."

Owen nods seriously and readies himself to step down into mundanity.

"Oh," Annette says, halting him mid-step. "If you do come back... bring candy."

●

The hard strawberry lozenge suffuses Annette's being with sweetness. She closes her eyes and leans her head back against the wallpaper in bliss.

"I'm sorry I couldn't get the good stuff," Owen says, crunching his own lozenge wastefully. "My dad gets drunk and eats everything good. All we had left was grandma candy."

"Shh," says Annette. "It's perfect."

"There's no candy here?"

"Shh," Annette says again, but after savouring the phantom of an imagined strawberry a moment longer, she opens her eyes and looks at the boy. "How many candy stores do you know with staircases inside them?"

"There must be a few," he says.

"And if I find one, maybe that will be the day I stop climbing."

Owen thinks about that for a minute, reaching into his plastic bag for another lozenge as though there were a limitless supply. "What's above the geese?"

Annette shrugs. "I'll know when I get there."

"Yeah, but you must talk to people. Someone must have told you *something* about what's up there."

"If they'd been up there," she says. "They'd still be up there. It's a one-way climb."

"What do you mean?" he asks. "Why?"

"Why?" she scoffs. "You expect me to know the why of this place? Do you know the why of your world? I imagine there's something magical about up. Up is a place that doesn't exist on its own. Ten thousand years ago, some person was in some place—some real place—and the thought occurred to them, why shouldn't there be another place above this one? So they built some stairs and the universe was reshaped, transmuted into a new geometry where there is always some new place above. That's where we are. Above. And when you're above, the only way you can go is up."

Owen's eyebrows squeeze together and his forehead wrinkles. "That's not true. We were up and then we came back down."

"You can go down a *bit*," she says. "How far up do you reckon we were before?"

"I *reckon*," he says, putting inexpert parody on the word, "about 50?"

"We were exactly 74 stairs up from here when you nearly chased a gosling off into the void," she says. "You learn to always count. The magic number is 223, and don't bother asking me why. 223 steps you can descend and then, on the 224th, the great staircase twists around you, your organs turn inside out, and you find the step you thought was down is actually up. You're climbing again. And so you can keep moving forever, never to see the same stretch twice. Or you can find a place that suits you and stop, knowing that you've shrunk your horizons to nothing. Almost everyone eventually stops."

"How many steps have you climbed?"

"That answer will cost you another piece of candy."

Owen passes over the whole bag. "You can have them all. They're gross as—"

Annette abruptly raises her hand for silence. Footfalls on carpet. Not an easy approach to hear, but her subconscious has long since catalogued every conceivable stairsound, tuned her alertness to them exquisitely.

From her pack she retrieves the multitool and flicks out its blade. *Get ready to go,* she mouths silently to Owen, inclining her head meaningfully to the boundary between the stairs. In a crouch, she peers around the edge of the shield wall, knife in hand.

Just abreast of the statue, a woman with shiny black hair leads a young girl—smaller still than Owen—by the hand. With her other arm, the woman clutches an infant to her breast. Mother and girl both are heavily laden with packs of goose leather. Hatred boils in the woman's harried eyes when she spies Annette.

Annette stands and calls down. "You're the lady who thought pottery could stop me."

"You tried to kill me," the woman says.

"I didn't though. You're looking for Darius."

The woman looks meaningfully at the steel blade in Annette's hand. "What did you do to him, you witch?"

"I sent him climbing."

"Then you're going to let us follow him." It's not a question. Annette nods and shuts the knife.

As the family trudges past the lean-to, Owen stares at the little girl, transfixed. She raises a hand slightly to wave at him, a constrained motion kept carefully below the line of her mother's angry gaze.

Annette draws a foil wrapped lozenge from the bag and holds it out to the girl. "You'll love this."

The girl begins to reach tentatively for the offered candy, but her mother yanks her roughly away by the arm. And then they are gone up into the switchbacks of the back kitchen stairs.

Owen watches after the family long past the fading away of their footsteps.

"Forty-seven million, two hundred and ninety thousand, three hundred and two," says Annette, breaking the silence.

•

In a shallow rock pit under the Greek sky, Annette coaxes a meagre fire from dry olive branches. On the once-shield-now-table beside her, an omelette of goose eggs waits in her prized copper pan for the flame.

Owen had been scandalized when Annette first started gathering the eggs, but he'd relented once she'd asked if he would prefer to make an expedition to his house for supplies. They couldn't subsist indefinitely on high fructose corn syrup and artificial strawberry flavouring alone. Besides, the eggs would be back tomorrow. The exact same eggs.

They'd been two days on the hillside. The old man in the hut had taken their measure from afar the previous day and then gone about his business. Annette had evaluated him in turn and appraised him a runner indeed, a solitary courier anchoring himself between worlds so that he may bridge the information and trade divide between Fiorentini below and whatever lay above. No threat from his person, Annette had concluded, for surely the old man was not party to Fiorentini's most closely guarded secrets.

Then, that morning, Darius himself had reappeared from the concrete stairs above, unarmed and clothed not in the garb of a soldier but in a clean white Oxford shirt and grey woolen trousers. He'd waved meekly at Annette and Owen—as though to contend that bygones were truly by and gone—and then proceeded to the hut, where he'd been let in after a single knock.

Now, while the omelette bubbles and fills the spring air with a savoury aroma that rumbles Annette's stomach, Darius finally emerges from the hut, casts one furtive glance down towards their encampment, and then disappears up-wards again.

"He didn't go far," Owen says.

"They never do."

"There must be something good up there."

"There always is. Eventually."

"What do you think he was talking to the old man about?"

"It doesn't matter," Annette says as she serves half the omelette into her only bowl for Owen. "That's the true blessing of the long climber. Whatever it is that concerns those two, that concerns those down in Fiorentini, those in the settlement above, it ceases to exist in just two hundred and twenty three steps."

As they eat—Annette straight from the pan—Owen finally says the words that have been lurking in the air for days. "I want to stay. I want to be a long climber."

Annette looks up from her eggs to take the measure of his conviction. His shoulders are set in a flimsy performance of confidence. His eyes meet hers and he holds her gaze without looking away, though she can see him sweating from the effort.

She shrugs and turns her attention back to her meal. "You're going to need your own bowl."

"You're not going to tell me I can't?"

"You're your own person."

"I am," he says uncertainly. "Do you think it's a good idea?"

"Absolutely not."

●

After they've eaten and cleaned up, Annette quickly ventures back down the back kitchen stairs, to ensure that no new surprises are brewing below. Upon her return, she settles in to read for a spell. It's a daily observance and she's skipped it twice now. She can't let herself get in the habit of letting habits lapse. All her routines are survival strategies, she reminds herself.

She demands an hour of silence from Owen. He manages about ten minutes. She's honestly impressed.

"Is that a *paper* encyclopedia?" the question finally bursts out of him.

She makes an exaggerated show of patiently closing *Unified Field Theory—Wallonia*, thumb holding her spot halfway down Uranium.

"You would prefer clay tablets? It's heavy enough as it is."

"Haven't you ever heard of the Internet?"

"Heard of it? Yes. But only from people who made the wrong decision when they chose to climb."

That shuts him up for a while. When she reaches Uranus, she takes pity and begins to read aloud.

"—from the union of Gaea and Uranus sprang the Titans, the Cyclopes, and the Hecatoncheires. But Uranus so hated his children that he imprisoned them inside Gaea's body. Distressed, Gaea fashioned a sickle of diamond and gave it to the youngest Titan, Cronus, who she then freed, encouraging him to exact vengeance upon his father."

Owen's hands have gone still, gripping tightly the bit of goose bone he had been fidgeting with. Annette carefully keeps her voice level, not betraying that she too is struck to the heart by the story. The encyclopedia always surprises, offering what is needed in unpredictable ways.

"The next time Uranus came to lay with Gaea," she continues reading, "Cronus ambushed his father and castrated him with the diamond sickle. The blood that spilled forth from the severed testicles of Uranus begat the Furies, the Giants, and the Nymphs."

"Fucking right," Owen says under his breath.

Annette is about to forge on into the downfall and exile of the sky god, but her narration is halted by a movement higher up on the stairs. The old runner has emerged from his hut—at least Darius didn't murder him, Annette is relieved to see—and he is making his way slowly down the hill towards them.

Annette slips the single heavy volume back into her pack. With a look, she conveys to Owen the need to be ready for anything. The boy's hand goes to the haft of Darius's spear, but she shakes her head once no, not yet.

Indeed, as the man draws near, he seems anything but a threat. His gait is slow and deliberate, his posture unworried. His wispy white beard catches the sea breeze like grass, giving him the aspect of an old unkillable tree. Set deep in his walnut visage, two dark eyes pool amiably.

Annette stands—staff in hand—and greets the man while he is still a dozen wide steps above, the tone of her voice friendly, but also conveying clearly that he is quite close enough. The old man stops and considers them for a long moment.

"You're long climbers then," he says at last, his voice gruff but clear.

"I am," Annette says.

"We both are," Owen quickly adds.

"Well, when are you going to get on with it then?"

"Soon enough," Annette says. "Are we unwelcome here?"

"A long climber asking if she's welcome," the man laughs. "Now I've heard everything. You know full well that you're not. Beggars and thieves the lot of you."

"Do you see us begging? Do you see us thieving?"

"Ask the geese, I reckon," the runner says. Owen stifles a laugh and the old man frowns at him before continuing. "I've climbed a long way myself. I've known enough long climbers to know not to trust anyone who never looks back, who runs away from every problem and leaves every consequence behind. What you do here today is lost to you with tomorrow's climb. Unaccountable. Your mess ours to clean up."

Annette glances at the warm cinders of the fire pit. "The hill will heal itself soon enough."

"You know that's not what I mean," the man says.

"I understand you," Annette allows. "We'll be heading up this evening."

"Very good then."

The old man scratches at his beard and does not move, as though he is quite happy to wait right there for evening to come.

"That man who came to your house this morning," Owen pipes up. "What did he want?"

The runner weighs the question and evidently decides it will cost him nothing to answer. "The same. He wanted to know what I knew of you two. I told him long climbers weren't worth knowing. He's a refugee from Fiorentini below. More mess, but he's sticking around to face it. I can respect that."

Owen opens his mouth to say more, but then tightens his lips of his own accord. Annette smiles inwardly in approval. The boy has sound instincts for the long climb.

Annette bends down and opens her pack. From one of the small inner pockets, she withdraws a tight-wrapped linen sachet, no larger than an acorn.

"We're not running away from anything," she says. "Not really. It's just that we're not running towards, either. The climb itself is home. It's the purpose. It's the gift. Yes, I may beg when I have need and the people are kind. Yes, I've stolen when I had need and the people were not. But I always hope, on this eternal pilgrimage, that I can honour the beauty I find without needing to make it unduly my own. That I can give as much as I take."

She tosses the sachet up to the man. "It's nutmeg," she says. "From a tree half a million stairs below."

The man catches the spice packet and holds it up to the sun briefly before pressing it against his white bough of a mustache and inhaling deeply. His eyes focus beyond the horizon.

"Sri Lanka," he says wistfully. "The name's Arjuna. Take all the time you need."

•

They're in the back kitchen stairs again, for the last time. Evening has come. Annette pauses at the final corner before the bottom, as she has on every one of her cautious reconnaissances since Owen's return. Reassuring silence has greeted her every time. Anticipating quietude, Annette almost rounds the corner before consciously registering the faint sounds of distant conversation. She holds up a finger to Owen, signaling stillness.

Though Annette can not make out the words that are being said, the voices sound casual and unworried to her ears. Gossip. Small talk. A laugh. And then the almost imperceptible sound of boots stepping from carpet to concrete. She risks a quick peek around the corner and catches a glimpse of two bronze spearpoints disappearing down the Underground stairs.

They're patrolling now, Annette takes note. She castigates herself for having tarried this long, knowing what danger might soon come from Fiorentini. But no longer. She and Owen will push these places below them quickly now, one step at a time.

"You know what you need?" Annette asks for the third time. "A sturdy backpack. A knife. A multitool would be better. A blanket. A bowl. As much nonperishable food as you can carry."

"Yes," Owen says. "I know the list."

"But quickly," Annette says. "If it takes you too long to find something, forget it. The stairs will provide. Eventually."

Owen shifts from foot to foot nervously. "Look—" he begins, and Annette knows immediately what's coming.

"It's the right decision." As she says it, she hopes it is true. Though she'd been deeply uncomfortable with his zeal for the long climb, though she had feared the regret and recrimination that might be a week or a decade away, and though she'd been continually vexed by the way he casually complicated her every routine, she is gutted to now face the prospect of carrying on without his companionship. It's a flavour of loss she hasn't tasted in a very long time. Her tongue abhors it.

Owen wavers meekly still, grasping for words. "I want the climb," he says. "I want it more than anything. But if I'm not there, I think he might kill her."

Annette's chest swells with something halfway between pride and fear. "It's been a long time since *Conifer—Dystopia*," she says. "But, as I recall it, things don't end happily for Cronus."

"I'll be okay," he reassures them both, unconvincingly. "I won't forget you."

"You will and you won't," Annette says. "There will come a time, not long from now, when you will convince yourself that I was a dream. That this place was a flight of youthful imagination. But I will be here, I will be real, and I will be thinking of you."

Owen nods, his eyes quivering one incautious thought away from tears. He starts to say something, but thinks better of it. Instead, he reaches out, touches Annette's hand for a moment—as though cementing her corporeality in his memory—nods again. Then he turns, takes one step down, and is gone.

Annette is alone. As she has always been. With a rap of her walking stick on the mildewed pine, she turns and resumes the long climb.

Step by step up the back kitchen stairs, she chases the familiar meditative rhythm of the climb. This is what she was made for. She has always done this alone. Her legs are pistons and they drive the world into focus. Up. Up. Up.

But it is not as it was. Where once her mind was empty, clean, sublime, it is now cluttered with concern and misgiving. She involuntarily concocts cascading variations on how Owen's story may play out, in search of one that will let her sleep soundly in the coming nights. She doesn't find it.

The distraction of this fractal tragedy carries Annette six stairs higher than where she would have otherwise halted. Something is amiss, her instincts have been screaming for half a dozen paces, and by the time her mind registers the warning it is too late. She is out in the cool dusk air of the hillside, exposed.

Darius steps from behind an olive tree, crossbow in hand. There is no hope of retreating to the switchbacks. The string of the bow is taut, bolt loaded and ready. His eyes are apologetic. His finger, resting lightly on the trigger of the crossbow, is not.

"Where's the boy?"

Annette takes in his clean shaven face, his neatly combed hair, his pristine hiking boots, and his freshly laundered clothes. "You've done well for yourself up there," she says. "And quickly."

"What can I say?" Darius shrugs, the point of the bolt never wavering from Annette's heart. "I'm charming."

Suddenly, it all makes sense. "You did it, didn't you? You did the very thing you were willing to kill to prevent me from doing."

Darius smiles sadly and Annette continues, piecing it together out loud. "You told them Fiorentini prepares for war. Did you say you were a conscientious defector, climbing of your own accord to prevent a slaughter?"

"It was the best option you left me."

"And Arjuna, this morning. You came down to get your story straight. To ascertain how much he had seen. Would you have killed him if he'd known the truth?"

Darius's smile is more pained now. "I don't know. I'm not what you think I am."

"You are though. You're weak and you're scared. You'll justify anything as necessary. But it isn't. You could just fucking climb."

"I have a wife!" He's angry now and she sees the muscles in his forearm tensing. "I have children! The climb would kill them."

Annette's survival mind is spinning fast, calculating which direction to dive when the trigger pull comes. There are no good ones. "It was her idea, wasn't it? She sent you to kill me. To make sure that no other stories catch up to you."

"Where is the boy?"

Annette is reaching for an answer that will buy her more time, time in which Darius might make a mistake, might lower his weapon for just an instant. But before she can find one, she hears light footsteps coming quickly up the back kitchen stairs and her heart sinks.

"Annette!" Owen's voice is urgent, terrified.

Against every long-honed instinct, Annette turns her back on the crossbow and welcomes Owen into her arms. He is shaking. She holds him tight, keeping her body carefully between him and Darius.

"He has a gun!" Owen says into her sleeve. And then Annette hears the other footfalls below.

The man who rounds the corner of the stairs is heavyset and breathing hard. He exhales clouds of sour whisky, his face red with exertion and burst capillaries. His bare feet slap the pine treads. He wears only underpants and a stained Metallica t-shirt.

"Get your hands off him," he shouts, gasping between each word and waving the menacing black pistol all around for emphasis. "And get the fuck out of my house!"

The horizontal rays of the setting Greek sun in her eyes, Annette tries to envelop Owen completely, shielding him somehow from all sides. She glares at the man and wills him to drop the gun. "This isn't your—"

The crossbow bolt buzzes by Annette's cheek like a hornet and lodges itself in the gunman's left shoulder with a wet thump. She throws herself off the stairs, lifting Owen fully into her arms as she does so. They land in a bruised heap amid the rocks. Startled geese take to the air, abandoning their goslings.

She hears but does not see the gunshot, her body curled tight over Owen like a shell. Glancing back through the gap between her elbow and her knee, she sees Darius drop his crossbow and sit down heavily on the flagstone stair, both hands clasped over his stomach.

Annette rolls quickly backwards, her hand finding her ficus walking stick among the pebbles and her body spinning athletically as she rises. The long end of the staff whips in a deadly arc through the air and cracks hard into the hand that limply holds the still smoking pistol.

The gun discharges into the sky as it flies free of the man's grip. He shakes his injured hand in the air and curses—"mother*fucker*"—but his wide horrified eyes never stray from Darius, dying before him.

His pickled mind is still catching up to events when Annette's *inquartata* turn brings the butt end of the staff around to strike him square in the chest, knocking every whisper of air from his lungs. He drops to the ground like a sack of offal, a pitiful squeak stuck halfway in his throat.

The sun dips below the line of the sea, painting the hillside red.

Owen rushes to his father's side and howls. "He's bleeding! He's dying! Don't die you—fuck! Help him!"

Annette kneels and tears the punctured sleeve, exposing the wound. The crossbow bolt is lodged deep in his arm, just below the shoulder joint. It looks like it could be stuck in the bone, and she fears it may have nicked an artery as well. Blood wells out in heavy red pulses from around the shaft. The injured man whimpers.

Annette rips the bloody t-shirt asunder, tearing a thick strip of cotton for a tourniquet and exposing a great expanse of pallid and flabby torso. As she ties the fabric tight around the arm, just above the wound, she accidentally jostles the bolt. Owen's father releases a horrendous shriek that sends the returned mother goose winging again for the sky. When

Annette looks back down, she sees that he has passed out from the pain, his breathing shallow and ragged.

"Is there a hospital near your home?" Annette asks Owen.

"In town," he says. "Almost an hour away."

"Shit."

"There's a doc…" The words come thinly from Darius' lips. Annette and Owen both turn to where he sits in a growing pool of his own blood, face white as a bleached bone and body swaying like a dead tree in the wind.

"Up above," Darius continues weakly through a burble of blood. "There's a doctor. A good one."

"I don't think a doctor will be able to help you," Annette tells him.

Darius chokes out a pained grunt that might be a laugh. "No. For him."

Annette looks back to Owen. "If we take him…"

"I know."

Annette nods. She points uphill to the hut. "Go quickly then. Get Arjuna. Tell him I need help cleaning up a mess."

As Owen sprints up the wide flagstone stairs, Annette fetches the one-time shield, one-time table, and carries it over so that it may serve one final role as a stretcher. With a groan, she heaves and drags the limp—but still breathing— body of Owen's father onto the planks.

By the time Owen returns with Arjuna, Annette has re- trieved a length of strong nylon rope from her pack and tied it firmly to the joins of the pine boards, fashioning a rudimentary sledge. One single loop of rope crosses Owen's father's bare chest and winds under his armpits, holding him fast. The pistol is heavy in her pocket.

"What happened here?" Arjuna's eyes are wide as he takes in the scene of mayhem and bloodshed, the strange fat man stripped down to his undergarments and lashed, bleeding, to the rotting pine.

"A misunderstanding," Annette says.

Arjuna leans down to take stock of Darius' injuries, but the dying man waves him away.

"This one can still be saved," Annette says, gesturing to Owen's father. "Will you help me get him to the doctor?"

Without saying anything more, Arjuna takes up the rope with Annette and slowly they begin the arduous climb. The sledge catches on every stair—Owen running alongside to guide it free each time—but it holds together and they gradually put more and more of the hill below them. When they reach the doorway to the parking garage, their clothes are drenched in sweat and their hands are bloody welts of rope burn.

Looking down to the base of the hill, Annette sees Darius—a child's doll at this distance—silently slump over and then lay still in the twilight. They pause only a moment before proceeding up the dim concrete steps of the garage—somewhere in Lagos, judging by the signage—the sledge trailing steeply behind them like an infernal anchor. As they labour, Annette mumbles an ancient stair blessing for Darius, one she first heard from another long climber some thirty million stairs below.

Eight steps, a wide landing, eight more steps, another landing. Stop. Breathe. Climb.

At the fourth landing, as she and Arjuna catch their breath once again, Annette puts her hand on Owen's shoulder, leaning on him more heavily than she had intended.

"How—" she wheezes. "How many steps up are we? Have you been counting?"

"Two hundred and seventeen," Owen says without hesitation.

"Your mother needs you."

Owen's stoic expression crumbles and he throws his arms around Annette's midriff, squeezing her so tightly she fears her aching spine might crack.

"Don't let him die," Owen sobs into the sweat-soaked shoulder of her tunic.

"I won't," she says. "I promise."

Owen extricates himself and takes one long last look at his father, impotent and pitiable on the planks of the back kitchen stairs like a plucked chicken on the butcher block.

Without saying anything more, he turns and is away down the long slope of the hill, taking the natural incline of the rock and scrub in quick easy strides, eschewing the stairs. Down down down into a future of futile missing person reports and complicated grief. A future as a man with a secret that keeps him one foot ever in dream. Cronus, young god of the righteous harvest, the turning seasons, may his reign last forever.

And then he is gone and Annette and Arjuna are climbing. Eight steps, landing, eight steps, breathe.

•

She can see why people stay, why Fiorentini readies for war. In all her years of climbing, she can't recall encountering a more auspicious confluence of stairs. They call it Cháng-ê and it is a paradise.

The lower part of town is somewhere in the foothills of China's southwestern mountains, locked forever in time at the height of the mid-autumn mooncake festival. Paper lanterns in all shapes and sizes hang from posts bracketing the carved stone stairs, each smooth step several paces deep, a serene meander up the gentle slope. The homes alongside the stairs are simple, rustic, charming, and sound. Ming dynasty. Chickens and pigs root in garden pens, slaughtered for each evening meal and rising again like the warriors of Valhalla each morning. In the predawn chill, the canopies of thousand year tea trees rustle above like a great green blanket.

This idyll stretches for 112 glorious steps—of which Darius, she realizes, never saw more than half, tethered below by his doomed perfidy. It then gives way to a vision of the sort that long climbers whisper only wistfully about in the late hours of the night. Twenty two broad white stairs, with newels of steel and banisters of oak, swoop in a curve through the centre of what a striking overhead sign declares to be the main showroom of Macy's Herald Square, Manhattan.

A pair of young men lounge all day long on the stairs with hooked telescoping poles, ready to reach into the forest of early twentieth century capitalism arrayed below in racks, shelves, and display counters. Angora shawls, expensive leather shoes, typewriters, evening gowns, the finest jewelry and timepieces, whatever a climber desires, they will hook it in from the void in exchange for a single local coin. And Annette's pockets had been heavy when she first encountered this cornucopia, having yesterday sold the gun that killed Darius—and the ten unspent rounds—to Cháng-ê's armourer at the very first price he offered. He'd been eager to buy it, frantic as he was overseeing the hurried construction of crossbows and spears for the coming war.

After settling with the doctor and filling her pack with dried goods from the market stall, Annette had still been left with more money than she could spend in months. And her destination was far above the tender of this currency, on a timescale measured in days. It had thus been no problem at all to pay for a little hookpole shopping. A sturdy new rucksack. A new pair of boots. An alpaca wool blanket both lighter and warmer than the tattered rag she'd been carrying. Even a brimmed hat with a feather in it, which she would surely discard in a week's time when she ceased to be amused by it.

And, above New York, a greater wonder still. The upper reaches of Cháng-ê extended into the heart of Bombay, a narrow spiral staircase climbing shelf by shelf through the stories of a cramped antique bookseller of exquisite taste. Annette had been tempted to dump her newly purchased food supplies directly over the railing, to load her rucksack entirely with words.

As she picks her way down now through the early morning sounds of lower Cháng-ê, the weight of her restraint sits lightly on her shoulders. The jerky and dried fruits—and the hefty bag of candied ginger—remain ensconced in her rucksack, accompanied by just a few thin tomes and a single more substantial volume. The greatest treasure of the day, *Wallpaper—Wuwei*.

Annette takes a seat on the stairs in front of the little house that serves as a school for the children of Cháng-ê. Classes will be starting soon for the day, lessons drawn from all the collected knowledge of Bombay. Jealous of the school-children, Annette digs the encyclopedia from her pack and treats herself to a few paragraphs of Wandering Jew (*Tradescantia fluminensis*) while she waits.

The cockerel across the way coughs up a strangled morning crow, stamps its feet in embarrassment, and then tries again. A clear and piercing cockadoodledoo cuts through the morning, setting sleepers grumbling and feet shuffling up and down the length of Cháng-ê.

The students begin to arrive, chattering, jibing, shoving, laughing. Among them, one girl lumbers morosely, eyes obscured by raven curls, feet still catching uncertainly on Chinese stone where they expect Italian marble. When she spies Annette, she scowls and turns away. But Annette is not ready to leave her alone. Not yet.

Moving to block the girl's path, Annette retrieves from her pocket a silk kerchief knotted around a heavy knot of coin. She crouches and presses it into the unwilling hand of Darius's daughter. "Hold on to this for me, until your mother is ready to accept it."

"She hates you," the girl says. "We don't want your money."

"It was never mine."

"She's talking to the chief again today," the girl warns. "She's going to convince him to hang you after all. You'll see."

"She won't have any more luck today than she did yesterday, I'm afraid," Annette says. "The chief trusts Arjuna's word. And nobody hangs a long climber. Why bother, when we exile ourselves."

"I hate you, too." But she pockets the coins nonetheless.

•

The killer sleeps convalescent on a low bed, a heavy cotton bandage swaddled tight and thick around his wounded shoulder. Sweat beads on his liver spotted brow and he writhes fitfully in a well-deserved unhappy dream, but his stubbled cheeks have a healthy redness to them. The doctor's garden is well stocked with traditional medicinal species, which he has put to expert use.

"Hey, Uranus," Annette says, nudging the sleeping man's flabby midriff with a boot. "Wake up."

He stirs, grumbling. "What did you call me?"

"You'll get used it ," she says, holding out a small jug. "Now drink this. The doc says you might get the shakes otherwise."

He sits up with a groan, takes the jug, and sniffs it skeptically. The tang of fermented rice lights up his eyes and he takes a long and thirsty swallow. "It's watered down," Uranus complains, smacking his lips.

"Yes. We're weaning you off. Now get your boots on. We've already lost too much of the day. I want to put five thousand stairs below us by dusk."

He takes another greedy pull of the rice wine before responding. "Why won't anyone tell me where I am? Where's my son? And I'm not going anywhere with you."

"You're above. He's below. And yes you are. I promised Owen I'd keep you alive and there's a war coming to these parts. You're no warrior."

His face twists into an ugly expression, easy anger, practiced vitriol, latent violence. But Annette is not his usual adversary. She does not quail. She simply stares at him with steady patience and honest pity, an immovable pillar of stair-hardened muscle.

He deflates entirely, withers into the bed, and begins to sob. "What have I done?"

Annette sits beside him, hip to hip. She lifts the jug from his hand and takes a single sober swallow. She adjusts her hat to a more sympathetic angle.

"You were a shit father," she says. "I expect you'll be a shit climber and an even shitter companion. But you have all the time in the world to learn."

Uranus—lost still, but getting used to it—blinks his eyes and stretches his stair climbing legs.

---

**D.F. McCourt** became proficient in English at an early age and has relied exclusively on that one skill ever since. He chooses to live in the French-speaking parts of Canada.

**Ian Li**

# *Memorized|Mesmerized*

I see reflected in the digits of pi
the quizzical stares of strangers
wondering what compels a child
to memorize lifeless strings of numbers.

But they've never felt the rhythmic urgency
of reciting digits, spilling them from their tongue
before they trip over each other, rolling waves
that lap soothingly at their spiky neurons, pulsing
like primeval music.

For the numbers I speak under my breath
like quatrains of flowing verse
are whispered promises that familiarities
might bloom into new discoveries,
a reassurance that we'll never know this universe precisely
but that doesn't mean we shouldn't try.

---

**Ian Li** (he/him) is a Chinese-Canadian writer of speculative fiction and poetry. As a neurodivergent economist and developer, he also loves spreadsheets, statistical curiosities, and brain teasers. His writing is published or forthcoming in *Orion's Belt*, *Abyss & Apex*, and *Worlds of Possibility*, among other venues. Learn more at https://ian-li.com.

**Dora M Raymaker**

# Play by Numbers

## 1. The Plan

The Parlor night club looked a little different in Eric's city of monsters than in my city of magic but seeing it always put a smile on my face.

I'd come to visit Eric, my almost-alternate in this parallel world. I was refining the physics equations for how I slipped realities and wanted his input. We had different histories, and saw solutions in different ways, but he was the only person I could share the maths part of me with because we had the same maths brain.

Unlike my city of neon deco and subtle whispers of magic, here rampant biotech made a city of vampires, shapeshifters, and bioluminescent eyeballs that functioned as streetlamps. Sticky vines, engineered into disturbing filigrees, gave the place a dark, oily look.

Both manifestations of the city were hungry. Only in this one, hunger wasn't lack of bread; it was lack of blood and flesh. Those who could afford it ate blood pills instead of each other, but here on the poor side of town I kept the collar of my leather turned up to hide my neck.

In any reality, The Parlor was my home. The bar never ran dry on account of the distillery in the basement, and the ground-floor club played our bands. The second story served as an office and community space plus a few bedrooms. I climbed up there, into the warm light. Ava, the club manager, laughed with our friends over a board game. Someone strummed a guitar, conferred, strummed again, working out a tune. We might not have had enough to eat, but we had each other, and we had our art, and everything glued together.

Eric looked over as I walked in, feeling the heat between us.

That sounded like a cheesy way to say we wanted to bang each other, which we did, but I meant temperature too.

Our physical attraction was a physics attraction, the effect of my imperfect duplication across manifestations of the city. Eric and I were so close to doppelgangers that we almost spontaneously combusted when we touched.

He came over grinning, stopping just before proximity made sucking face inevitable. "Hey Mac."

He ran a hand through the short, natural spikes of his blond hair as I pushed back the slippery hank of black that always escapes my ponytail. The simultaneous gesture made us look like two sides of an imperfect mirror.

I grinned and relaxed into my scene. "Hey."

"It's good times we've made here, isn't it?" Eric looped his thumbs into his belt.

"Fuck, yeah." I felt too many good things at once to do more than swear.

Then Eric said, just as casually, "Too bad we're going to lose it all."

My rational brain took a moment to process Eric's words, and by then my feelings had already expressed themselves in a, "FUCKING WHAT?"

Everyone turned to look at me.

"Shit. Sorry." I spat between my fingers to ward off evil as the attention turned away. "What do you mean 'going to lose it all?' I mean, that's not the fuck going to happen."

"Let's talk." Eric nodded toward his bedroom.

I followed him into the vertigo of what, in my city, was my bedroom. Eric's colorful artwork plastered the walls instead of my black-and-white band posters. An empty jar of blood pills sat beside a vial of what looked like actual preserved blood and the tip of someone's finger. I didn't want to know what that was about. Everything in this city from door locks to property deeds to bus tickets worked on some kind of biomatter. Eric's mathematics notebooks stacked in neatly categorized piles instead of scattering randomly over the floor. I accidentally but maybe on purpose toppled a stack with my boot.

Eric sat on the edge of the bed. "This building is owned by a thug named Joe Toley. He owns half the neighborhood, and he's been squeezing us, so we have to choose between paying rent and buying food. Everyone's still friendly tonight, but we're walking up to that line after which the neighborhood eats itself."

I stayed by the door to keep the heat of our connection down. Now that he mentioned it, there was an extra-hungry edge to the room. I twitched my collar. "Fuck, why didn't you say something sooner? Like, last time I was here. Or the time before that. You know I'd help."

Eric shrugged and looked away. "The shit we live with, you know. It goes unnoticed like air until we can't breathe."

I nodded; I'd been there. "Tell me about this Toley thug."

"Toley's tacky but he fancies himself plutocrat material. He wants to play with the ruling poshes across the river, even though they'll never have him. He noticed they visit our club, and decided the best way to capitalize is to price us out, starve us out, just get us out, and install his tacky shit instead."

"But the whole reason poshes come to this side of the river is because of us." I never could wrap my head around the short-sightedness of people scrapping for power. I mean, there was zero reason for my indignation because I know power gives people tunnel vision. Exploiting that is why I'm a decent con artist when I can keep my poker face.

Eric rolled his eyes. "I know that; you know that; the poshes across the river know that. There's a reason their art is dead and ours is alive. But Toley doesn't know shit about art. He just wants into the plutocrat club."

I frowned. "So, where's Toley vulnerable? Let's clean him out. Cut off his hands so he can't touch you or anyone else again. I mean, it's not like he could trace anything to you if I do the dirty work. We might have to burn my non-identity to take him down, but who cares. He can't reach me in a different reality."

Now that I knew what the problem was, I didn't know why it was a problem. Eric and I done bigger jobs together than neutralizing and redistributing wealth from some low-level sleaze-ball landlord who wanted to build a sad empire on the turf no one else wanted. Nothing made for a better fall guy than not existing—or for a better getaway than slipping to another reality. Only a handful of people knew the secret existence of the multiverse and Toley wasn't one of them.

"Well, I've thought about that. Besides the rentals, Toley's income is from a casino he owns—" Eric started.

"Well, there you go! We can—" I tried to finish.

"But the vault's got security that's a hundred percent monster-proof," Eric finished.

"Monster-proof how?" I asked. I should have been suspicious of his conviction given how scrappy he was. But I had taught him everything he knew about this kind of job. I figured I'd notice a hole he hadn't.

"The casino is built on an accessible part of the undercity." Eric pulled out a notebook. He flipped a few pages of maths before turning over a blank page. He began sketching, talking through the drawing.

Eventually he tossed the notebook to me so I could look at the map without contacting his hot hands.

What Eric had drawn and described was a newer structure built on an older foundation. Maybe from a Renaissance era villa or something more Baroque. But that sat on top of ancient Roman catacombs worked into the even more ancient volcanic tunnels and aquifers beneath the city.

I was familiar with the tunnels. Over millennia, they'd been used for everything from transferring goods between noble families, to military operations and smuggling, to storing potatoes. The tunnels below Toley's Casino bottomed out at the water table, into what looked like a natural cave. Great for a getaway if not for the miscreated ivy, formed into grotesque and impenetrable rubbery limbs that regrew faster than anyone could cut, blocking the tunnels from the vault.

Plenty of people in this manifestation of the city possessed supernatural strength, speed, or constitution. Many could shape-shift into animals, in whole or in part. A few I'd known could shape-shift into other people. And the vault security Eric had detailed, from those biotech ivies to the reinforced steel door with the goo-moat that could dissolve the most constitutionally enhanced infiltrator, was, as far as I could tell, designed to keep all of them out.

"Uh, you know," I waved the notebook at Eric, "I'm not a monster. I'm magic." I wanted to do something cool like snap my fingers and make a flame appear to punctuate that statement, but the truth is I'm not very good at magic. Or, at least, not very subtle or witty at it. It takes me a while to prepare—I need to crunch a lot of numbers—and even then, I need a hit of adrenaline to get over the last hump of disbelief. I get plenty of adrenaline when I break into vaults, so that shouldn't be a problem. And I had plenty of time to do the maths. I was already calculating how to magic my way through the security in the sketch.

"Yes, you certainly are magic," Eric grinned coyly.

I stuck up my middle finger and, grinning back, wiggled it suggestively.

But Eric sighed. "You could bypass the vault security, but we have no way to get you down there. They've got surveillance eyes and mobster-goons protecting their investment tip to tail, so unless you know how to pass yourself off as one of them in the next few hours we're out of time. The rent's due tomorrow."

"Which you could ignore and spend the money on food. Or you could pay, but then, uh..." I didn't want to come right out and say that everyone in the neighborhood would eat each other because Eric was sensitive about things like that. "If we don't act in the next twenty-four you lose the community one way or another."

"That's the sum of it, yeah. We need a speedy solution."

I stared at Eric trying to formulate some plan to take the vault in time, but nothing happened. "Okay. Do they have poker at Toley's casino?"

"Yeah," Eric said.

"We can hustle that," I offered.

"Or be hustled by it. The house edge is 4.379 percent, over eleven tables, in the past three months."

I whistled. "That's almost three times higher than it should be. The house is fucking cheating." I didn't question Eric's numbers. He, like me—because we are, in fact, imperfect mirrors of each other—is a colored-number synaesthetic and maths savant. Not just savant with the numbers. With the theoretical stuff too. But his numbers are colored all wrong. He'd probably tell me 4.379 percent was red and purple instead of its actual teal swirled with ambers. Which is why I don't ever ask.

"We could use those odds," I said, "to make some mobster at the table notice and then the mob can take Toley down. Then Toley goes away for good."

Eric shook his head. "Won't work. The reinforced steel vault door? The live security? He can't afford that. He's in the red with the mob for it and repaying the debt from the skim. He focuses his grift on safe marks only."

I was still confident. "Whatever grift he's got going on, we can still take him at the table. Especially if he thinks I'm a safe mark. We can exploit that. Hustling poker is how I paid my own rent for years. It's not the vault, it's not a permanent solution, but it gets you out of the immediate shit and makes Toley hurt a little in the process. More importantly, it buys time to build a permanent solution. Let's get us some seats at that table."

The plan made sense, but also hustling poker near-tops my list of favorite things. The maths of the game are hot fucking balls. Just consider the juicy variables: there's counting cards, yeah, but also counting the number of players, chips, and hands over time; there's the amount of information held by each player; the order of the deal; and more. Those variables feed statistics to calculate likely outcomes, dynamics to approximate the movement of the play over time, and game theory to anticipate player strategies. And, being maths savants, Eric and I could juggle all those dimensions at once and converge them without compromising our poker faces. The only thing hotter than sex with Eric is maths with Eric.

But the fun doesn't stop there. Because the key to a successful card hustle isn't just using numbers to decide one's own play. It's using them manipulate the other players and control the game. Someone who controls the maths can exploit the amount of information, for example by colluding with another player. Or by manipulating players' perceptions to change their behavior. Or, my favorite, controlling player expectations to introduce surprise. The simplest example of this is acting like a rookie when you're really a master. Cheating by surprise is the most satisfying cheat of all.

Eric broke my maths swoon saying, "No, let's get you, Mac—not us—a seat at that poker table. Because Toley knows my face."

Disappointment collapsed my grin. "But conning together with you is half the fun."

"Anything with you is all of the fun," Eric said. "But don't worry. Toley's goons won't let me play because of my skill with numbers, but they will let me in to spend cash at the bar. More importantly, no one connects your face and mine. I could feed you information from the room and share the computational load on the maths." Eric rose from the bed and took a step closer to me. He rocked back and forth, and the heat between us pulsed in the binary code we'd invented for communication. "And that's hot, right?"

My grin came back. "Shit fucking hot. No one at that casino has any idea that I'm almost you or how we can exploit that with proximity."

Eric licked his sharp teeth. "You caught my thought. Just like we have the same brain."

"Just like." I moved closer to him. The air molecules stirred between us, through the physics that let me slip realities.

Then in a hot snap we were sucking face and all the rest.

## 2. The Game

Joe Toley's casino was named Joe Toley's Casino. Because Joe Toley's favorite thing in the whole world was Joe Toley. There was a gold fucking bust of Joe Toley smack in the center of the lobby. I knew it was Joe Toley because it had a huge plaque proclaiming it Joe Toley. I knew it wasn't real gold because no one had stolen it. Toley was wealthy but not even close to as wealthy as plutocrats who ran the city. He just wanted everyone to think he was.

Deeper in, the walls showcased paintings of Joe Toley and the card backs featured Joe Toley's gold bust. This provided incentive to avoid the bar and its disturbing offerings because I didn't need to feel even more nauseated.

Eleven poker tables scattered about a blocks-long space broken by structural columns and drink bars. We didn't have a casino like this in my reality, but we didn't have a Joe Toley either. Weird plant-things with rotating, whirring eyeballs watched for cheating.

I was fine with them watching. The kind of cheating we had planned wasn't anything a biomechanical eyeball—or any eyeball—could see.

Eric had pulled the starting ante from the rent kitty. He'd told Ava the truth of it; instead of deciding between rent or food, we were going to clean up at Toley's poker table. She trusted us and our work from the more complex jobs we'd pulled off before.

For my part, I traded my black jeans, band tee, and leather jacket for Eric's clothes from high school. He'd had a rod up his ass back then and I felt awkward in dress pants, a button-up shirt, and a tweed jacket. I wouldn't remember what I was wearing once my mind was in the game, and for now appearing out of my element was good for the con.

We'd entered separately, brown forty-seven minutes apart. Eric had been working the room, like he was on an end-of-the-world bender since it would be exactly that if we didn't succeed at this job.

His cheeks were flush with blood and booze by the time I found him, all the way in the back. I watched him charm a girl in a fancy dress. I deduced her attachment to the dude at an adjacent poker table. Eric's attention was on her for one reason only, and that was to tell me which table to work.

I pointed to an empty chair and asked if I could be dealt in.

"This is a pro table," gruffed the dude who was burly, ugly, and wearing way too much expensive metal.

I blinked like I was trying to decide if "pro" meant me, tapping into the itch of Eric's tweed jacket for authenticity. "Five-card draw?" I asked without much authority since I knew it wasn't.

"Stud." The house dealer corrected mechanically without appearing to look up from his shuffle. But I knew how this shit worked, and he'd already made me. Hopefully as a mark, not as trouble.

Five card stud is a good variation for my style of con. It consists of one card down—the hole card—and four cards up. There's a lot of information on the table, statistical calculations have a small margin of error, counting cards is helpful, high hands are rare, and most of the play comes down to human behavior. Someone might show a promising hand face up, but whether it's a win or a whole lot of nothing depends on the hidden card. This means the real game is players trying to convince each other that they have a winning card in the hole.

All I had to do was teach them my false tells, learn their real ones, and use my edge from the maths to control the play.

The other player at the table said to the dude, "Aw, let him play. Game's no fun with just you and me." If dude looked exactly like one would expect at a poker table, this woman looked exactly the opposite. She couldn't have been more than five feet tall, baby-faced and cutting a bony line in a glittering dress. The dress had been repaired so many times I worried both it and she would disintegrate if I exhaled.

"Nah. It'll be too short a game," Dude scoffed. His eyes reflected light like a cat's.

"Aw, are you scared of him, Lui?" Wraith-lady winked at me, showing pointy vampire teeth.

"All I'm sayin', Ketti, is it's early in the night. We should keep practicing on each other and wait for better." Dude—whose name was Lui—clearly knew Wraith-lady—whose name was Ketti. They advertised collusion, but animosity showed in how they held their bodies away from each other. Since the game was simple, any cheating by the house would need to happen in collusion with the dealer, which made at least one of the two mob and in on it. My bet was both. The dealer might stack the deck in their favors to clean me out, but they were in competition with each other for the remainder of the pot.

I sat, itching at the dress pants, and checked for exits. Usually, I hid that habit because it reeked of vulnerability. Now I advertised it; they'd assume my nerves were for the game. I spotted a little door fifteen feet away and relaxed. It wasn't marked "EXIT," but it had the look of leading to something besides a closet on account of the plants—normal-looking plants—framing it.

Less normal-looking plants ivied along the walls like electrical wiring. They sprouted tiny blue eyeballs where they touched the ceiling, pivoting unblinkingly.

I tried to put the eyeballs out of my mind. They weren't going to see me do anything but who can concentrate when they're aware of hundreds of tiny eyeballs all over the fucking ceiling.

I dug into the pocket of the tweed jacket and dumped my chips on the table. I never stack them both because it unnerves people and because I always know how much I have on account of the colors of the numbers. My not-stacked stack consisted of two thousand five hundred in red, yellow, and blue chips. It wasn't shit compared with what the others had, but enough to keep me in the game if I built cautiously at the start and saved the big wins for later.

Eric, laughing with the girl, pulsed heat between us in an encoded message that confirmed my general assessment of the house cheat. He further narrowed it to an exploit called Double Duel, which uses shared information instead of a stacked deck to con the mark. Double Duel requires two colluding players, and it's useful when one has a hand almost as good as the other's and they duel it out to artificially raise the pot. Then, after the game, they share the spoils. Or, in this case, share the spoils with the house.

That made things even easier. We'd use vanilla statistics with the deck. We'd use game theory and dynamics for the play. Eric would handle spying in the holes and crunching the dynamics. I'd handle the game theory and putting everything together with the statistics.

With a nervous cough, I opened the ante with its token twenty. Which is yellow even though I used red chips.

The dealer, a bland man who I'm sure would be my match in a clean game, dealt the first round of cards—the hole cards—face down. Everyone looked in their hole and bet. The dealer dealt the remaining four cards face up. Between each round of dealing, we bet.

I used the initial hands to get a feel for the table and set up my false tells. Eric, entertaining Lui's girl, had a good view of my opponents' holes. They barely turned up the corner of their cards to peek, but Eric had quick eyes and between that and the statistics I had a good idea of who would win each round before the deal ended.

I threw early hands, making amateur mistakes and winning just enough to keep myself in the game.

Since my opponents played against me for the house, I could treat them like a single player as far as strategy. But they also competed with each other—a second two-player game nested within the house-versus-Mac game. Ketti made bold moves, quick to raise and quick to fold. She responded to my false tells but I sensed I'd need to be careful; her plays were shrewder than she advertised. She wanted us to think her heart was on her sleeve when it was really in a tiny box on the other side of the city buried in ice.

Lui gave little away and nudged the bets around in tiny increments, only going big when certain he had the winning hand. He was less responsive to my tells but more predictable in his reactions.

I needed to watch the dealer most. He was focused on me and counting cards. I caught him signaling, accurately, to Lui and Ketti with his style of deal about the odds. I doubted he was savant like Eric and me, but if I played one too many hands, he'd be onto me like I was onto him. I leaned back and forth to Eric to make sure he was aware of the dealer's parameters. That would change the dynamics.

Then I got serious. This was the sweet stretch with low suspicion and high gain.

Eric darted around the girl teasingly as the dealer lay down the hole cards, angling to see their values and pulse them to me. In the hole, the dealer gave Ketti a queen of hearts and Lui a jack of diamonds.

The dealer signaled the odds were equally poor for everyone this hand, an assessment I agreed with.

In my hole, I received the king of hearts.

Ketti was in front of the dealer. She opened with a typically higher-than-necessary bet which caused Lui, typically, to scowl at her. When he scowled, tiny extra hairs grew on his forehead. They looked more insectile than feline. He saw Ketti's bet and I followed.

Ketti's first face up card was a king of diamonds, and Lui's a king of spades. That made my odds of multiple kings poor, but to my pleasant surprise, I received the king of clubs. Two kings for me. My odds of winning just went way up. No one else knew my hole; they still thought I had an equal chance at crap.

Eric reassured me that my risk of exposure remained low.

Ketti bet similarly to her first round. Lui and I saw her.

On the third round Ketti got a queen of clubs and Lui an ace of spades. This opened new vistas of con for me. I pulsed my intention to Eric, and he confirmed my safety.

Now Ketti, with her pair of queens, had become my unwitting Double Duel accomplice. Her pair was one notch below mine, and she had every reason to think it would be the winning hand.

Lui was in the awkward position of maybe getting a pair of aces, so he'd need to stick it out instead of folding. With an ace-king-jack, he could also try to trick me into thinking he could get a straight. He knew he wouldn't, but I'd let him take me for a pile of chips that way earlier, when setting up the hustle.

All I had to do was keep Ketti raising the pot in her duel with me and keep Lui thinking he could scare us into folding with the threat of another ace or the appearance of a straight. Even if he lost to Ketti, keeping me in would mean a big win for the house.

I got a ten of clubs, but my hand was no longer my focus. My two kings were set and the best anyone likely to get, given the maths. I pretended to be super-excited about my ten, as though I might have a chance at a straight of my own and raised hugely.

Ketti licked her lips, certain I'd lose to her queens, saw my raise, and raised again.

Expressionless, Lui saw and raised on his phantom aces and straight.

I saw their raises and waited for the fourth card.

This time, Ketti got an eight of spades—in other words shit—and Lui got a jack of spades—not shit, but that pair of jacks wouldn't beat Ketti's pair or mine. He didn't lose the appearance of a straight though, and with three spades showing he could pretend to a flush, even though it was out of reach on account of the diamond in the hole. He could still get another ace, which remained the possibility that would tank me. He might think his jacks were good, too.

The dealer gave me a three of hearts. I gave my tell that I'd gotten a disappointing card and now had shit in my hand. Like, oh no, that straight I was convinced of getting just fell through. But I'd made bad decisions earlier trying to bluff my way through losing hands, so I saw Ketti's huge bet.

Last card down, Ketti got a four of clubs. She kept her gloat over her pair of queens.

Lui got a two of hearts. He was now betting on his pair of jacks.

I'd won the moment Lui failed to get another ace. But I accepted my nine of clubs and kept signaling that I had shit in my hand.

Ketti bet an enormous wad.

Lui folded.

I called.

Triumphantly Ketti turned up her hole card.

"Oh, wow," I said, turning up my king in the hole. Blinking, I said, "I think I won after all."

Ketti cursed vividly, though the dealer's face didn't move at all.

I worked the sweet spot like that for a while.

But the longer we played, the more I worried at the dynamics. The dealer continued to focus on me with subtle but increasing intensity. I threw a few hands, but it didn't cool him down. I had to leave before they realized my moves were a hustle. I sent more frequent queries to Eric.

Eric, tickling the girl, kept telling me the dynamics were safe.

But Eric didn't know poker like I did. Maybe what he thought was safe wasn't. I had more than enough in my stack to give Ava. I was done.

I made a few bad choices to cover my ass, folded, and was about to step away with my huge pile of beginners-luck loot when the door between the two plants opened and Joe Toley stepped out.

He looked just like his portraits, only shorter, skinnier, and older. Behind him came three thugs with the bushy look of werewolves or wereweasels or whatever fucking werethings this reality produced. The thugs slithered to the fore, focused on me.

I focused on Eric for help from his vampire reflexes.

But Eric focused on Toley and Toley focused on Eric, and the kind of focus they held was of collusion.

Eric smiled at Toley with his sharp vampire teeth like they were best fucking friends. "As ordered, Joe! One magician from another reality!"

The bottom dropped out of my world along with my jaw. "What the fucking fuck, you told this fucker there are other fucking realities? That's fucking secret!" I screamed at Eric.

Toley smiled at Eric. "And as requested, unlimited food and a job in my enterprise for as long as your magician produces."

I had already slight-of-handed my biggest denomination chips into my pockets and risen with fists swinging as Ketti, Lui, and the dealer dove for the sidelines.

But the werethugs were faster and one of them cuffed me in the back of the head so hard I face-planted into the table before I'd finished winding my blow.

## 3. The Deed

I was stunned.

Eric and I had collided like gravity the first time I'd slipped to his city. We had the same brain, the same bedroom, the same friends, the same maths notebooks. We were so close to the same person we almost spontaneously combusted in cosmic maths-sex when we touched. How could he sell me out to a tyrant bent on destroying our community? I'd die to protect my friends, and almost had, more than once.

But there I was, arms pinned back by literal monsters, and Joe Toley's triumphant face shoving its sweaty self into mine. Eric stood at distance examining the vial of blood-and-maybe-a-finger from his room and salivating so he could avoid looking into my eyes. And the truth sunk in that despite our similarities, I didn't really know Eric.

"...get you somewhere less public and see what you can do." Toley's words started making sense as the stars and disbelief from the pair of blows cleared.

I could see the points of Toley's teeth. They weren't vampire teeth. They joined together into a serrated monotooth. There were a lot of were-animals in this version of the city, but those teeth didn't remind me of any of them. He was some other kind of monster.

"Oh yeah? You get shit from me, you fucking monster." I spat blood and tried to get a read on him, but my perception wobbled from the hard cuff.

"We'll see." Toley jerked his head at his goons, who tightened their grip.

I made my weight go dead.

They still carried me by the shoulders through the little door so fast most of the room didn't even notice an altercation.

We went down stone steps that felt like they would never end, just get older, colder, and slipperier.

Eric followed, sliding the little vial of blood between his fingers, like a card trick. I could feel the heat of him even as the ambient temperature chilled and equilibrated into the purple-gold sixty-two degrees of underground.

We stopped in the office from Eric's notebook. Eric hadn't drawn the specifics. Presumably because he didn't know them, though now I wondered. The dimensions of the room were spot on.

I'm guessing it was a root cellar but now it held an oak desk so blocky I could build a house from it. The desk sat at center, so Toley could perch in the chair with the thugs around him. They carried me to the opposite side and dropped my shoulders.

Eric stood behind Toley. He held up the creepy blood vial and winked, like he was toasting my capture. Like he extra-wanted to rub in his betrayal with a blood-and-finger chaser.

"Here's how this is going to work," Toley said. "Show me magic and I'll show you hospitality. Get me into the plutocracy, and I'll get you whatever you want. Your pal Eric says you're hungry, too. We've got plenty of bread here, don't we, boys? We've always got plenty of eats for loyal men with skills."

The thugs nodded and grinned. Eric grinned too and licked the pointy ends of his fangs.

Unfortunately for Joe Toley, I was hard-wired to disrespect authority, even when it wasn't in my best interest to do so. Which, in this case, it certainly the fuck wasn't.

I gathered defiance in my mouth and when it was good and juicy spat a long, bloody wad straight into Joe Toley's mean little eyes.

When I came to from the resulting much harder cuff, I recalled the dungeon from Eric's notebook because I was in it.

It wasn't on the path of the vault, but it was on the layer beneath the root cellar and above the catacombs which led to the vault.

They'd chained me with medieval hardware to the wall, and my hands were numb from being over my head for who the fuck knew how long. It's not like I could look at my watch. My head ached but I'd had worse concussions.

A nest of eyeballs watched me from the lower left of the cell. I couldn't give them the finger because of the chains. But I made them a silent and solemn promise that they'd get theirs.

Magic is something everyone has in my reality. However, not everyone is equally good at it on account of variations in talent and skill at focusing will. Just like maths, most people can calculate. Some might have talent for more. But only a few have the talent and skill to be certified triple-A computers like me.

As for magic, I do have talent. But I also have as much skill as a ten-year-old does at algebra.

I had used my magic to make things cold before though, so I knew how that worked. Drawing on maths to focus my will, I conjured the equations for how water changes from solid to gas if the conditions are right—the mathematics behind how frost and hoar frost form. The conditions in this room weren't right, but this was magic, magic focused by physics but realized by my will and the genetics of my reality. I intoned the equations like a spell, "Q equals mc-delta-T, where Q is energy, m is mass, c is heat, delta-T is temperature change."

Nothing happened without adrenaline to push me past my general disbelief in magic. So, I reminded myself I was chained to a medieval dungeon wall and panicked.

Cold blue light flashed from my palms and the chains above me snapped off the wall from cold as the bars of the cell frosted over.

Fuck yeah!

My hands thudded in front of me. I was bound by standard police-issue cuffs threaded through a chain forged by giants in the year six-hundred and three. My magic is big and blunt. Anything I tried to do to the cuffs to free myself of the broken chain was going to take off my hands. Luckily, I knew how to pick that style of cuffs if I could find a scrap of wire and time.

Free of the wall if not of the chain, I stomped the living fuck out of the nest of eyeballs in the corner with my biker boots.

The eyeballs had seen me; there was nothing I could do about that. But I was counting on Toley's complacency to buy me a head start.

Focusing my boot on the flash-frozen bars, I kicked them the fuck out and fled the shatter.

A cave-in had left only one way to go, so I ran in the direction of the vault. I felt ridiculous in that square-ass outfit with the dress pants and tweed, sprinting with my hands shackled in front of me, and cursing as my wrists flayed from the pull of twenty pounds of giant medieval dungeon chain.

I passed by the stairs leading up to the root cellar and the casino where Toley and his goons would tackle me. Instead, I headed through the door on the other end.

Immediately, I tumbled down a set of stairs.

Pain thudded from every direction until I squared my boots and shoulders with the walls and stopped my momentum.

Fucking Eric didn't mention there was a fucking set of fucking stairs on the other side of that fucking door. He probably hoped that if I escaped, I'd break my fucking neck. I'd break his fucking neck if I managed to get out of here.

There was no time to assess damage because I had to get up and keep going.

Time and shifting earth had worked at the passage, and the steps were uneven, crumbling, or missing. The chain shifted my center of gravity, making balancing hard.

But I made it to the bottom and into a low, tight corridor smelling of damp with walls of unfinished earth. Gnarls of tree roots poked out and omnipresent eyeballs lined walls lit by glowing fungus. I kept my distance. The way things worked here, that fungus probably wanted to suck my blood and gnaw my bones.

I ran again. My hands were slick with blood from the cuffs, but not slippery enough to slide free.

Another century into the past I reached the shelves of the catacombs.

It didn't matter that bodies no longer reclined on them. Bodies once had and that memory never left a place.

A root caught on the sleeve of my tweed, and I yelped because there's not a lot of difference between a tree root and a reanimated skeletal hand.

I reached the monster-proof door to the vault.

A fountain of thick, green goo recirculated up the rock walls to drip back down into a moat extending two feet across the stone floor. It would melt anything else that touched it.

The modern edges of the vault door jarred against the thousands-year-old stonework. An encrustation of oily vines and what looked like bits of beef sat where in my reality a lock would have been. Eyeballs swiveled to watch me along the low ceiling, just out of reach of the goo. This time I gave them the finger with my cuffed hands before I punched them out with double fists.

Eric had described how the door was impregnable to super strength and super lock-picking. Made of reinforced hollow steel with reinforced steel edges, it sported steel strike plates and five-inch steel screws in steel hardware. I could have bought the whole neighborhood food for life with this much steel. It was impervious to prying, kicking, and battering ram. The monstrous meat lock needed to taste Toley's blood and biometrics before it would even think about opening.

The one thing the door was not impregnable to was physics.

The equations I'd started planning in Eric's bedroom poured into my head.

The door was too thick and the meat-lock too resilient for frost. I needed entropy, the natural tendency of things, over time, to move toward randomness in absence of new energy. It's the physics that makes a bowl of steaming, delicious soup into a dish of cold, unappetizing slurry. Except it would take millennia for something like this door to reach thermodynamic equilibrium naturally.

I modeled entropy as the door's capacity for disorder over its capacity for information—that which held it together. "Disorder equals $C_d$ over $C_i$," I muttered, and imagined the atomic cohesion of the door. I imagined deep, into the molecular level, the particles in the cold steel bits and the warm organic bits slowing down and falling apart. Turning into tepid, unappetizing slurry.

I waited for the fear.

I knew it was coming; I'd calculated for it.

I heard footsteps and there it was. Adrenaline spiked and a purple light flashed from my palms. The vault security, which Toley had sold himself to the mob to obtain, melted into tarry goo.

I leapt over the mess and into the vault.

The vault was part of the ancient catacombs. It had smooth walls and a low ceiling. Along the far end, a cut-out overlooked the dark lapping of the water table. I'm not sure why. Perhaps as part of an ancient viaduct. So much history lay beneath the city, in any manifestation of it.

The monster ivies over the egress were a creature purely of this manifestation. They extended over the opening in a lumpy grid. They looked more meat than plants, like a mass of flayed appendages. They glistened wetly and churned slowly. My stomach turned.

As for the contents of the vault, Toley had taken little care to secure his wealth. Either he assumed no one would get past the monster-proof door and its moat of corrosive green goo, or he'd run out of patience for caution.

Gold goblets and Baroque paintings, stolen or taken as gambling debt, tangled in jewels and loose paper money.

A pile of furs slithered from their heap to the floor.

On a broad table, a stack of legal folders sat beneath a vase with the patina of ancient Roman glass. I saw more arti-facts—vases, jewels, armor.

Toley's hoard wasn't anywhere near the size of the pluto-crat hoards I'd seen, but it was still more than any of us at The Parlor would hold in our lifetimes.

I wanted to pocket some of the small shit but the foot-steps outside neared and I still needed to take care of the gro-tesque plant-thing between me and the exit. All this wealth lying around everywhere, and I couldn't do shit about it. I had to be content with smashing some of it to the ground.

I found a paperclip on one of the legal folders and pulled it off. It was exactly what I needed to get out of the cuffs and loose the twenty pounds of giant medieval torture chain.

But I couldn't do shit about that either. I had the scrap of wire but not the scrap of time.

I reached the exit, trusting Eric's untrustworthy map because I had no other choice. As I neared, the ivies unsheathed thorns thicker than my arm and sharper than an ice pick.

If Eric was right, those plants re-grew so fast as to almost defy thermodynamics—and they fed from a source I didn't know enough about to cut off. What I needed this time was enough force and speed to punch through and be gone before they regrew.

I could magic that kind of explosive force. It was, in fact, among the first kinds of magic I'd ever done. But I had to wait until the last pants-pissing second because that's how much adrenaline it took.

The urge to flee fluttered toward panic, but my brain wasn't yet convinced that I was about to die.

Toley entered first, face red and eyes bulging. He had a gun in his hand, but his hand wasn't a hand. I mean, like, he literally had a gun inside of his hand, or his hand transformed into some kind of meat-gun or some shit. I didn't even know what I was looking at.

The three goons surged around him. The seams of their clothes busted as they transformed into the most butt-ugly wolves I'd ever seen.

And last, making me hot all over, came Eric. His vampire teeth glinted brighter than the golden goblets and I wanted to punch him in those teeth as bad as I wanted to bang him.

He banged into the table with the legal folders, and I heard the Roman glass vase shatter to the ground as he took them and shook them at me.

As Toley's handgun—gun hand? whatever—leveled on me and the weregoons closed the distance, I became convinced I was about to die. Pure terror trumped reason.

But not before I'd turned a spring green hundred and eighty degrees.

As the defensive spell came out of my palms to flatten everyone in the room, it hit the plant-bars point-blank instead.

I felt the rush of air as it reflected back into the vault, hopefully slowing down the goons.

I was through the hole so fast the only thing the thorns snagged was the heel of one biker boot; the boot slipped off.

Icy water shocked me so hard I didn't realize at first that I was sinking fast despite kicking hard.

This should not have been a surprise.

I mean, the giant fucking chain was functionally a giant fucking boat anchor.

Panic began to re-trigger the spontaneous defensive magic I'd used on the bars.

I imagined numbers so I wouldn't blow myself up. All the numbers with the calmest colors. Counting by factors of two I could get a lovely array of soothing greens, blues, and violets. Two, four, eight...

I bent the paperclip into a violet forty-five-degree angle, and then stuck it into the keyhole on the cuffs to make a purple ninety-degree kink at the tip.

I inserted that end into the lock, pointing outward from the center of the cuffs. Applying force counter-clockwise I concentrated on pushing the double-lock bar into its double-lock slot—which is what a key would do if I had one.

I started to see stars and wanted to inhale so badly I almost lost the paperclip.

Eight, sixteen, thirty-two...

I fumbled the first attempt but felt the tension in the lock, so I got the click of release on the next quick try.

The edges of my vision darkened.

Thirty-two, sixty-four, one-twenty-eight...

Everything came down to numbing fingers and that paperclip in the dim light from above as the chain cleaved me to the bottom and the darkness closed in.

I removed the wire from the lock and replaced it, this time facing inward to the center of the cuffs.

Applying force clockwise now, I pushed the lock bar away from the ratchet arm.

The darkness became complete.


## 4. The Aftermath

Water lapped on a tiny underground beach.

The water glowed with algae. It mixed with the sand. The sand glowed.

I figured I was dead until I rolled over and vomited two lungfuls of water.

At least this far underground the water was clean.

Concussive headache, lacerated wrists, waterlogged lungs, and a livid assortment of whole-body bruises—I'd had worse before but needed to get moving or I'd hypothermia to death.

It was a straight shot out of the caves and into the city, at least according to Eric's map.

Fucking Eric.

Fucking Eric who sold out the fucking community to fucking Joe Toley for a fucking thug job and a fucking pint of fucking blood! What the fucking fuck!

Rage cleared the haze of almost drowning, and the one thing I knew for absolute, ice-clear certain was that Eric was going to pay for what he'd done. I would shit inside his maths notebooks. I would set his bed on fire. I would make sure he was never welcome in the community again. I would take down Joe Toley just to cut Eric off if it cost me my fucking life. No one hurts my friends.

Eric wouldn't be living above the Parlor anymore. But he'd come back to collect his maths notebooks. That much I could count on because, regardless of our epic differences, we still had the same maths brain. And when he did, I would be there. Magic trumps monster and I'd have the adrenaline for any spell I wanted. So, I made my way to the surface and through the city streets, and back to The Parlor.

At least I still had those chips I'd palmed in my pocket. They were enough to pay Ava back for the money she'd fronted and save the club for another month while we came up with a plan.

Two hours later I arrived, damp, bleeding, limping on only one boot, and pissed as shit.

Halfway up the stairs to the second story, I felt the heat of Eric's presence. Probably trying to sneak out with his maths notebooks before his betrayal got loose. I grinned at the rage I was going to extract.

I yanked open the door.

Ava wooted and tossed a big bucket of shiny paper into a party. Silver sparkles rained down.

People passed around a jar of blood pills—the expensive kind that would keep vampire folks nourished for days.

A three-piece band started in the corner.

And in the center of the room, like the man of the fucking hour, Eric beamed.

"Mac's here! Excellent! Bring out the cake!" Eric fist pumped.

Everyone turned to me and clapped.

I did not clap. I strained every ounce of my near-zero will-power to keep my distance from Eric and gathered my maths. I knew the physics that made the two of us cosmically horny when we touched. I could cast a spell to dampen the effect just long enough to land a solid one across his jaw without any urge to kiss him.

Eric's smile dropped as he heard the numbers coming out of me. He knew what they meant. But he didn't move.

Ava stepped between us. "Hey, chill Mac."

"Ava, get back," I snarled. "Don't you get it? He traded me, you, all of us, to Joe-fucking-Toley for fucking blood pills. Eric sold us out."

Ava looked at me like I had grown another head.

Eric looked confused. "Wait, you think what?"

I lost control of the spell.

The music stopped. Everyone's confused body turned to me.

Eric's confusion crumbled to mortification. "Oh no! I'm so sorry. I figured—we have the same brain—"

Ava shook a fistful of legal folders at me. "He didn't sell anyone out. This wasn't about blood pills," she said. "Look, deeds."

"Deeds?"

Ava nodded. "Deeds to the club and casino. Deeds to Toley's other properties in the neighborhood too. We scored his finger and blood a little while back, and that's the biomatter we needed to transfer ownership. We just needed you to get to them. It's not like the authorities look hard at paperwork from this part of the town, and Toley's going to be up past his eyeballs in late payments to angry mobsters. Especially since we own what's left of his vault."

I saw the indentation on the folders where I'd pulled off the paperclip.

It all made sense. The barrier to magicking my way into the vault, Eric had said, was getting there in the first place. Me, the unwitting inside man and fall guy all in one. The Roman glass vase shattering to the floor of the vault as Eric snagged the deeds while Toley and his goons focused on me, and I focused on escaping. Eric carrying around a finger and blood in a vial as if I would understand what it was for.

Except I wasn't from here. So, it didn't read to me as "keys to the deeds" at all.

I was angry all over again. "Why the fuck didn't you tell me the fucking plan, Eric?" I pointed at my bootless foot.

"I ran the numbers," Eric said, holding up one of his notebooks. "The odds if I let you in at the start were too high, and not in our favor. But I really did think you'd figure it out. Or trust there was more going on, at least."

"Oh yeah? And when, exactly, did you run those fucking numbers? You didn't know I was coming. I was with you until you left for the casino."

"I ran them weeks ago, because I knew you'd come. Mathing together is just too sexy to resist. I'd hoped you'd come sooner. I wasn't lying about the rent being due tomorrow."

"But you would have lied about the rent being due if I'd come sooner," I frowned. I didn't know what to do with my anger. Was I still angry at him? I made a snarly face and demanded, "I want to see those fucking numbers."

He held the notebook toward me.

I yanked it from his hands and retreated fast so we wouldn't end up sucking face.

Across multiple pages, in Eric's annoyingly neat handwriting, I read through the variables he'd plugged into his mathematical models. Some were about me—my emotional reactivity, my success at the poker table, the parameters of my magic. Others were about Toley, or the casino, or about the goons at the casino. He'd run a simulation of the heist on paper a good two dozen times, and I had to admit, his calculations were as flawless as mine would have been.

"You don't have a lot of confidence in my ability to do magic without feeling like it's life-or-death," I pointed to one of the parameters.

"Do you?" Eric raised a brow. "Was I wrong?"

I scoffed because he really wasn't. "And this here. You were banking a lot on Toley being hyper-focused on me and not paying attention to what was going on behind him."

"Again, was I wrong? The only thing I didn't calculate right was that you'd trust I was still on your side all the way back in Toley's office when I held up the finger and winked."

"I thought that finger was your lunch, Eric. And you could have looked for me in the tunnels."

"I had to escape with the deeds. The goons made me the moment you blasted the ivies. I barely made it out." Eric pointed to what I realized was a nasty shiner across his face with what I realized was a bandaged arm. Given vampire healing, that meant something. "I really am sorry about the boot. And, uh, what you went through."

I was still angry. But I was impressed by Eric's maths. I was also proud. Eric had never run a con before he'd met me.

Cons and maths, they have a lot in common. Just like me and Eric. Given these numbers I would have done the same.

"I'm still fucking angry at you," I said and stepped on purpose into his personal space to hand him back his notebook.

"I still sort of deserve it." Eric knocked the notebook aside and gave me a tentative smile.

I brushed his hand.

He yanked me with vampire speed to his room.

In a hot snap we were sucking face and all the rest.

**Dora M Raymaker,** PhD, is an Autistic/queer/genderqueer scientist/author/multi-media artist and troublemaker whose work across disciplines focuses on social justice, systems thinking, and the dance between hope and fear. Dora is author of the novels *Resonance* and *Hoshi and the Red City Circuit*, and short works in Spoon Knife anthologies.

**George Wehrfritz**

# *Records of Every Days*

## 1/10

Pining for her I remember the gold Cordoba, its capacious rear seat once formative in our relationship. A Chrysler product, the hand-me-down I drove off to college in tangible embarrassment, a freebie. Mom's first new car ever, acquired in my childhood after the family split, adding mechanical disappointment to the mess we'd landed in. Dad, having been consulted on her impending purchase (they were speaking again by then), made his views clear. "Piece of crap," he said at the dealership. "For Christ's sake be practical and get the goddamn Buick."

Mother didn't waiver. No goddamn Buick for her. She loved the television commercial with Ricardo Montalbán touting the Cordoba's "fine Corinthian Leather," which sounded Old World the way he pitched it. Continental and seductive. To Dad's point the Check Engine light began flashing at intervals before the new car smell had surrendered to children and dogs. But that interior, wow. Classy and European to the end.

Mom's next car was an Infiniti. Made in Japan, artifact of the First Nuclear Age, a vehicle for corporate warriors landing Mothra-like and incandescent to level Detroit and thereby reclaim a conquered nation's dignity. Mother just wanted a car that would run forever which that one didn't do either despite the implied promise, though it clocked 159,577 trouble-free miles before the transmission dropped on Highway 99 just south of Sacramento.

Entropy. Impermanence. Dust in the wind.

## 2/10

T. Yoshida's artistic transmutation also postdated atomic war. His abstract woodblock prints burst Godzilla-like from murky depths amidst unstable isotopes washing downward into the sea. They evoke astral phenomena still centuries from discovery, chart inner worlds boundless and subatomic, Whovilles within Whovilles on paper mulberry. A handful prefigure integrated circuitry. The grandest reveal extraterrestrial mesas and monoliths bearing glyphs undecipherable even by Google—almanacs, metaphysical musing, salty dark matter limericks even; dispatches lacking standardized font or point sizes lost for a time in translation. Rendered as components of numbered sets. 3/13, 9/30, 28/50, 63/100, etcetera, etcetera. With titles like *From a Star, Night*; *Abstruse*; *Transcendence*; and the totemic *Records of Every Days*.

T. Yoshida's contemporary critics found his midlife metamorphosis jarring. Modern art historians credit humankind's obsession with the space race at the dawn of the television age.

Abridged timeline: *Astro Boy*, 1963-66, 193 episodes; *Thunderbirds*, 1965, 32 episodes; *Star Trek*, 1966-69, 79 episodes.

## 3/10

T. Yoshida created more than 300 nonrepresentational woodblock prints between 1952 and 1975. His first, *No. 1*, conjures an aircraft or space capsule disintegrating in the stratosphere. His last, *Should Not Use*, depicts an atomic plume. Their sepia colorways suggest burlap covers on an encyclopedia concealing the cosmos.

T. Yoshida passed late in the last millennium, second patriarch to a family art collective spanning three centuries, head of a workshop with a bread-and-butter repertoire including images of Mt. Fuji as viewed from numerous perspectives in various seasons and sold year-round to tourists. His abstracts answered an inner calling, embodied the *sosaku hanga* ethos of individual artistic expression. Popularized first with Japan's American occupiers including my wife's father Gordon, they rose into the Jetstream to encircle the planet like carbon 14 from Castle Bravo.

"What do you see in these?" I asked him early on. Gordon thought for a long moment then replied: "Infinity."

## 4/10

Being impressionable I adopted Gordon's viewpoint on the spot. Yet true understanding required time without signature; space to take full measure of T. Yoshida's perspectives on perpetuity, the slivers, slim vistas, peeks through perceptual peepholes honed by a Japanese master now three decades gone. Each reflecting newfound freedom following the death of his own disapproving father; each rejecting traditional themes and folk impressionism.

Eventually I grasped the interchangeable relationship between energy and matter. Eventually I realized serendipitous alien contact could not be ruled out.

## 5/10

Reposed in my distressed Gio Ponti wingback chair, I imagine procuring a complete edition of a single abstract Yoshida creation, 1/50 to 50/50, say, to test a nagging theory of mine. If surreptitious interstellar alien contact followed nuclear war late in the last millennium, and if the point of contact was/is T. Yoshida as I have come to suspect, these prints might not be exact copies dashed off willy-nilly per the tyranny of Adam Smith, but instead subtly discrete works, stealth mono-prints comprising pages of a single encoded story, i.e., a book. Perhaps even a trope. Galactic star map with a wormhole onramp conveniently positioned mere light-seconds from Earth maybe, or the *Complete Idiot's Guide to Kitchen Fusion* for a carbon-based ecosystem with gravitational attraction of 9.81, or the exact time and date a comet the size of Kansas will drop like a dead transmission outside Sacramento.

The possibilities (being boundless) include humankind's comprehensive salvation via science, technology, the One True God, whatever; or annihilation under same said forces.

Yet as latent, motionless potential energy, the random pages from different books that currently adorn every wall inside this forsaken house must temporarily suffice. Until a monkey replicates T. Yoshida's entire catalogue.

## 6/10

My Gio Ponti survived the last millennium, survived also Gordon's habit of napping mid-Marlboro, yet it has come to resemble a burst chrysalis, its implied Monarch free. Left front leg cracked and glued. Back corners shredded, various scratch posts never good enough for Elvis, Clark, Clarence, Kita or Taj. Cats, two batches, the last of which died right here in my arms after 17 cantankerous years. Rose brocade faded; armrests spackled with burns, coffee and wine; cushions sagging, wool batt and hemp thread liberated at various stress points. This chair won't last forever (Milanese designers long ago having rendered "timeless" a mere cliché), though it will remain unto dismemberment at the center of the universe just like every chair ever manufactured.

Until it outlasts me, as I have the woman for whom I pine.

## 7/10

"I can't do these trips anymore," my sister informed me at the end of her last visit.

"I understand," I replied. Then we said goodbye.

We'd driven out to the coast the previous afternoon. Her rental car's satellite radio kept replaying an ad for a

Bartender-*something*, a product which, per the sketchy description recited too quickly, sounded like a Mr. Coffee device that mixes cocktails at the flip of a switch.

"Where's all the liquor come from? Thing must be *huge!*" I'd barked into the dashboard infotainment system to defend matter's conservation, as one acclimated to solitude does.

"Seems they've invented a replicator," said my sister, a Trekkie since age five. Her theory: a band of Gen Z inventors skittering between parental garages in some Silicon Valley suburb, seeking only to disrupt Happy Hour and TGIF, created this robotic bartender yet somehow failed to grasp that their unicorn conjured spirits clear or brown from thin air as if by magic.

"Which Scotty down in the engine room could've told 'em," she riffed, shifting to a brogue we'd been slaughtering since childhood. "Ye cannae change the laws of physics! Ner'er mix matter and anti-matter cold!"

## 8/10

My wife adored sci-fi too. A fondness inherited (along with height and cryptanalysis) from Gordon. The last book she read featured rival clans of rogue AIs locked in warfare for eternity. Which in general plotline tracked our favorite space opera, *Battlestar Galactica,* with its treacherous Cylons, convenient resurrections, and star-fighters resembling Medieval scythes and crescent—motifs prominent in some of T. Yoshida's grandest prints. Examples of which we'd once clustered together family portrait-like along a hallway, even calling them "The Cylons."

Occasionally, when inclement weather dashed a planned weekend outing, say, my wife would ask "Move art?" And we'd set about rearranging our T. Yoshida prints by color, by creation year, by themes as we imagined them. Only once did this pastime go somewhat awry. It happened when she reframed another print retrieved from storage years after the inheritance, a giant work called *End of Summer*, number 10/13, dated 1960.

"What do you see?" I asked her as we unwrapped it.

Having just then read the name and being suggestible by nature, she replied: "Summer, you know, the lifeguard, run down by a dune buggy on Malibu Beach."

"Do tell," I said.

"Here, her contorted head and short hair. There, poor girl, her crushed heart, flattened lungs and ample bosom—"

"—kinda ruins it for me," I replied.

Still, we hung *Summer* in the dining room, where her unfortunate accident proved a handy conversation starter whenever a dinner party threatened interminability. For context, we'd reference years spent posted to a failed communist republic still sufficiently wary of "foreign friends" to sequester diplomats within guarded compounds. Ours, a late Soviet monstrosity, featured dodgy steam heat, brown grass guarding a broken fountain, and a basic satellite link with entertainment options deemed suitable for sanctioned expatriates, meaning *BBC World*, golf tournaments from Dubai and *Baywatch* (a show, we soon recognized, with near-universal appeal).

## 9/10

*Records of Every Days*, 16/18. Pencil signed. Dated 1959. Dimensions: 85 cm X 55 cm. The composition depicts two steles with graphic ornamentation and/or astral-geometric mapping and/or text in unknown script. The smaller resembles the lead carriage in a bullet train aimed skyward. The larger stands taller by a factor of 3.28 and presents a beak-like protrusion near its apex. Juxtaposition evokes parent and child. Alternately, a rocket with its sky bridge deployed awaiting cosmonauts. Alternately, monoliths bridging time and space (see "The Sentinel of Eternity" by Arthur C. Clarke, published in 1951). Lines/roads/vectors meet at hubs/cloverleaves/interchanges. Precision, crispness, fine chronometric movements within totem cacti. Each rendered in black and red, pigments pulverized into powder liquidized in porcelain bowls, color brushed onto blocks and pressed into paper using coiled rope. Light oxidization from exposure to atmospheric pollution. The backdrop shimmers, a *moiré* curtain in rare charcoal silk, or ancient silver chainmail looted from a vault beneath Luxor.

*Records of Every Days.* The title connotes a diary. Occurrences preserved, catalogued, sorted. If accurate, dispersal of 17 additional *Records* into the Jetstream has obscured something important. Evidence of an advanced alien species capable of interstellar travel possibly.

Caveat 1: clusters of uncountable atoms observed by the human eye for long enough will appear to move like ants, whose highly organized colonies exhibit "social life as it might evolve on another planet," the late biologist Edward O. Wilson once wrote.

Caveat 2: Once, in Central Asia, we became lost in the Silk Road ruin Yarkhoto, eating dates and drinking mint tea from canteens.

## 10/10

The thing about infinity: there's a goddamn lot to consider. Even in one's own living room. Where, as gravity besets the Gio Ponti like taxation, the grey fellow cradled within its stub wings and tired brocade cabbage roses, pet-less and alone, naps. Beside a bookcase where Jorge Luis Borges conjures a religious manuscript with countless pages and Kobo Abe traps lovers in a village beset by vast sand piles relentlessly bearing down. So much to take in: castaways who mustn't cease digging; a cursed tome without reference points; T. Yoshida's inestimable imagination on fibrous sheets in ink and mineral dyes transferred via planes of wood carved from trees with tight graining still visible, against a father's dying wish.

My house spins. I write, being, technically, still a writer, aware that even a monkey could sharpen the story fogbound inside my brain just now if given enough time, recalling how Bill Murray became, in the end, a good person in that film about groundhogs. A train whistle hoots. Quitting time somewhere close by. Or have I left the television on? Hope does not, just now, spring eternal. Gio Ponti's chair envelops tired bones and I sink into an infinity pool of sleep. Fretting a sibling unable to travel anymore, awestruck by an artist who rendered forever in two dimensions so beautifully, pining.

I remember the gold Cordoba. And her.

---

**George Wehrfritz**, a retired journalist, began writing short fiction during the pandemic. His recent work has appeared in *Periscope Literary*, *The Sandy River Review*, *Written Tales* and *34th Parallel*. He lives in Salinas, California.

**Dani Alexis Ryskamp**

# 809.93592, "*Autobiography: Librarian*"

*"At the broadest level, the Dewey Decimal Classification system is divided into ten main classes, which together cover the entire world of knowledge." - DDC 30 (1989), xxviii*

Birth (mine): 304.63092477417. (Humor: 152.41)

Parents: 306.874. See also 305.90653.

Depression (mental state): 362.25
    Depressive reactions 616.895
        Medicine 616.8527
            Social welfare 362.25

        *See also* Mental Illness.

Adulthood: 305.24.

152.41: Love. It's funny like that.

Married persons: 306.872
    130: Happiness.
    001.9: Spurious knowledge

*"001.9 and 130 both pertain to topics in the twilight realms of half-knowledge, topics that refuse either to be disproved or to be brought into the realm of certain and verifiable knowledge."*

(153.12: memory?)

(154.3 daydreaming)

(152.41 hope)

Admissibility of evidence: 347.062

    Intersections 338.13 (urban 388.411)

    Motorcycle accidents 363.1259

    Negligence 346.032 (injury 346.0323)

    Hospitals 362.11

    Family 306.855

    Fear 152.46

    Death 386.9  biology of 574.2 philosophy of human 128.5

    Grief 155.937

    Grief 155.937

    Grief 155.937

152.41: Love. Humor. Hope.

---

**Dani Alexis Ryskamp** is a retired propagandist and current librarian. Her work has appeared in *The Atlantic, Disability Studies Quarterly*, and previous Spoons Knife. She is currently battling an AI for her right to eat.

**Nick Walker**

# Counting to Five

Out behind the row of shotgun houses where I lived was an empty lot overrun with weeds where all the kids played, and at the farthest corner of the lot was a big old gnarly tree. One day when Aunt Flo came out on the back stoop and called Katy in for dinner, Katy didn't come. For a couple minutes nobody could find her, and then finally Mikey spotted her in that tree, way up in the top branches. We all goggled at her and a couple of us cheered, cause no one we knew ever made it that high before. The cheering cut out pretty quick, though, cause Aunt Flo went storming across the lot screaming at Katy to get down from there this instant.

Aunt Flo stood at the foot of the tree shouting up at Katy, but Katy didn't even notice. She'd found something, maybe a beetle or caterpillar, and she was so wrapped up in studying it that Aunt Flo might as well have been shouting from the moon. Aunt Flo shouted at Katy for a bit, then shouted at the rest of us for not keeping an eye on Katy even though we all knew damn well that she was special and couldn't be let alone, then shouted at Katy some more. And when Katy still didn't take any notice of Aunt Flo, that's when Aunt Flo stomped back inside and got Uncle Al.

Uncle Al was the biggest, scariest-looking grownup any of us had ever seen, six and a half foot tall with fists the size of a kid's head. He was Aunt Flo's brother and he'd moved in a few weeks earlier after getting out of prison. We'd heard the grownups talking about it. They said he was so tough that one time in prison a whole gang came after him at once and he just looked at them and told them he was going to count to five, and they'd better be out of his sight by the time he finished. And sure enough, they were, because none of them wanted to find out what happened when Uncle Al got to five.

Uncle Al stood at the foot of the tree and called up to Katy in a voice so loud and slow and dangerous that every kid in the lot froze up like some animals freeze in the headlights of a car. "Katy," he said, "you climb back down here right now." That voice would've stopped a stampede of elephants, but Katy was special. She just kept on looking at her beetle or caterpillar or whatever it was she'd found up in those branches, and took no notice of Uncle Al at all. And that's when Uncle Al said, "Katy, I'm gonna count to five."

For a few seconds there was dead silence in the lot, and then Uncle Al said, "One."

A couple of kids started to cry. Uncle Al said, "Two."

We were all frozen in place, terrified of what Uncle Al was going to do but unable to look away. When Uncle Al said "Three," one kid broke free of the spell and went running for home.

"Four," said Uncle Al, and all the kids held their breath.

Uncle Al said, "Five."

There was total silence. The world stood still. Not even the wind dared to blow. We looked up at Katy, who still hadn't noticed Uncle Al. We looked at Uncle Al, who was squinting up through the branches at Katy.

It was Mikey who broke the silence. He was the bravest kid of us all, but when he spoke we could hear his voice shaking. "Mr. Uncle Al?" Mikey said, "S-sir? What... what are you g-going to do?"

Uncle Al slowly turned his huge head and looked down at Mikey. Then he looked back up at Katy, then down at Mikey again. "Do?" he said. His brow furrowed, and Mikey took a step back. Then Uncle Al shrugged his shoulders. "Damned if I know. That's all I got, kid. First time it hasn't worked." He gave Mikey a smile. "Guess she'll come on down when she's good and ready. Hope old Flo ain't too mad." And he strolled back across the lot and went inside.

---

**Nick Walker** is a mild-mannered scholar and psychology professor. His nonfiction work includes the book *Neuroqueer Heresies*, and his fiction has appeared in a few previous volumes of *Spoon Knife*. Together with fellow author Andrew M. Reichart and artist Mike Bennewitz, he's co-creator of the urban fantasy webcomic *Weird Luck* at weirdluck.net.

**Jay Cherrie and Dean Gloster**

# *Numbers Guys*

Leon, the boyish 51-year-old CEO of several companies and one of the five richest men on Earth, was 20 minutes late for his scheduled meeting with "the Guys," and he was nervous about it. They'd helped him numerous times—ending the union organizing at his electric car company, persuading a battery supplier to put his orders first, quashing community opposition to his rocket launch site, and even changing the view of an SEC commissioner. But this was the first time the Guys had called for a meeting with him, instead of him calling them for help.

They weren't the kind of guys you let sit out in the lobby, where they'd be seen, so they'd been ushered into his office. When Leon finally opened his office door, he was astonished to see Big Frankie sitting at his desk, in his chair.

Walking in beside Leon, his assistant Harrington gave a little concerned gasp.

Leon's office was huge, with a panoramic view over Sand Hill Road. The chair was deliberately higher than his guest chairs and the couch with a coffee table under an original Monet painting. The walk up, across the expensive carpet toward the Aeron chairs, was meant to intimidate, but Leon hadn't experienced the full effect from this side before.

Surprisingly, Big Frankie didn't seem embarrassed about sitting in his chair.

"Uh—" Leon started, waving a hand. *Get out of my chair.*

"It's important to avoid misunderstandings," Big Frankie interrupted, smiling and welcoming Leon in, as if it were Big Frankie's office. "See—me, sitting in your chair. Could be misunderstood as a lack of respect." He showed no sign of moving. "Like, say, being late for a meeting. If we didn't know better." He smiled again, as if to say, all is forgiven.

Leon's main contact with the Guys had been someone named Tony "Hands". Who also had a last name. Santini? Leon's sense was that Big Frankie was Tony's boss.

"Where's Tony Hands?"

"Hands couldn't make it," Big Frankie said. "He died. Of an accounting error."

Standing behind Big Frankie were two old guys and one young, who looked like a newly-minted Stanford MBA, except in a dark suit instead of tech world dressed for casual Friday. Leon was sure he'd misheard, in the middle of taking this all in. "Died from an accounting—?"

"Well, not directly. First there was the error, then the discovery, then lack of a good explanation. Then loud noises." Frankie shrugged. "Ultimately, probably heart failure." He turned to one of the guys behind him, as if for confirmation.

The man nodded. "After losing that much blood, it's usually heart failure."

Leon also had another personal assistant, Tanya Ayotte. He started texting her.

"See," Big Frankie said. "Lesson in life. Even if your name is 'Hands,' don't have too much of other people's money stick to your fingers."

Leon blinked at him. Was that a reference to Leon's XSLA compensation package—all $34 billion of it—that had just been approved by the board? Leon finished his text and hit send: *What happened to Tony "Hands" Santini?*

"You can put away your phone." Something in Big Frankie's expression changed, and the air in the room felt five degrees colder. "You were invited to Tony Hands' funeral."

*Right.* It finally clicked into place. Almost no one had his phone number, but the contact he listed as "the Guys" had texted three times about some funeral invitation they'd snail mailed. He'd ignored it, wondering—was he supposed to send some truckload of flowers?

Big Frankie sighed, as if embarrassed to explain something simple. "Basic respect. We're in business with you. You send a representative." He looked up at the suspended ceiling. "When I was coming up, I spent sometimes four days a month going to funerals. Showing respect. But we make allowances." Frankie waved both hands generously, then gestured with one of them to the youngest guy. "My nephew, Mikey. College Kid. Graduated Stanford University, then Business grad school." He beamed, every bit the proud uncle.

So, the kid *was* a Stanford MBA. What was he doing working with the Guys?

"He tells me we should excuse some lapses," Frankie went on, "because you don't pick up, what do you call it?" He turned to the young guy.

"Social cues," College Kid said. "Cultural cues for appropriate behavior."

Big Frankie nodded. "This—" he waved around, taking in the whole scene "—is a lesson in avoidable misunderstandings. You should have sent a representative to Tony Hands' funeral. Basic respect."

Then he rose. Waved Leon into his own chair. "Lesson over. Have a seat, Rocket Boy. We've got a proposal."

Leon tried not to bristle. The Guys had nicknames for everyone, and Rocket Boy was his.

The pitch memo was only five pages, starting with a one-paragraph executive summary and bullet points on how it would support the XSLA stock price, the exact format Leon insisted from his staff. The Guys were well informed. According to the pitch, the final budget reconciliation being negotiated that week in DC would result in the addition of a new line-item for "space junk removal"—a pilot program to demonstrate a technology to remove junk satellites from orbit and "the feasibility of kinetic de-activation of operating satellites".

The Guys would provide the orbital maneuver modules, or OMMs. Leon's XSpace would launch them into orbit— for a fee, including a profit margin, paid by the government. There would also be a licensing agreement with XSLA, his electric car company, for a variant of the radar and visual tracking solution to help orbital units dock with junk satellites to push them into decaying orbits. And—more important—that would provide revenue for XSLA to beat Wall Street earnings estimates to buoy the stock price.

Maneuverable space vehicles were ridiculously hard to make. "What are you using for the OMM?"

One of Big Frankie's guys handed Leon a lengthy design document. There was something familiar about the schematic. Not just the propulsion system and the elegant compactness, but even the style of the drawing. "Who designed this?"

Frankie smiled broadly. "Two guys. You've heard of them—Spassky and Bromwell."

Leon's assistant Harrington did his intake of breath thing again.

Spassky and Bromwell had been chief engineers at XSpace at the beginning. They'd quit over Leon's supposed interference with design decisions and over his proposed noncompete agreement. Annoyingly, they were still talked about by the engineering team in reverent tones. *Spassky would have... Bromwell thought...* Neither Leon nor his private investigators had found out where they'd gone. If Spassky and Bromwell were involved, this was probably the real deal.

"And the revenue model...?" That was particularly unclear.

"Every time we take a drink, you get a taste," Frankie said.

At Leon's blank look, he added, "You get your beak wet."

After an awkward silence College Kid said, "There's a ten percent revenue participation for XSLA car company, structured as a licensing fee, but providing you discretion under the LLC documents for timing, to allow XSLA to beat earnings expectations in key quarters..."

"I get that." Leon let annoyance creep into his voice. "But revenue from who?" Beyond the initial government funding, who would pay for satellite removal? The deal memo also mentioned a pilot program for a kinetic package to make satellites inoperable. That was easier than satellite docking—just hit it with something at high speed, and a $400 million satellite instantly depreciated to zero. Did the Guys think the CIA would pay them to destroy satellites? The CIA budget was black boxed, but too small for major expenses like satellite destruction.

Frankie held up a hand. "There's 380 satellites up there, if you count only the GEOs."

The satellites in high geostationary orbits around the equator, fixed in place above the spinning earth.

"Lot of 'em cost close to $500 mil." Frank added. "Difficult to replace."

No kidding. There were only one to three launches of geosynchronous satellites a year, and a long waiting list.

"We're numbers guys," one of the big men behind Big Frankie said. He looked more like a pro wrestler in an Italian suit, with a long scar on one cheek. "We wouldn't be doing this unless we were *highly* confident about the money."

"It's called 'protection'," Big Frankie added. "Like insurance. But more...proactive." He smiled at College Kid.

"We target market segments with high replacement value assets," College Kid said helpfully, "otherwise difficult to fully insure."

"Exactly." Big Frankie said. "High replacement value."

Was Frank going to threaten trillion-dollar telecommunications companies? "You can't... just destroy people's satellites." Maybe it was a mistake to include Harrington in this meeting.

"We'd rather not," Big Frankie agreed. "And most people see the value of the insurance we offer, making it unnecessary. A hedge against an irreplaceable loss." He and the Guys behind him all shared smiles, as if that was part of some private joke. "The smart ones will be willing to pay a small part of the satellite's cost, to protect the value of their assets. I assure you, we've *thoroughly* tested this business model."

If something did happen to a couple of geostationary satellites, that would—interestingly enough—make XSpace's launch services more valuable. Leon frowned anyway. "This whole thing is contingent on the U.S. government agreeing, in last-minute budget negotiations—"

"This week. Happening now," Big Frankie said.

"—to pay for it all, and you getting the government contract."

"Yeah. We will. We got what you call a—" Frankie turned to his nephew.

"First mover advantage," College Kid said.

"Yeah. That." Frankie beamed. "We got the hardware. You got rockets to put 'em in orbit. 'Course, you're not sole source for that. There's other rich guys with their little rocket companies. Bald Amazon guy, and even that Musk clown, who likes Russians." Frankie shook his head. "We don't like the Russians. Bad history when they moved in on us, in New York." Then he smiled. "And we've done business with you before."

Many times. And each of the nearly dozen times the Guys had solved a problem for Leon, Leon had contributed a slug of XSLA car company stock into an LLC he owned, 60/40 with the guys. Because Leon formally had control over the

LLC, Leon never had to disclose those transactions as insider stock sales, which might have spooked investors.

Leon's phone dinged. Tanya.

*Tony "Hands" Sabatini was shot to death ten times at close range. Police suspected that there was a message-sending aspect to the shooting, because he was shot, among other places, in both hands. And in the mouth.*

She'd linked an article. Leon would read that later.

"I'm going to have to check with my government affairs guy..." Leon said. How could there be a huge satellite contract in the federal budget he hadn't heard about?

"Of course," Big Frankie said. "Call your guy. But this is the only time we've asked for something. It's important to us."

Leon nodded. "Excuse me." He stepped out to make the call. Harrington went with him.

●

Out in the hall, Leon handed his phone to Harrington. "Get me Ackerman." Gil Ackerman was pretty tied in, given the importance of government contracts to XSpace and of electric car subsidies to XSLA.

It took only seconds. People became available when called on Leon's phone.

"Gil, what's going on?" Leon filled him in on the proposal, and how it was based on space junk removal appearing, at the last minute, in a budget deal.

"That was floated early," Ackerman said, "but never got out of committee."

"So, what are the chances?"

"Slim." Harrington's voice made it sound *extremely* slim. "I mean, there's last-minute horse trading, and nobody's going to see the final version of the bill until the day of the vote. I guess chances are non-zero. But it's not in the House version *or* the Senate's. So, I don't expect some new satellite junk removal or killer satellites in the budget. Say, less than one percent."

Even if he signed, 99% of the time this deal wasn't going to happen anyway. It was throwing a bone to these scary guys who'd been useful in difficult situations. Like Big Frankie had said, they hadn't asked for anything before, which made Leon nervous. Leon hit end call.

Some decisions were hard. This one seemed easy. "What d'you think?" he asked Harrington.

"They've been helpful before," Harrington said, "and if the government funding doesn't come through this week—" He shrugged. "—you're giving them the sleeves off your vest."

Harrington had a knack for putting into words what Leon was already thinking, which was the biggest part of why Leon still kept him around.

●

When Leon re-entered his office, he was pleased to see the Guys sitting respectfully in his guest chairs and on the couch, instead of on his desk chair, which he promptly occupied. "This deal is contingent on Congressional budget approval this week. And on your being selected for the contract." He leaned forward.

Across from him, Big Frankie nodded. "Understood."

"And is subject to board approval."

"Please." Big Frankie gave him a *don't fuck with me* look. "You got the board on such a short leash they pee on the sidewalk. You got them to approve *your* pay."

Was the $34 billion compensation package a sore spot with the Guys? If so, it was good to do this sleeves-off-his-vest deal to placate them. Leon cleared his throat. "Also, you leave Chinese satellites alone." China provided half of XS-LA's finished car manufacturing, along with all of the microprocessors for U.S. models.

Big Frankie waved a hand. "We thoroughly understand the impact of messing with China on our XSLA stock value. You can absolutely trust us, Leon, to act in our own financial interest."

"We are," the muscular guy behind Frankie reiterated, "numbers guys."

Leon smiled and reached across his big desk to shake hands with Big Frankie. "Gentlemen, we have a deal."

●

Leon got the same thrill at a launch he got from watching Formula 1. The sheer power and the stunning sound were part of it, and another piece was wondering if some spectacular catastrophe was about to occur. He'd seen a lot of his rockets go up—and some go sideways and down—but today was different, because Big Frankie and his guys were here to watch. The Guys' satellite was—by far—the heaviest of the seven in the payload today, because of its internal fuel-and-maneuver capacity and two OMMs.

•

"T-minus 8." The speaker crackled. "Raptor 7 on internal power."

They were at Launch Operations, gazing into the pre-dawn darkness, close enough to see the steam-like clouds venting from the two-stage Raptor 7 launch vehicle on the pad.

Leon had yet to meet the Guys' satellite project director, Chiara Bianchi, who was reported to be very hot. He glanced down cargo row, the line of monitors for checking payload.

There. Dark-haired woman. Super cute. Even more attractive than his third ex-wife, and definitely younger. "I'm going to say hi to Chiara."

Big Frankie neatly intercepted him by stepping in the way. "Key-ar-ah," Big Frankie corrected, looking pained. "Not 'chee-'. The ch is a 'K' sound."

"Oh, like Kitty," Leon said.

"You think it's hard for women in tech?" Frankie didn't move out of his way. "Our organization is what College Kid here—" He waved a hand. "—calls even more 'male-dominated'. You find a woman running an important line, you know she climbed over a huge pile of bodies to get there." It was hard to tell if Frankie meant figuratively or literally.

"She sounds interesting." She also looked shorter than Leon. Leon liked that.

Big Frankie sighed. "I bet you're already thinking what kind of number you're going to run on Chiara, thinking she's a 'Kitty'."

Leon tried to compose his face into something resembling an innocent look. His reputation must have reached even the Guys.

"T minus six minutes," the calm voice announced. "Stage one fuel loading complete."

"Kitty, maybe." Big Frankie continued. "But not the house-cat kind. More like lioness. Last guy who pulled stuff with her is still missing...." Frankie trailed off, then shook his head. "It's mostly not my business how you conduct 'staff meetings' or what meat is involved."

It was well-known Leon had fathered four children with four different subordinates.

"But Chiara means 'bright,' Rocket Boy. So don't do anything stupid." Frankie made a sweeping "be my guest" gesture and stepped aside.

At Chiara's launch station, Leon began, "Hi, I'm—"

"I know who you are." Chiara's eyes barely flicked to him before they returned to her monitor. "I'm a little busy here, champ."

"I'd like to have a look at the final schematics for the payload." Leon stood closer to her than necessary, but she didn't look up again. She was definitely hot, with black hair cut short enough that he could see part of her slender neck. The twenty or so status bars she was monitoring were all a reassuring green.

Chiara clicked briefly on a tablet to pull up the schematic and then slid it across the workspace, positioning it so he'd have to retreat to stand over it. To Leon's surprise, on the schematic even more parts were redacted, with only a notation of the unchanged weight.

"What are these new components in black?" he asked.

"None of your business." She said it without heat, like telling him the Earth was round.

"Well, it quite literally is my business, isn't it?"

"Piss off," Chiara said, "and step out of my space. I've got a list of shit to keep track of. That list does not include your hormones or your questions. Frankie!" She raised her voice. "Can you reposition Rocket Boy so I can concentrate?"

"All right, all right." Leon backed away. "I get the message."

"I doubt it." Chiara went back to staring at her monitor. "But you will."

●

"Liquid Ox top-off complete. T-minus four minutes."

Leon was back at the big front window, next to Frankie. This was the dangerous phase. The rocket was a complicated set of tubes now completely full of powerful explosives.

Even Big Frankie looked nervous, staring out into the darkness at the tall, lit-up rocket.

"Relax," Leon told him. "Trust my technology."

"Your technology," Frankie snorted. "I'd trust it better if you took better care of your difficult messengers."

"My what?" Like some of the other things Frankie had said in that New Jersey-or-whatever accent, Leon wasn't sure he'd correctly heard the man.

"Messengers. With bad news. Some guy tells you your launch pad is messed up, you take it personal and fire the guy.

Word gets around. Next guy you ask, how's it going with fixing the launch pad? He says, 'Great, boss!' whether it is or not."

"Flight termination system to internal power." Now even the voice at launch control sounded stressed. "T-minus three minutes."

"Let me tell you a story, Rocket Boy. When I came up, Louie 'the Duke' Graziano headed our organization. He asked everybody two things: First, can you tell me something I don't want to hear? Second, what's keeping you awake nights, worried we don't have an answer to?" Big Frankie turned to Leon and fixed him with those scary, deep eyes. "So, some kid tells him early: The Russians are here, hungrier than we are, they haven't gone soft, and they got help offshore—their whole country is a criminal enterprise run by ex-KGB guys."

Big Frankie looked out into the darkness, frowning. "So, we packed up. The other families fought with the Russians and lost ground, then got taken apart by the Mayor and the FBI, then lost everything. Instead, we cut deals, sold off, turned things into cash, and figured out how to infiltrate the government, so when we slugged it out next time, we'd be on home turf."

Advice exactly not applicable to the tech world, which was about the 100x return on the upside, not about cutting your losses, a rounding error on finances at the end of the day.

"All tanks at flight pressure. Go for launch."

Frankie sighed again, as if he could read Leon's thoughts on his face. "The point, Rocket Boy, is you don't know what you don't know. You should ask your people what you *don't* want to hear. That would give us more faith in your technology. And in you."

"Four, three, two, one...ignition!"

Orange bloomed at the base of the rocket, a boiling carnation of fire. The satisfying crackling roar hit, loud enough Leon could feel it in his chest. The rocket rose, slowly, then faster, as the connecting gantry toppled to the right. The Raptor 7 accelerated smoothly up and out of the huge observation window.

Leon pivoted to the huge video screen in the corner. The camera, shaking slightly, was trained on the bright dagger of flame as the rocket crackled up, up, up through the clouds, arcing into the sky, the bright gold flames, now trailed by blue ones, like a halo. It had passed through maximum atmospheric pressure already. The plume spread and lengthened in the lighter upper atmosphere. A perfect launch.

•

"Fifty meters," Bobby Razor said, counting down the approach. "No doppler, no change in orientation." It was two months after launch, and their OMM was closing on the Insat-1A in geostationary orbit over the Indian Ocean. The Guys were in a side control console room at Leon's XSpace facility. Aside from Leon, they were the only ones with access to this room. They'd picked a day when Leon was in Europe.

Big Frankie didn't expect the target to maneuver—it hadn't in 40 years—but this was practice for the Chinese satellites later. Those later approaches would be accompanied by a release of shredded aluminum chaff at lower altitude, to mask what was happening from radar.

Fingers, a man with a narrow face, rubbed his hands together and then gently touched the control joystick, his eyes on the big flatscreen with the video feed and the radar info.

The next part was tricky. There was a quarter-second delay in round-trip messages to the OMM in geostationary orbit, so the operator had to allow for that lag.

*But we got the right guy for that,* Frankie thought. He and Chiara were in the back of the room, on a little raised platform, watching Bobby Razor and Fingers at their consoles. Fingers was a skimmer, who could throw a pair of dice so one of the cubes slid all the way across the craps table and just barely bumped the back wall before it came to a stop, with the chosen number on top, while the other cube bounced enthusiastically. That meant the odds on a bunch of the bets on the table were six times more likely to come up.

Fingers was good with making sure where things ended in the near future.

Insat-1A now filled about a third of the huge viewscreen, a partly hollow box with raised bumps on the bottom. Two solar panel wings stuck out, attached by y-bracing that looked like arms. The angle of the two solar panels didn't quite match.

Chiara snorted. "That is one complete cluster of a fuck-up satellite."

It was. The solar panels had only partially extended, and the stabilizing boom never deployed. A valve problem had drained its fuel. When it went inactive it didn't even have fuel to push itself into a dive toward the atmosphere and instead had been orbiting space junk since.

"Twenty meters," Bobby Razor said.

They were approaching the satellite from its underside, positioned to jam incoming S-band and C-band radio transmissions with overwhelming static.

"Say, you got five minutes left with the chaff cloud." Big Frankie pushed start on an old-fashioned stopwatch. They'd probably have lots more than that when they made their move on China, but it was good to practice fast and smooth.

It took Fingers less than three minutes.

He wrapped the two extruder tentacles around the struts holding the satellite's solar panels and maneuvered the OMM so its cushioned nose was flat against the junk satellite's side.

"Accelerating." Fingers sounded happy.

Which was really more like braking to the junk satellite, slowing its orbit so gravity would pull it down.

"It'll be breaking up soon enough," Chiara said, as if she could read Big Frankie's mind.

They were about to earn their proof-of-concept fee from the government. Frankie smiled. Imagine that. The government, paying his guys. They'd jettison the two extruders and maneuver to strike again. But Insat-1A was slowing and falling now, and would be atmospheric toast. Big Frankie gestured to take in the whole room and the sky beyond. "I always liked fireworks."

●

To great fanfare, Insat-1A burned up on re-entry over the Pacific.

Mysteriously and maybe not coincidentally, an object traveling at high speed struck the Russian Luch-2, turning it into a debris field. The Luch-2 was broadly suspected of carrying anti-satellite weapons. Reading the news, Leon thought, *the Guys eliminated the competition.*

Leon tried the questions Big Frankie suggested, asking at meetings for bad news and asking what kept his managers awake at night. The results were astonishing. He learned more in four months about his companies' most critical issues than he had in four years of meetings and operating reports—including that supplies of key components from China had all recently become just-in-time deliveries, with no cushion of parts in inventory.

Three expensive telecom satellites stopped functioning, apparently victims of similar collisions with fast-moving objects. None were insured, but there was talk anyway about the two major satellite insurers not writing new policies, and also charging a "supplemental risk" premium to continue coverage. There was supposedly a new insurance company entering the market, but no one knew anything about its backing.

A press release from the Guys' venture describing how these "sudden failures" underlined the critical need for removing space junk, which could otherwise "lead to loss of expensive and hard-to-replace satellites." *If that was the work of the Guys,* Leon thought, *why bother creating a docking vehicle, when they could just smash satellites from a distance?*

Serious revenue rolled in under the licensing agreement. Forty million in licensing fees for XSLA in the first quarter out of the LLC, modest compared to other sources, but providing a whole new category that allowed the company to beat analysts' estimates.

Alarmingly, Leon was now dodging angry phone calls from telecommunications company CEOs. He'd have Harrington respond with the polite statement that XSpace was simply in the satellite launch business and did not monitor what telecommunications companies—or anyone else—did with that payload.

July brought a second launch of a different satellite supplied by the Guys into low earth orbit, with almost everything on the schematic blacked out. It was the final item covered by the expenses-plus-profit terms of the government appropriation, but the publicly-available launch materials listed it only as an "XSpace supplemental communications package."

•

Right after that launch, Leon insisted on a conversation with Big Frankie. Two of Frankie's guys went with him, but waited outside when Leon stepped into one of the conference rooms down the hallway from launch control. It was furnished with a long table of blond wood surrounded on three sides by bland art, the fourth side a panoramic window onto the launch site, sunny in the late morning, now empty of its rocket.

There were no OMMs in this payload, and it wasn't headed anywhere high enough to reach the satellites in geostationary orbits. "I don't understand what you're doing—"

Leon started, which was fairly breathtaking. He'd almost never used the words *I don't understand.*

"Rocket Boy," Big Frankie clapped him on the back. "After you catch the whales, you go after tuna."

Leon looked at him blankly, then said, "Oh. Low-earth-orbit satellites."

Big Frankie beamed, as if proud of him. "Exactly. Might cost only $500,000 each, but there are thousands of 'em."

Including hundreds of Leon's XLink communication satellites. Were more angry CEOs going to call? He looked at Frankie with alarm. "I'm worried that this is getting out of hand—"

A loud knock shook the door, and the muscular guy with the Italian suit and the scarred cheek stepped in, without waiting for an invitation. "Sorry, boss," he said to Big Frankie, without looking at Leon. "Important return call. Telesat." He handed a phone to Frankie.

"Gotta take this," Big Frankie said.

Leon wasn't used to people taking calls while they were in a meeting with him. Telesat provided broadband to most of Canada. When their geostationary satellite was launched, it had more communications capacity than all the other satellites over North America combined. Apparently, unlike him, Big Frankie *was* taking calls from communications company CEOs.

"—Garrett, it's not a threat," Big Frankie was saying. "It's a sure bet. You can pay for the insurance, and I guarantee nothing will happen to your bird. Or, you can decide not, in which case, consider your bird cooked."

What the person on the other end of the phone said, for a Canadian, didn't sound polite.

"I thought after the last incident you'd have a new appreciation." Big Frankie raised his free hand in a half shrug. "But maybe we should talk *after* the next time there's a collision. Be a shame if something happened this week, though..."

Frankie listened for another minute. "You have our wiring instructions. We'll have some coffee, and if it goes well, we'll be calling it a day instead of keeping ourselves busy, if you know what I mean. And I think you do."

Leon was in a state of shock. Although he'd heard the scheme outlined, he somehow never thought the Guys could really start a protection racket in space and call it "insurance". Yet, here he was, watching it in action. And oh, shit. He was involved. "Uh," he said. "You need to not mess with China."

Big Frankie clapped him on the back again. "We fully understand the importance of China to XSLA. And the exact nature of our investment."

It wasn't until later that Leon thought about the ambiguities in that statement.

•

Harrington's face looked especially pale the morning he met with Leon.

"Something's going on," Harrington said. "Somebody's massively shorting XSLA." Shorts sold shares they'd borrowed, instead of actually owned, betting that a stock's price would go down sharply before they had to buy shares back to repay the loan.

Leon shrugged. They'd always crushed the shorts before, because if the stock price went up, the shorts faced huge losses.

"It's a record amount, Leon. And it's none of the usual players. XSLA shares are down nine percent in early trading, on high volume."

Well. It would be a perfect time to find some unanticipated revenue from the licensing deal to announce. Leon reached for his phone.

•

Big Frankie had suggested they meet at his brother Carmine's house in Hillsboro. It was large, like the other $8-million-plus McMansions along the tree-lined street, but as Leon looked around the dark living room, he thought *cheesy dump*. Clearly, Carmine had learned his decorating skills at the School of Tony Soprano. It was odd to be meeting at the house of Big Frankie's brother, but Leon figured it was to stay out of public view, which seemed reasonable.

"Have a seat," Big Frankie waved to a nearby gold velour chair.

"No, thanks." Leon hoped this meeting wouldn't take long. "My watch says I haven't met my stand goal yet for today."

"Suit yourself." Big Frankie shrugged. "But I'm guessing at some point you'll want to sit. You're worried about all the short-selling. Did I use that term right? Short selling?"

Big Frankie's face gave nothing away. Did he know something? "Not especially *worried*," Leon said. "Concerned. In the end, we've always crushed the shorts. But to create a short squeeze it would be nice to have good earnings news."

There was a long silence, which made Leon finally look away from the prominent gold crucifix on the wall to study Big Frankie's face. Somehow, Frankie's usual annoying faint smirk now looked more like a shark's grin. It unsettled Leon, a message triggering something deep in his limbic system. *Be afraid.*

"Good news?" Big Frankie shook his head, then looked at the other wall as if there was invisible writing on it. "I'm thinking there might be bad news."

Leon's phone buzzed. It began as a couple of text alerts but then, like popcorn in the microwave, it was hard to tell one buzz from the next. And the alarm Leon had only heard twice since he'd had the phone. A car horn honk, signifying that the XSLA stock price had dropped over ten percent in 10 minutes.

"You may want to look at that thing," Big Frankie said.

With a practiced motion, Leon whipped out his phone and scanned the alerts.

"Oh, shit." He sat down.

China had shut down all XSLA manufacturing in their country and stopped all shipments of XSLA parts to the U.S. With the prior shift to just-in-time delivery of key components, that meant that all U.S. manufacturing would stop within two days.

The car horn honk alarm sounded *again.* Another ten percent drop.

China had announced the changes would be "permanent" if they didn't reach a new agreement with XSLA, in their sole discretion. The XSLA stock price was in free fall.

"Shit indeed," Big Frankie agreed. "Last night, we pushed two Chinese GEO satellites into decaying orbits," Big Frankie said. "Nothing we can't fix. If we want. Soon."

Leon opened his mouth, but no words came out. XSLA stock was down thirty percent in just minutes. If it went down another ten percent, there would be a margin call, and banks would start foreclosing on shares Leon had put up as collateral for buying his social media company. When that foreclosure became public, it would trigger another public shareholder panic selloff.

"We're in discussions with China," Big Frankie went on.

"You said—" Leon's voice went up an octave in the space of those two words. "—you wouldn't mess with their satellites."

"No." Big Frankie's voice was steely. "I said we knew messing with China would hurt the XSLA stock price. Let me tell you a story about my Great Uncle, Harry the Horse."

Leon did not want to hear stories about Anyone the Horse. But apparently, he needed Big Frankie's cooperation to fix the stock-price free fall. He gritted his teeth. His phone made the car honk noise again.

"Harry made the legal Nevada sportsbook bets for a syndicate tied into college trainers." Big Frankie waved a hand, to indicate a big circle of people, as if they were all scattered through this big living room among the dark furniture. "In the pros, they got required injury reports—what players are probable, doubtful..." He looked at Leon, as if giving him a rating. "... or out. But there's no system for college. So, if you know what other people don't, you can bet before the point spread moves. Then, you have the trainer announce there's a problem, and bet the other side, *after* the point spread moves." He paused, as if waiting for Leon to catch up. "College Kid tells me you call this 'arbitrage'."

What did this have to do with the XSLA stock price and China? "What—?" Leon's voice was an almost incoherent gurgle.

"Rocket Boy." Frankie shook his head, as if disappointed, like he'd expected Leon to be a faster learner. "You don't have to know how the game ends, as long as you know which way the point spread will move. We'll meet with you in five days, in your office, to discuss a fix. But excuse me. I got money to make."

•

Leon's phone honked twice more on the drive back to the office.

•

China wouldn't talk to Leon. He'd gotten terse messages, first that they were negotiating with "the true parties," and then that "a deal has been made." China publicly announced that "agreements in principle have been reached" and would be disclosed when "confirmed in writing." The two diverted Chinese satellites were returned to their original positions. In the meantime, over the five days before the scheduled meeting with the Guys, the value of all XSLA's outstanding shares shrank by over 400 billion dollars. A huge chunk of that money ended up in the pockets of the short-sellers who'd started the crash, selling borrowed shares at the top, and then buying them back for a fifth of the price. The Guys.

•

That morning, a delegation from China was waiting in another conference room to sign agreements, but they'd insisted that Leon meet first with the Guys, "who will explain the deal".

The deal memo on Leon's desk was even shorter than five pages. Below the terse executive summary, it said XSLA stock price would likely rebound somewhat after the supply chain was restored, but he had to give up his share in satellite project revenues, which would instead go to China, to ensure continued parts supply.

The taste in Leon's mouth was like wet ashes. The stock price would never get back to the earlier highs, because XSLA had never been priced by the numbers. He'd been selling an idea—the stock that only goes up, in the future of transportation. Now it was just a carmaker, except tiny compared to the big ones, and with no dealer network. Leon looked across his desk to Big Frankie and his guys.

"How could you do this? You were...*shareholders*." They'd had a forty percent interest in an LLC that held hundreds of thousands of shares.

"Shareholders?" Big Frankie stood and loomed over him. "You got a lot of nerve. You think I'm some kind of *scungille*?"

"A big snail," College Kid translated helpfully. "Slow, not very bright guy."

"You think I'm some kind of *mammalucco*?"

"A patsy," College Kid said.

Leon shook his head. If there was a patsy in the room, it wasn't Big Frankie.

"You call us 'shareholders,' but under the agreement, we can't sell those shares to get real cash. They just sit there." A vein throbbed on Big Frankie's forehead. "You call us 'shareholders' but don't even consult us, when you vote 'our' shares to increase your pay by 34 billion for practically a no-show job, because you're running two other companies."

The throbbing vein could not possibly be good news. Leon wondered if he should call security, but the cut of the Guys' Italian suit jackets was designed to conceal shoulder holsters. He did *not* want a shootout in his office. He glanced at the Monet on the wall.

"I take *my* time," Big Frankie continued, "to educate you on respect and running an organization. And do you take that opportunity to come back and apologize? No. Do you ever ask me to tell you something you don't want to hear? No."

"College Kid," Frankie asked, "what did we warn Leon?"

"We specialize in assets with a high replacement value."

"Yeah." Frankie nodded. "Like the stock price of a company that sells a battery-powered car, whose stock sells for 87 times earnings. Oh. Excuse me—*used* to sell at 87 times earnings, but now sells for 14 times earnings. Maybe you should have paid us protection, Rocket Boy."

Leon didn't even want to read the rest of the three pages. "So, what's the deal?"

"We promised not to launch any more OMMs," Big Frankie said.

There was no way Leon would launch another satellite for the Guys.

"And turned over control of our two OMMs in high orbit to the Chinese," Big Frankie added. "Now that they have almost no maneuver fuel."

*So, you gave them the sleeves off your vest,* Leon thought. "There are laws," he said slowly and distinctly, "against insider trading."

"Laws." Big Frankie laughed. "You bring in the law, it goes bad for you. A chunk of the shares we borrowed were the LLC's. Yours. Any investigation, I guarantee, wraps around to your front door."

Right. The LLC agreement prohibited selling shares. But not lending them. When they'd met five days earlier, Big Frankie had said, *short selling. Do I have that term right?* The Guys had played him.

Leon read the memo, outlining the agreements waiting for him in the other conference room. He felt like he'd swallowed a stone.

•

Of course, nothing in the memo addressed whatever the Guys had launched into low earth orbit.

•

The new control room was more cramped than the one back at XSpace, but it had the comfortable lived-in look of a bachelor apartment for a dedicated console gamer, with a small refrigerator and a microwave. A still-warm pizza sat on the conference table in the middle. One entire wall was taken up by a huge monitor and crowded computer equipment.

"No change, no orienting for maneuver," Bobby Razor said.

He and Fingers were both looking at the radar rangefinder. This was a head-on pass.

Fingers gently closed his right hand around the joystick. The whizzing patterns of the low earth orbit satellites made for more difficult intercepts. Kinetic kills, though, with just a tungsten projectile, were much easier than docking.

"Target acquired."

He tapped a button. "Fire one."

There was a several second delay.

"Yeah! Trackable debris." Bobby Razor sounded like a guy cheering for a touchdown. "That's a kill."

"Good-bye, Russian satellite." Fingers sat back in satisfaction. "Hello, space junk."

•

Leon watched from his car as the last of his office furniture came out the door of his former HQ. Wall Street loved cost-cutting through down-sizing and letting employees go. Leon didn't. Even his $34 billion compensation package was almost all in stock grants, now worth less than the taxes on it when it was granted. For years he had only watched his numbers go up. Now he probably wasn't even on the list of the 100 richest humans. He felt hollow. He had no mechanism for processing this new version of his world's math.

•

Frankie settled back in the seat of his stretch town car. Most of his peers had long switched to overgrown SUVs, mostly armored. But Frankie enjoyed this touchstone to the past. It helped him remember the fundamentals: A little pressure here, a threat made good there—all starting a stream of income, steady and predictable. Business looked good, along with both sets of books, and the competition was in check. He basked in the glow of winning the numbers game. He relaxed his shoulders.

Maybe he was too relaxed. Otherwise, he might have noticed the car with a diplomatic number plate following, two cars back.

---

**Dean Gloster's** checkered past includes being a law clerk at the U.S. Supreme Court and doing stand-up comedy. He is now a full-time writer in Berkeley, California. His YA novel *Dessert First* is available from Simon & Schuster, and his short stories have appeared in *Spoon Knife 6: Rest Stop* and *Spoon Knife 7: Transitions*. He is at work on two more YA novels and makes anti-authoritarian ramblings on Bluesky at *@deangloster.bsky.social*.

**Jay Cherrie** is an old soul in an old body who lives in Alameda, California. He worked in a casino and a hotel before spending 43 years in banking technology. Now retired from IT, he does some consulting and catches up on other interests. One of those interests turned out to be a bit of writing. Jay can be found on Threads as @jayscherrie.

**Sarah Teresa Cook**

# Three Observational Poems in Six Words

**On the refusal to feel difficult feelings**

As fast as I could,
red-handed

**On mustering up some hopefulness after a long year**

Star-shaped, you turn
toward the moon

**On the obligatory self-referential nature of poetry**

Made myself a stanza too long

---

**Sarah Teresa Cook** is a neurodivergent writer, poet, and creative mentor. She lives in Oregon and publishes For the Birds, a Substack newsletter about writing, resilience, and the natural world. Learn more at sarahteresacook.com.

**Rachelle Stein-Wotten**

# *The Future's Potential*

Reference Number: 241x032xx1

**RE: Important Land Status Information**

Dear Wildlife Member:

Our records indicate you are the last wild-born northern spotted owl living in a valley of what we call the lower Fraser Canyon region, others call Nlaka'pamux Territory and you call [not provided]. <u>This is to inform you that we have recently approved a land status re-designation in your future generations' possible homes.</u>

>>Your current traditional home that our scientists have identified as your best chance of survival and only place to live due to the fact that you require old-growth forest where we understand you mostly consume flying squirrel and pack-rat, interferes with approved cutblocks.<< These are areas that our researchers, in consultation with our supporters, have identified as profitably preferable.

Our legislation requires we identify and map what is to be known as your *core critical habitat* in order to preserve the continuation of your bloodline, and species overall. We understand that without this core critical habitat, the likeliness of you producing offspring is lower than if you did not have it. Recently we have introduced a new designation that, while not legally required, provides a new layer of description: *potential future critical habitat.*

Potential future critical habitat are lands that we consider a possibility for you and your future, potential offspring.

(A reminder that our biologists captured your three children from the past two years, the last ones you produced before the death of your mate, so that we could integrate your bloodline into our captive breeding program. This program is located at a multi-million dollar breeding centre in a municipality you may or may not be aware of known as Langley. The state-of-the-art facility houses 30 owls and is funded by our government at no charge to you.)

We understand from the scientific community that your future offspring require habitat. As your progeny are at this point only a potentiality, we have thus assigned these lands on our maps—see attachment 4—as the aforementioned potential future critical habitat. If, in future, you successfully rear owlets again, this land will be recorded by our government as critical for their continued survival. But, if by an undetermined timeline they are not confirmed present, we reserve the right to remove the habitat for alternative benefit—see attachment 5b for detailed projections from our economists and lobbyists.

(Our records indicate a male spotted owl living in the area that we call the Utzlius watershed was unsuccessful in locating a mate and has not been located by members of our team and therefore been designated as missing and/or dead. If you have contact with this individual, please tell him to identify himself at the nearest government facility.)

Our recovery strategy for you and other individuals of your species (have you seen the last male of the Utzlius watershed? Tell him to contact us.) agrees to maintain *sufficient critical habitat* for your survival. As such, we will cease human-caused threats such as clearcutting *where spotted owls are detected*. In other words if we see one of you, we will stop removing your homes. <u>Thus, it is critical you show yourselves to the nearest government official.</u>

*The Northern Spotted Owl Breeding Program has dedicated 15 years to caring for its population of spotted owls. Please be aware that three individuals from our captive program have been released in your area and are equipped with GPS backpacks, at no cost to you, so that our experts in your ways can track their movements. Up until the time of release, they have been fed euthanized rats and mice. Please support their integration into your community.* >>Update: One owl has been injured and recaptured.

If you have questions such as how and when decisions on whether potential future critical habitat will be transferred to core critical habitat, we are pleased to inform you that a schedule of studies will make such a verification by 2083. If you do not expect to be alive any time between now and 2083, please designate a future relative with whom the government may notify of any changes.

The future potential of the northern spotted owl is important to us. >>*Update: The other two captives have died. The bodies have been relocated to our breeding facility for necropsy. We will not be releasing further information at this time.*

Your cooperation and interest in this matter is appreciated. Any inquiries must include your reference number. Please do not respond to this notification.

Yours sincerely,
The Government

Referenced material, with thanks to the reporting of Sarah Cox:

Cox, Sarah. "Old-growth spotted owl habitat removed from federal maps after talks with B.C., docs reveal." *The Narwhal*, March 15, 2023 https://thenarwhal.ca/bc-spotted-owl-habitat-removed.

Cox, Sarah. "Canada's Trans Mountain pipeline destroys spotted owl habitat feds have vowed to protect." *The Narwhal*, March 17, 2023 https://thenarwhal.ca/trans-mountain-spotted-owls/.

"Joint statement on death of two spotted owls released into the wild in 2022." Government of British Columbia, May 12, 2023. Press release.

---

**Rachelle Stein-Wotten's** writing has appeared in, among others, *The Temz Review*, *Counterflow*, JÓN Magazine, and *The Belladonna* and her sketches have been performed in Vancouver and Seattle. She writes and eats mostly vegetables from her home on Vancouver Island.

**Marilia Angeline**

# *raw*

maybe I'm raw and I can't be
refined or molded when I break

the mold just by breathing
and I am not flawless

sculpture— because I speak up
and they could never bind my feet

when I know the art
of walking away

and I can't be measured
in measures;
how dare I be
imprecise...

how dare I be?

how could I not—

dare
to
be

**Marilia Angeline** is a poet, writer, actor, and transformation coach based in Los Angeles. She holds degrees in Creative Writing & Literature and Drama from The University of Michigan. Marilia's work explores themes of neurodivergence, voice, femininity, and spirituality/mythology. Her poetry has been featured by the City of West Hollywood, *Myth & Lore*, *Apparition Lit*, and is forthcoming in *NewMyths*.

**Jenni Brooks**

# One, Two, Three

Joy bounces up and down, up and down, up and down. She lifts up her arms, fingers stretched so wide she almost can't feel them. She can barely feel the rest of her, either. Her body's weightless, like she doesn't have one. Like her hair has dissolved, her legs have melted, and she no longer has a physical form. Hearing herself squeal, she claps her hands, made out of playdough. They don't have any bones. She'd do this all day if it was up to her. This or swimming, or running. She pretends not to hear Mrs. Fisher tell her to stop. It's time for lunch.

Joy jumps around with her back to her. Not yet, she thinks. But Mrs. Fisher leans on the trampoline, tilting it. Losing her balance, Joy slows.

'Joy, come on.' Mrs Fisher grabs her hand.

Joy snatches it back. Her legs and face have grown back. She can feel her hair as well. Buckling over, she clutches her ears.

'Joy, come off the trampoline. Come on. I'm going to count to three.' Mrs Fisher gets a toffee out of her pocket. Joy can hear the cellophane crinkling. 'One. Two...' The thought of it makes her feel sick; she's had so many of them since the start of term, but Mrs. Fisher won't stop until she's come down, and put it in her mouth. She does it slowly, her body a cumbersome creature. Mrs. Fisher presses the toffee in her hand. 'Good girl,' she sings, 'that's it.'

Joy humours her, smiling wide. She drools as the toffee glues her teeth.

•

Joy hates the lunch hall. It smells like wet biscuits and feet. The other pupils don't seem to like it, either; their faces contort, as their one-to-ones try to make them eat yogurt. Sometimes, Joy can hear a collective groan, like a choir, when she comes in, complete with cymbals of dessert spoons hitting the floor. There's always a few pupils tossing theirs about. Their TAs will pick them back up, maybe wipe them with a paper towel. There's no point in washing them or getting a new one; they'd be at it all day. Giving their students the spoons back, they'll tell them to try again.

Joy wonders how many times she'd have to toss her cutlery for them to just give up. So far, she's up to three. She hopes to get higher one day. She probably already is, but she always gets distracted and loses count. She doesn't know what comes after 10 anyway. The rest of her class usually get stuck after seven. They've been working on it for months.

Leading Joy to a seat, Mrs. Fisher puts a bib on her, tying it around her neck. She doesn't pull her hair through. It's stuck there, tickling her. Rocking a little, Joy tries to scratch her neck. She hopes Miss won't notice and try to get her to stop.

A young woman comes with a meal tray, putting it in front of Joy. She mutters something to Mrs. Fisher about how she's supposed to be shadowing her.

'Oh yes. You must be *Duh...*' she trails off. 'New TA?'

'Yes,' she smiles. 'I'm Daiyu. You can call me Di, if it's easier.'

Mrs. Fisher chuckles, muttering something about how she's glad she has a nickname. Pulling her lips in, Daiyu smirks. She turns to Joy, smiles briefly, then looks away. Joy's glad. She seems better than the other newbies, who can't resist staring until she smiles back. Which she never does, she just grimaces, but they seem to take what they can get.

Mrs. Fisher goes through the lunchtime routine with Daiyu, telling her about the foods that Joy won't want to eat. Pasta, egg, baked beans, which funnily enough make an appearance on her tray.

Scraping her chair, 'Oh sorry,' Daiyu says. She goes to take it away, but Mrs. Fisher stops her, her hand on her arm.

'No, it's fine. It's good.' She says it might seem cruel, but Joy's diet is very limited. It's the same with a lot of the kids. That's what this programme is for; otherwise, they would have to be tube fed. 'That's what happens in a lot of the other schools.' Picking up the fork, Mrs. Fisher hands it to Joy, taking the fidget spinner off her. Joy found it in her pocket while they were talking. 'Come on,' she says. 'Then you'll get it back.'

Joy throws the fork. One.

Mrs. Fisher picks it up and hands it back to her. 'Try the beans.' She rubs her stomach. 'Hmmm tasty.'

Joy wonders if she's ever tried them herself. They don't look tasty. They look rancid. The skin on them makes her palms sweat. She throws the fork again. Two. This time, Mrs.

Fisher picks it up and hands it to Daiyu. 'Put some pasta on it. Try her with that.'

Daiyu does, but she looks at it tentatively, like she's going to gag herself. She hands it to Joy, apologetically. Joy almost doesn't throw it, out of respect, but it slips out of her hand. 'Three,' Joy says, as she rocks. 'Three, three. Three, three.' She can't get her mouth to say 'Th' though; she spits slightly as she pronounces 'F.'

Picking up the fork, Mrs. Fisher delights. 'Yes, Joy! That's how you say free.' She raises her hand, trying to give Joy a high five. When Joy doesn't accept, Mrs. Fisher leans forward, slapping it lightly anyway. Rocking harder, Joy snatches her hands away, wringing them together. 'You have to praise them, if they use their words. It's how they know to carry on doing it.' Handing Daiyu the fork again, Mrs. Fisher tells her to give Joy some egg this time. 'Give her a thumbs up if she complies.'

●

As they clear up, Mrs. Fisher asks Daiyu, 'So, what got you interested in this line of work?'

'I'm autistic.' Daiyu gulps. 'So I can empathise with the kids.'

Frowning gravely, Mrs. Fisher takes off Joy's bib. Joy breathes out, swaying in relief. 'The kids that are here have it a lot worse than you. This might not be what you're expecting.'

Joy watches Daiyu. 'What do you mean, worse?'

Mrs. Fisher looks down. This has got to be good. Joy kind of wishes she had some popcorn now, if the hulls didn't break off and stick to her tongue.

'You're level one, aren't you?'

'And you can tell, just by looking at me?'

Mrs. Fisher fishes in her pocket, giving Joy her fidget back. After leading her and Daiyu into the hall, she locks the door behind them. Skipping ahead, Joy zooms up and down the corridor, shaking her curls off her face. While she's stimming, she hears Mrs. Fisher mutter something about Daiyu undermining her. 'We've got to be a united front, you see.'

Daiyu smiles a fake smile, because, like Joy's, they all must be. Joy wonders if she's expecting a crisp for it, or one of her toffees, or a sticker. She mutters an, 'Of course,' and Joy spots a speck of saliva fly out of her mouth. It glints and lands on Mrs. Fisher's shoe. Joy wonders if it was on purpose. She means, *she* drools all the time. She doesn't even realise it's happening, until she feels that the top of her polo shirt is soaked. Maybe Daiyu's the same. Joy watches her staring at where the spit has landed. Mrs. Fisher hasn't seemed to notice. She just heads into the office, opposite, to get out Joy's file. Daiyu stays in the corridor with Joy. Her back against the wall, she lowers her head. Joy thinks she can see a glimmer in Daiyu's face as she spins. As she rotates again, it's gone. Daiyu wipes her mouth with the back of her hand.

Coming back out, Mrs. Fisher shows Daiyu Joy's file, telling her what to put in it after mealtimes. Joy wonders if she timed it right, she could send the papers flying. She spins closer as Mrs. Fisher fishes the papers out. Just lightly, Joy nudges Daiyu and Daiyu bumps into Mrs. Fisher, harder than she had to. Bullseye. The papers fly, floating onto the floor like leaves.

'Sorry,' Daiyu says, 'that was my fault,' as Mrs. Fisher puts the folder down and tuts. As Daiyu crouches down and helps her pick them up, Joy runs around, trampling on the pages that are left.

'Joy, stop!' Mrs. Fisher says. A few of the papers rip under Joy's feet. Once they've caught them, Miss gives Daiyu a toffee. She tells her to give it to Joy, if she can get her to go to the sensory room.

Daiyu unwraps it. As Joy runs back toward her, she sees Daiyu examine it. 'We're going in there,' she says, pointing to the room where Mrs. Fisher's going. When Joy goes with her, Daiyu offers the toffee, but Joy keeps her hands by her sides. She genuinely couldn't stomach another one, even if she wanted to. Putting the toffee in her trouser pocket, Daiyu motions for Joy to chew. Joy pretends to, happily, stomping her feet, clapping her hands. Mrs. Fisher turns back to the pair of them. 'Awesome, Joy!' she croons. Zooming through the door she's opened, Joy jumps onto the bean bag with the spaghetti lights. Running them over her eyes, she looks at Daiyu through them.

'Second time lucky.' Sitting down, Mrs. Fisher gets the file out again. Daiyu tries not to laugh at Joy playing peek-a-boo with her.

●

Tuesdays are one-to-one language days: a group of eight pupils per classroom, plus eight teachers, and three TAs. What's Mrs. Fisher going to have Joy type this week, as she hands her the AAC device? To be honest, she thinks it's a bit rich she has to respond to each question, when there's not even a symbol for *Fuck off.*

Mrs. Fisher starts her off on a 'easy' one. 'How are you doing today?' She pokes Joy in the centre of her nose, and then does the same to her own. Joy knows she wants her to look at her face, but it's like staring at the sun. She looks at the wall behind her instead, which seems to be enough. Mrs. Fisher gives her a thumbs up, and asks her the question again.

There are only two symbols for this question, but there might as well not be. Mrs. Fisher takes Joy's finger, hovering it over *Good.* When Joy presses it, Miss says, 'I am glad.' She gives her a crisp out of the open packet. They must have run out of toffees at last.

The session goes on for hours. Months. Joy looks at the clock, even though she can't read it. The other students must be feeling it too. She sees Marcus flip his device, and scratch the TA who goes to pick it up. The other teachers gather around, debating whether to put him in a restraint.

He seems to calm down, briefly, until Mrs. Taylor comes over. She tells him if he uses his words, they can stop and take a break. 'Come on,' she says. 'It's easy. Press *Stop*, and then we'll stop.' But it isn't easy, because if it was, Marcus wouldn't be flailing and baring his teeth. The teachers take him to the floor in a MAYBO restraint, as he thrashes and squeals. It is a terrible song. Joy puts her hands over her ears. As their hands grip Marcus, she feels them gripping hers too, like they did the other week, when she was too tired for OT, and the lights were too bright, but they wouldn't let her stop.

After Marcus leaves, Joy can't concentrate. No one can. A couple of pupils try to stand, but their teachers won't let them. Not unless they press the button for *Walk*. Joy can see Daiyu in the corner, tapping her foot. She looks pale. Mildly green. She gets called out to speak to the Head.

When she comes back, she doesn't look relieved. The others do. Their eyes might be red, but Joy can see that their breathing is slower. Daiyu's isn't. Her lips are pulled in; she's not speaking. She's letting Mrs. Brown, whome she's shadowing, work with their student, as she sits there, holding it in. Joy hopes they don't break her. No one stays here for long. The ones that do have been here for years. They probably came with the school. Were trained by Hans Asperger himself.

Mrs. Fisher pokes Joy between her eyebrows again. Joy shudders. Wipes her off. 'Joy, come on. You're doing so well. What do you want to do next week?' Mrs. Fisher points at the screen.

Joy sighs, looking through the options. There's the park. She could run in the park. But then again, there's swimming. Her hair's not attached to her body when she's underwater. She goes to press it, but her finger slips. What, no? She didn't mean *Cinema*. The dog paw smell of popcorn. The yapping and squealing in the 10am autism screening. The fact that they only show Disney or Pixar films. Not a thriller like she'd prefer.

'Great, Joy! I'll tell Mrs. Taylor,' Miss says. She hands Joy another crisp. Joy takes it and chews it miserably, as Mrs. Fisher gives her another thumbs up.

•

Parents' Day. Joy heard them mention it this morning through the staffroom door. They were talking about the protocol, about how to get it over with, painlessly. They told the pupils on Monday morning, but the staff aren't reminding them today. Still, Joy doesn't know what good that's done. They should've know they wouldn't forget. Even the ones that can't read calendars are being egged on by the ones that can.

By 11 am, a cloud of them wait by the windows, watching the cars arrive. The teachers tell them they've got lessons. They can see them at break. Their mummies and daddies will want to see them trying their best, following the rules. It's a losing battle. The teachers are drowned out by vocal stims. It's a glorious ode. Joy is in the centre, clapping her hands, conducting. She tries to push through to the front of them, to see her parents' car arrive. It doesn't, but they might be late. She's not seen them in so long, but she remembers their car is a specific beetle skin shade of blue. It has a scratch on the side of the back door, from when she threw that fit over the ice in her drink. It was too cold. They looked like plastic blocks. She'd forgotten they would melt.

She often forgets things like that. Like rain's from the sky, not a hose, or that it won't be night forever, even when she wakes up and it's still dark. But she remembers the sandalwood in her mum's perfume, even if she doesn't know that word. And her coiled hair, and her black skin, a deeper shade than Joy's. And her dad's pale skin with a mole on his shoulder, with a hair on it Joy liked to pick. She waits for them all morning and afternoon. The other kids get plucked out one by one. Joy looks up whenever the door opens, but it's never for her.

At the end of the day, Joy sits in the sensory room, as Mrs. Fisher and Mrs. Taylor do their paperwork. Sitting on the bean bag as usual, Joy plays with the spaghetti lights. 'You know, if one were mine, I dunno what I'd do,' Mrs. Taylor says. 'I mean I'd love them, of course I would, but I couldn't imagine if they couldn't talk.'

Mrs. Fisher nods. Gesturing to Joy, she lowers her voice, 'I'm just glad they live in their own little world.' She flips the page, scribbling something down on it. Asks Mrs. Taylor if she knows what time tea's gonna be. She hopes it won't be late because of Parents' Day. She's been doing overtime every night this week.

Joy pokes her tears with the ends of the spaghetti lights, watching them blur, like spilt oil catching light.

·

'Three for the autism screening,' Mrs. Fisher points to Joy. 'She has a CEA card.'

'Oh,' says Daiyu. 'So do I.'

Frowning, Mrs. Fisher hands the card to the man on the till. 'We can't use them both,' she mutters. 'You're the carer here. You're not disabled.'

Daiyu sighs. 'I know. I just wanted Joy to know, for solidarity.' She smiles at Joy, flapping her hands lightly. Joy does the same, wiggling her fingers. Mrs. Fisher tells them to stop. She gives Joy £20.

Joy doesn't know what to do with it. Is it for the popcorn? For her to keep? She tries pocketing it, but Mrs. Fisher says no. She tries giving it to Daiyu. No again. 'Hand it to the man,

Joy.' What man? There's lots of them walking past. Joy looks at them. One. Then another. She balls the note in her fist and hums.

'It's OK, Joy,' Daiyu says. 'Give it to the man at the till. Opposite you.'

Mrs. Fisher tells Daiyu to take Joy's fist. The one with the money inside.

'I'm not going to touch her.'

'Well she can't hear you when she gets like this.'

Joy thinks about getting on the floor, lying on it, peacefully protesting, but Mrs. Fisher grabs her wrist. Pulling her over to the desk, she opens Joy's hand until the poor man takes it. He does, trying not to look at them. He sorts out the change, handing it to Daiyu. She takes it before Mrs. Fisher can make Joy.

Once they get their tickets ripped, Mrs. Fisher tells Daiyu she's nipping to the loo. Daiyu leads Joy to the sofa outside the screen door. As she sits, Joy can already hear screaming, even though it's supposed to be soundproof. She sees Daiyu wince as she folds her ticket, then folds it again. Joy wonders if Daiyu would stop her if she ran. They could run off together, or sneak into another screen and watch something else. Joy's pretty sure the new thriller's playing opposite. She can see a glimpse of it as someone goes in. One of the TAs saw it a couple of days ago. She could hear her talking about it with Mrs. Price; they watched the trailer on her phone.

Joy wonders if Daiyu's thinking the same. She wishes she had her AAC device. She rocks, trying to pull the right words out her mouth. Her words. Any word. 'There. Go,' she manages, loudly, but she can't coordinate her hands to point.

Daiyu jumps and turns to her. She looks startled, but not afraid. Her eyes search Joy's trying to understand, but doesn't quite get there. Joy wishes she could pluck more words out to tell her, but her words are a stew of alphabet soup that she can't blurt out or spell. She rocks harder, as Daiyu watches her hit her head with her fist.

Mrs. Fisher comes back from the toilet. 'Sorry, there was a queue.' She points at Joy. 'What's going on?'

'I don't know,' Daiyu says.

'Well you were here.'

'I know.'

'Any smells? Lights? You know she's sensitive to those.'

Joy would like to tell Mrs. Fisher her perfume's painful. She's not supposed to wear it in school. She probably thought she could get away with it here though, what with all the other smells. Joy wants her to scrub it off, but she can't make her. She can't even tell her. She grabs a fistful of hair and pulls, chewing the clumps that come out.

Mrs. Fisher sighs, taking Joy's arm. 'We can't go in with her like this. We'll have to take her back to school.'

In the taxi, Daiyu tries to cheer Joy up. 'You know, I didn't want to see it anyway. If you want, we can get the DVD when it comes out.'

Turning around in the front seat, Mrs. Fisher puts her finger on her lips. When she turns back, Daiyu makes a babbling gesture. Joy would laugh at it, but she's too tired to get the sound out. She flaps her hands instead. Daiyu does the same.

Joy feels the wire of their connection again. She'd screenshot this moment if she could; if they'd let her have a phone. She closes her eyes tight instead, then opens them. She turns to Daiyu, who's doing the same.

•

Monday lunchtime. Spag bol. The worst kind of spag. It doesn't matter what they offer, toffees, crisps, Joy's not eating it. It's not like she can feel hunger, just like she doesn't know when she needs the loo. She sits on her hands, rubbing her pull-up through her school trousers. Classy. It feels full. She's not going to tell them she needs changing, pressing the button on her AAC device. She'll sit in it as long as possible, until it's rotting and giving her sores. Until those Ofsted people come.

'Come on, Joy, a mouthful.' Mrs. Fisher swirls spaghetti on a fork. Joy hums, flipping it. One. Fork and bol make a splat dong on the floor. Mrs. Fisher picks the fork up, and two. Joy does it again, clapping her hands, squealing. She can tell Mrs. Fisher's losing patience today. Her voice isn't as tuneful as usual. She scratches the finger where her wedding ring used to be. She took it off a week ago. Joy noticed it was missing when she took her arm. Her hand felt warmer. No metal band cooling it down.

Joy flips the fork again, stamping her feet. It's working. Mrs. Fisher's eyes are going to pop. Daiyu's sitting a few tables away, watching it unfold. Joy drops the fork again and again. One, two, three. One, two, three, until Mrs. Fisher stands, screaming, 'Will you fucking behave? All of you!'

The room is silent after Mrs. Fisher throws the fork herself and storms out. A rare feat at any mealtime, but then the noise starts again. It's a glorious uprising. A few squeals. A few stims. Joy looks at Daiyu through it. She doesn't join in, but her face is tight. Gathering herself, Daiyu tells the teacher she's shadowing she's going to check if Joy's OK. She gets Joy to stand. Her stench rises with her.

Leading her to her bedroom, Daiyu gets her a change of clothes. She takes her to the toilet, helping her out her wet ones. She's not as rough as Mrs. Fisher, or as tickly as Mrs. Taylor. She tells Joy what she's doing for every step and doesn't wrinkle her nose. As Daiyu turns to throw the wet pull-up away, Joy looks down at her body. She carries on looking, as Daiyu wipes her, and puts some Sudocrem on her behind. Joy points her toes as Daiyu asks for her leg, and puts the fresh pull-up on. After helping Joy into clean trousers, she leads her back out of the door.

Mrs. Taylor frowns at Daiyu when they get to the corridor. 'Erm, what are you doing?'

'Joy needed changing.'

'You need two staff members for that. Where are you meant to be? You're not supposed to be alone with a student.'

'I know, but there was an incident. I couldn't leave her on her own.'

Mrs. Taylor raises her eyebrows. 'What incident?'

'In the canteen.'

'What happened?'

Daiyu leans toward her. 'With all due respect, I don't think we should be discussing it in front of Joy.' She leads

Joy down the corridor, as Mrs. Taylor calls after them. Daiyu holds her hand out, offering it to Joy. When Joy accepts, they run, past Mrs. Fisher in the office, crying, as Mr. Bishop puts his arm around her. When they get outside, Daiyu jumps up and down. Joy does the same, shaking her hair. They sing a wordless song at the top of their lungs, their voices upright against the wind.

---

**Jenni Brooks'** short fiction and poetry has been published in *The Paul Cave Prize Anthology*, *Streetcake Magazine*, *The Phare*, and others. Her spoken-word film 'Women and Autism', won the Best Professional Short Film, in the National Autistic Society's Autism Uncut Awards, hosted at BAFTA. She is currently working on her first short story collection, and a novel, *Teggies*, which was shortlisted for The Book Edit Writer's Prize.

**Katy Vane**

# Aflare Again

The leaves, like daggers, danced on the branches above him. Lively green and cool to the touch, he imagined, reaching his hand out as if to pluck them one by one. *They love me, they love me not*, the earth, the universe entire: he knew how it would end.

Not the universe—that is ever continuous—but his relation to it; indifference or love didn't matter when both resulted in pain.

His feet pressed into the ground, seeking the coolness of relief. He'd walked only from his couch, to his backdoor, to this spot beneath the tree, and the joints of his toes and his achilles tendon were aflame, a splash of red spilling across the yellowing grass. One blade, like an epee, stuck through the space between his pinky toe and the next—an itch, welcome for the variety of sensation. He was all aflame, he thought, a continual burning, but his feet most of all.

He'd learned as a youth, from his academic mother, that there is a number greater than infinity. Not infinity plus one, as a child may try in a competition of love declared, or even infinity times itself, for any manipulation of infinity remains infinite. It is unchanging, in that way: although constantly adding to itself, the whole is still the whole. No, his mother explained, there is the continuum. *I love you to infinity and back* means taking steps, infinite steps, and counting each one. *I love you in continuum* means an unceasing slide toward love all-consuming, impossible to count each micro-space between the steps of infinity.

Infinity and continuum; it was the difference between the way his wrist throbbed, on and off though never ending, and the constant heat of his ankles. He watched his feet turn a brighter red, near neon against the whiteness of his legs. He watched the heat turn the chlorophyll of nearby dandelions into steam, which rose as a warning cloud above the earth. He streamed his hand through the steam, to make a signal for the leaves, an SOS they could read in the presence of moisture, then the presence of chill.

The universe was indifferent to him, he thought. In all its continuing fullness, there was no benevolence, but he could not ascribe malevolence, either. His pain, in all its chronic continuing, was less than what others suffered. There was always a calculation, when he reached this helpless place, a subtraction of his privileges from the fire in his joints. It added up to zero: a life of no worth, for in his pain he was unable to do a thing of good or ill—but not yet death, and never suffering (what he would count as true suffering). He imagined his equation lined up against someone with his pain but also, in addition, living in a war zone, in a famine, in a genocide. There were integers less than zero, he reminded himself, again and again. An infinity of integers, and a continuum when he allowed for decimals.

Yes, the universe was indifferent, and he loved it to infinity and back. The leaves, like daggers, danced on the branches above him; the wind, like a friend, waved through the wilting grass. He closed his eyes, bringing a cool shadow to his mind if nowhere else, and felt the transformation of his feet from skin and bone and mangled joints to only blood, blood that boiled. Blood that turned the stone of his body to liquid, to a lava that oozed through the grass, helping the summer sun in its quest to scorch all green life to the quick.

He was losing his feet, although he could still feel them; what used to take steps to reach was now a slow sliding across the earth. What once were his toes, and the blade of grass stuck between them, were now encircling the trunk of the apple tree beneath which he rested, turning the bark black and brittle. What once were his arches now flowed over roots, between rocks, reaching his neighbor's fence. It was a heat that would cover the earth in its love, because he had learned from his academic mother that love was pain. Her ex-husband, the topologist, said there was no difference between a square and the symbol of a heart; each was but a single continuous loop, never breaking or overlapping, and easily stretched into the shape of the other without the need for scissors or glue. The number of angles or sides was inconsequential to topologists. As too, it turned out, were the number of people in his relationship. Love is all-embracing, he'd defended himself: it did not change with the addition of lines. But that proof did not withstand his mother's testing.

His mother had been alone, now, for more years than he had kept count of. And he had been alone for (if he did the math right) nineteen years, his penultimate year of high school to the present. But the math, like love, was predictably difficult to follow when his feet were lava.

His mother, whom he had lived with once and lived with again, arrived home; her hybrid car had a quiet but particular electric whinge to it when it pulled into the driveway. The sound of her steps bypassed the front door and went straight to the yard gate. He thought he heard her ask how he was doing but, again, his feet were lava, and that made it hard to listen. She seemed to realize his state, that he had been translated—still the same shape, technically, but manipulated so by the pain that he was nearly unrecognizable. She, his mother, was logical by trade, but emotional by choice, and she sobbed a surprise between her lips and the palm of her hand. That palm became a cup with which she attempted to scoop handfuls of lava back to their untranslated state of toes and ankles, but even infinite pulls with her cool hands was nothing against the continual heat of his pain.

She took the clip from her hair, then, and let the rivulets of brown and gray fall against her shoulders. Her forehead pressed to the earth, like she was sending a prayer to the indifferent universe, and the strands of her hair spread across what had once been his feet. Her hair soaked the lava into itself, turning black and brittle but not breaking. She cleaned, and it was his feet she cleaned, a tress of hair catching between his pinky toe and the one next to it. And, when his feet were his feet and the lava was her hair, he opened his eyes and watched her walk to the base of the tree. Her hair over one shoulder and twisted around her wrist, she spilled golden water onto its bark, blew cooling breath as it found its brownness again, but not its firmness. All still felt brittle: the tree, her hair, the ligaments that held his body together so that it could not again become lava. The golden water flew from her hair, through the corrugations in the bark, under the arches of the roots, and beneath his body, holding him buoyant and painless. The water flooded over other plants: her artichoke that she always mistakenly called asparagus and her unhappy tomatoes; the rosebush that had once died and been cut down to the quick, but sprung anew of its own volition. The inundated garden shimmered in the light of the sun, and the grass, like a friend, danced in the waves.

His academic mother considered the futility of watering the backyard, better usually at fending for itself than taking to her tending. She turned off the hose. The state was in a drought, anyway, she reasoned aloud, and he could only nod from his sprawl in the shade.

Would dinner help? she wanted to know, after a moment of looking down at him with her dampened arms crossed over her stomach.

It couldn't hurt, he figured falsely, because pain could always be added upon itself.

She reached down, hooking her arm around his tender shoulders, and hauled him to standing. Their connection with the ground and the weight of his own body set his feet aflame again, but his mother helped him this time, and the steps from the backyard, to the backdoor, to the couch did not seem infinite. *I love you to continuum and back*, he thought, but did not say aloud, for the childish appearance of living with a parent in his thirties was already more than he could bear. Instead he said, Maybe just a smoothie, could you make smoothies?

I can make anything, she said confidently—and he believed her, for her calculations were rarely wrong, and never when they concerned herself.

Inside, he felt, there was less of the universe to love. There was the black table upon which he rested his feet, and the wrapped ice pack his mother placed atop them. There was his mother, whom he loved, though she had warned him again and again that love was pain. There was a belly, not full, but full enough that the meds wouldn't make him nauseated. And there was sleep, which was a way of leaving the universe, of leaving love and pain. For sleep was a kind of discontinuation, a gap of life, and the universe, as he knew, was continuous. He had learned recently, from his academic mother, that a discontinuous line could never join with the continuous. He slept, and he woke, and the universe ended and began anew, and yet was unchanged, because there was no difference between a beginning and ending when you were a circle—and he, as the universe and of the universe, was a circle continuous.

---

**Katy Vane** is a writer and artist based in Oregon. Her short stories have been featured in such publications as *Crab Fat Magazine*, *The Last Line Journal*, and *Peaches Lit*.

**K. Ann MacNeil**

# *Visit*

Your mother comes to you

as a mourning dove

on a frozen but melting wire,

as a barred owl

tall in the middle of

Ridge Road

after sunset,

where in warmer weather improbable

    dahlias,

      snapdragons,

and common,

    daisies,

      foxglove,

volunteers, all,

dot the road to the one grocery store

open

this late

this time of year.

My gran

sends

a dream of a pinching pixie,

urging me to scrub crevices,

so that I wake and add

mint

cloves

bay leaves

oregano

to our list;

a check out man at the Hannaford's tells me

"That's the third time this morning I've had that exact total:

$96.35,"

a pick four winner,

at least.

---

**K. Ann MacNeil** lives on the Hudson in northern Manhattan and on the Atlantic in southern Maine. Her work appears in *This Assignment is So Gay: LGBTIQ Poets on the Art of Teaching*; *The Still Blue Project: Writing with Working Class Queers in Mind*; *Love, Always: Partners of Trans People on Intimacy, Challenge, and Resilience*; *Closet Cases: Queers on What We Wear*; and *Sweeter Voices Still: An LGBTQ Anthology from Middle America*. *Salt*, a mini-collection of micropoems, has been published by Rinky Dink Press. Her chapbook, *Even*, is forthcoming with Bottlecap Press. She is deep-down grateful that her grown daughter checks in so regularly.

**Scott Nicolay**

# *Talking with Janet about Her Talking Boards*

"The Arabic numerals, and YES and NO.
What more could a familiar spirit want?"
—James Merrill
*The Changing Light at Sandover*

More than 500.

That's how many antique talking boards my friend Janet has in her collection. I'm sorry I can't be more specific, but neither can she. She *collects*, but she doesn't *count*. I refer to them here as talking boards because many of the earliest predate the dominance of the more familiar name "Ouija" by which most of us know these planchette-based oracles today.

Growing up, Janet never had her own Ouija board. Her family was Catholic, and her mother was in no way going to allow something like that in the house. Janet's cousin had one, however, and every chance she got, Janet secretly joined her for sessions with it. Not until she was in her late thirties, however, did Janet purchase a Ouija board of her own. Only she did not stop with one. Over the last decade and a half, her collection has grown to its current size, making it one of the largest and best in North America. Many of her boards are antiques and/or rarities, including everything from the obscure and somewhat infamous 1907 Nirvana Talking Board, of which only a few survive, to the Transogram company's controversial Ka-Bala of 1967, "The Mysterious Game that Tells the Future." The latter was a hybrid talking board and Tarot oracle with a large plastic eyeball at its center: perhaps the most occult children's toy of all time and the spiritual equivalent of the HAZMAT-level chemistry sets of my youth. I remember seeing the television commercials for that one during my preschool years, back before Janet herself was born, but I never saw one in the wild until the first time I visited Janet at her home and got the tour of her collection.

Allow me to clarify a major point before we proceed. We are *not* embarking here on a discussion of the ghosts, spirits, and/or demons that both the lovers and the haters of talking (or "Ouija") boards believe might emerge through their use. This narrative will not be one of demonic possession, a fear that was not associated with talking boards when they first appeared during the original Spiritualist era and became popular. That only developed later. My interest, like Janet's, is in the boards themselves, and in her relationship with them and the forces that have compelled her to assemble such a large and impressive collection. Although these are not demonic forces, I would argue nonetheless that our philosophy has only begun to dream of their implications.

Much of the impetus for the volume of "nonfiction Weird Tales" of which I hope this essay will someday become a part derives from my initial encounters, c. 2016–2017, with Object

Oriented Ontology (OOO) and related bodies of theory within the Material(ity) Turn. I developed a special interest in the concept of object agency and how this might apply both to my work as a writer of Weird Fiction and to my academic and professional discipline of archaeology. The realm of fiction contains many examples of objects with agency—some of them even possessed of that much rarer capacity, intent, as well. In the "real" world, however, one is hard-put to identify objects that do not acquire their agency from human actors: a process that anthropological art historian Alfred Gell described as "ab-duction." In Gell's model, a human agent is always the source of the agency that objects possess, especially *objets d'art*. Intent remains with the human actor. The obvious fictional example is Tolkien's One Ring. Yet even the One Ring, like Gell's canoe prows, ab-ducts its agency from a "human" actor, Sauron. It is essentially a variation of the ancient motif of the "separable" or "external" soul, which Stith Thompson identified as Folklore motif E710. Thompson reports this motif from Ireland, Iceland, India, and Africa. Many other examples exist from other lands and times, including the horcruxes of the Harry Potter novels.

What is important, and what interests me most, is that Janet's primary interest in her talking boards is as *objects*. Neither occultist nor spiritualist, she has employed fewer than a dozen of the boards in her collection for their originally-intended purpose. She doesn't buy her talking boards to call up demons or the dead. She buys them simply to have them—to paraphrase George Leigh Mallory's famous line about Mount Everest, "because they're there." And now they're in her house—something that doesn't seem to cause Janet or her family any spiritual unease—in fact, she also has a box of allegedly "haunted dolls" that she has gathered over the years (and regarding which she is appropriately skeptical). None of these things keep her or her family awake at night. Janet herself is an exceptionally grounded lady: self-possessed, confident, and very, very *present*. I think any spirits would have to work extremely hard to disrupt her equilibrium.

As for her collection however, anthropologist Sasha Newell has discussed the power—the agency—that certain objects and assemblages hold over the average American: materials kept in attics, crawlspaces, storage units. Things that one might look at only once or twice in one's life, but which one would never consider selling or discarding. These items have power; they dictate our decisions, sometimes at deep levels, like boulders in a field around which a farmer must plow. The family silver is a primary example. I know exactly where ours is in my mother's house, but I have never seen it in use. Newell compares these objects to sacred fetishes in West Africa, where he conducted his fieldwork. The primary difference between Janet's talking boards and Newell's examples is that she did not inherit them. She acquired her entire collection well into her adult life, and she did so consciously, deliberately, and systematically. But 500-plus talking boards, even in their "inert" state, with no spirits evoked, develop considerable *inertia*. Their cumulative mass creates a sort of gravitational force. Their orbit and Janet's orbit affect each other, although which is planet and which is moon remains unclear.

Although Janet grew up and attended high school in the same town as me, no more than a mile from my family's home, and she even went to school with my cousin Lisa, we never met until I reached out a few years ago looking for someone to interview about the Talking Board Historical Society on my Weird Fiction podcast, *The Outer Dark*. To be sure, I substitute-taught at our alma mater during her senior year in high school and mine at Rutgers College, which means that we likely passed in the hallways at least once or twice over 35 years ago. When we finally connected directly, we were both shocked to discover our shared hometown heritage. I left that town (and the East Coast) in 1989, but good ol' Middleburgh readily provided a solid basis for our early conversations. I think we really bonded, however, over our common interest in esoteric tropical fruits: mangosteens, ice-cream beans, Buddha's hands. We can talk for hours exclusively about our passion for different varieties of citrus.

Janet was not the first person I contacted to talk about talking boards on *The Outer Dark*. I had originally reached out to the then-current chair of the Talking Board Historical Society. He responded enthusiastically, but somehow, we never managed to coordinate a date and time, and our exchange of emails eventually faded and fell silent. My interest in interviewing one of the society's leaders began after I read an article regarding how they had raised money to place a headstone on the formerly unmarked grave of Elijah Bond in Baltimore's historic Green Mount Cemetery. Bond obtained the original patent for the name "Ouija." Since the society's successful effort, his grave has become the most-visited in that cemetery. I felt this would be an interesting angle for an interview, and my occasional cohost Justin Steele agreed.

When that original dialogue with the society's chair fizzled out, I returned to their website to consider the other board members. I noticed that the capsule bio for Janet, the society's treasurer at the time, mentioned that she was from New Jersey. I looked her up on social media and saw that we had a mutual friend—a college friend who remains very dear to me, in fact—so I wrote Janet a message, explaining my interest and informing her I would likely be in Central Jersey that summer. In that message, I mentioned my hometown and asked if she lived anywhere nearby. Communication on these platforms being what it is, it took several months before she saw my message and responded, but when she did, she mentioned with enthusiasm that she was not only a native of Middleburgh, but also a current resident.

Although I had originally proposed that we meet during my planned summer trip to the East Coast, by the time we connected I was preparing for a Christmas visit to my family. The first step therein was to meet her and her husband, aka "Big Daddy," at Kerwin's, our hometown's iconic local bar, a venerable watering hole older than either of us. Apparently, I passed this vetting process, which led to an invitation to visit her home and view her collection in person. This included dinner and the discovery that Janet is an excellent cook, leading to our ongoing culinary discussions. I also got to meet, albeit briefly, her three children—all of whom seem quite normal and well-adjusted, entirely free of any spiritual possession and/or undue worry regarding their mother's gigantic collection of occult artifacts.

Janet and Big Daddy bought a new home a couple years ago—a much larger place not far from Middleburgh but up in the Watchung "Mountains." Along with a pond and a small in-home theater, she will at last have room to display at least some of her most prized talking boards. In the old house in my hometown where I first visited, her boards were largely consigned to an alcove of the basement with limited display space, alongside other collections, including the aforementioned haunted dolls. Some gentle digging was required to reveal certain special pieces.

Some talking boards are so scarce that only a handful survive today. Obviously, these bring high prices when offered for sale, and the bidding wars they incite sometimes generate real acrimony within the small world of hardcore collectors. Some examples include the Nirvana board, the Russell Rucker board, the Mystifying Oracle board (a metal board, with an electric planchette that moves on its own when working properly—fewer than five of these are known to survive), and the Electra Board, on which the heart-shaped planchette is permanently attached to the center of the board, rotating to point to the letters and numbers which are inscribed in an arc above it. One of Janet's greatest prizes is the ultra-rare I-D-O PSY-CHO-I-D-E-O-GRAPH board manufactured by Theodore White in 1919, for which she has acquired both board and planchette. This is another of which fewer than five are known to survive.

Examples such as these exist at the very cusp of the crisis that provides the subject of Walter Benjamin's famous essay

"The Work of Art in the Age of Mechanical Reproduction" (originally "*Das Kunstwerk im Zeitalter seiner technischen Reproduzierbarkeit*"). Many of the early talking boards, regardless of the method of their production, very clearly retain the *aura* of which Benjamin wrote. Attractive wooden objects as suitable for home decoration as for spiritual dictation, they display evidence of both assembly-line manufacture and artisanal production. Janet also has a handful of homemade one-of-a-kind boards, which many artists continue to produce and sell on Etsy and other online shops, making the talking board market an ever-expanding scene.

Although her talking boards are the showpieces today, Janet took care in our conversations to emphasize the importance of the planchettes, which are arguably the more important component of the apparatus. The planchette "moves" across the board, selecting numbers, letters, entire words, depending on what the particular board provides. If the ectoplasmic appendages of unseen entities indeed contribute to the oracular process, they do so by moving the planchette, or at least by gently directing the corporeal hands whose fingertips rest lightly on its edges. Although we focus on "Ouija boards" or "talking boards" as the oracles, the boards themselves are static. Only the planchettes are active. These are deliberately manufactured to be light and semi-frictionless so as to facilitate their movement. Janet recognizes their importance, and she made a point of showing me significant planchettes associated with particular boards such as the I-D-O Board, for which she actually obtained the planchette before the board.

One historically important talking board that neither Janet nor any other private collector can own is the home-made specimen used by poet James Merrill and his beloved partner David Jackson to write the poems that became his epic sequence, *The Changing Light at Sandover*, the first part of which—"The Book of Ephraim"—was the final poem in his collection *Divine Comedies*, which won the 1977 Pulitzer Prize for poetry. Merrill and Jackson's planchette was a cheap blue-and-white ceramic teacup; presumably they used the handle as a pointer, as it lacked the sort of viewing window that Ouija planchettes possess. Both board and teacup—significant yet singular examples of talking board technology—now reside at Yale's Beinecke Rare Book and Manuscript Library, along with the few surviving transcripts of their sessions. Merrill supposedly burned all the rest. His board, though crude and lacking in any real artistry, nonetheless possesses a genuine *aura*, to which its existence beyond reach of all collectors must contribute. It occupies the apex of associational examples.

When we spoke, Janet described the appeal of collecting talking boards in terms of their variety, scarcity, and antiquity. She also mentioned the compulsion to *protect* the rarest boards. In this conservation interest, I find a tangential intersection with archaeology, where the preservation and protection of cultural resources is central. "Stewardship" is, in fact the first entry in the Society for American Archaeology's "Principles of Archaeological Ethics." Although considerable daylight exists between archaeologists and most private artifact collectors, the two communities do share common roots in the antiquarianism and "cabinets of curiosities" that became popular during the late Renaissance. Some archaeologists, myself included, still work to build bridges with collectors in the interest of preserving more of the archaeological record and its accompanying data, but suspicion runs strong on both sides.

Janet's talking boards, of course, are not prehistoric artifacts but historical objects, largely manufactured within the sphere of commerce, which means that the legal and ethical restrictions that apply to the sale of antiquities do not govern their acquisition. As mentioned above, talking board collectors can become combative over the rarer examples, and Janet is steadfast enough in her collecting that she has sacrificed a friendship or two while acquiring new boards. She accepts these tradeoffs with minimal regret, and given that in such cases she was the one who was expected to back down and surrender to *male* collectors, a sexist element seems present in the whole process. Here again we encounter the power, the pull, the *agency* of talking boards. The boards themselves, and not any undismissed entities residing within them, compel these high-level collectors to compete for their acquisition.

During my conversations with Janet, I came to realize that the crux of my interest is the moment when she went from wanting *one* Ouija board to wanting *all* the Ouija boards, or at least something on the order of *one of each*. Obviously, obtaining even one of each is nigh impossible, given that no one can know for certain exactly how many different talking boards have been manufactured over the last century and a half, especially considering all the variations, predecessors, and prototypes—as well as the one-offs and associational examples such as Merrill's homemade board and expedient dime-store teacup planchette. As someone who has collected many things during my own life, I understand a little of what the serious collector feels with each new acquisition. There must be something both comforting and terrifying about reaching the point that Janet has, having obtained at least one (and sometimes several) of *most* of the important talking boards, including a majority of the rarest ones. Then the collector stands forever on the edge of the unknown. The excitement of obtaining each new rarity becomes greater, while the opportunities themselves for those experiences become fewer and fewer and further between. The delightful shots of dopamine that such acquisitions bring become ever more scarce and elusive. I think all hardcore collectors must face this, at least unconsciously. However, we are not talking about just any collections here. We are talking about TALKING BOARDS, objects that supposedly afford the capacity for communication with entities from the spirit world. As Sasha Newell suggests, these items "reflect a cosmology of material entities as containers for spirit."

Expanding on the work of OOO, philosopher and "dark ecologist" Timothy Morton developed the concept of the "hyperobject," a class of objects whose scale can only be grasped statistically and conceptually. Hyperobjects are "massively distributed in time and space relative to humans." Among Morton's examples are "all the Styrofoam ever made," "all the plutonium ever made," and global warming. No one can see these things in their entirety, even though their effects and edges are observable, and each of them, like Kafka's creepy Odradek, will outlast anyone living today.

I would argue that "all the talking boards ever made" or even "one of each talking board ever made (with its original accompanying planchette)" represent examples of hyperobjects, if only on some lower end of the scale—the chart of all hyperobjects being a hyperobject itself. I think this is probably true for most collections that come up against a certain level of scarcity and expense. No one really knows nor can anyone really ever know how many unique talking boards exist, much as no one can ever really know how many record albums Sun Ra released during his career. Serious collectors claim somewhere between 100 and 200 of the latter, but because Sun Ra had his own studio and he pressed many of his records in limited editions, sometimes consisting of a single copy and often with variations, no collector can do better than to approach the total asymptotically. As with Janet's collection, no one was counting. Talking boards overall present a similar scenario for collector.

If collectors as committed as Janet are not assembling full-scale hyperobjects, their collections are at least something close: para-, ultra-, mega-, or simply *extra* objects. And this is where I will push a bit into the outré, into The Weird: I argue that Janet's collection of talking boards, as with the examples of hyperobjects that Morton provides, is "massively distributed in time and space." Perhaps not so massively as global warming or the magnetic field of Jupiter, another of Morton's examples, but her collection is far too large for her to hold any meaningful portion of it in her arms, or even to store it in a single room suitable for its full display. I doubt my readers will find that part of my argument difficult to accept. But aye, here's the rub: Janet's talking boards are also distributed in *time* as well, as I have no doubt that Janet's mental image of her collection includes boards she has *not yet acquired*. And isn't this true for other collectors at her level, whether their passion is for Sun Ra's discography, postage stamps, Sonny Angels, Funko Pops, comic books, baseball cards, handbags, or wine?

Certainly, a potential danger can sometimes accrue to such four-dimensional thinking, associated with the point of diminishing returns. What if new acquisitions fail to meet expectations? During my senior year in high school, an older friend experienced a mental breakdown and was temporarily institutionalized. After several conversations regarding his circumstances, he eventually revealed to me that the roots of his issues extended back to his own adolescence, when he waited eagerly for but was ultimately disappointed by something anticipated as life-changing and special that he purchased via mail order, as we were wont to do in those days. When his purchase finally arrived, it somehow failed to fill whatever internal emptiness he felt in his life at the time, and that became the beginning of a years' long downward spiral. What exactly was the nature of the delivery to which he had assigned so much importance? "Pictures of racecars." Although I have never fully understood how this impacted my friend so severely, I had already done enough collecting that some sense of the situation's existential horror has penetrated and lingered with me for over four decades. The disproportionate nature of his disappointment and its outsized effect on his life struck me as a cautionary tale that led me to take a step back from some of my own collecting activities for a time. I have long since devolved into more of an accumulator than a collector, primarily of books.

I expect my friend's case represents an outlier of sorts though, and I have long since lost touch with him, so I don't know if and how well he was able to recover from his issues at that time. I hope he is living a good life free of any long-term distress over those inadequately-satisfying pictures of racecars. What a thing...

Obviously, a line exists where collecting crosses over into unhealthy obsession—now sometimes labeled "hoarding"—but I don't see Janet as anywhere near that edge, despite the extraordinary number of talking boards she has acquired and her occasional willingness to ruffle feathers during her acquisitions. Her focus is on her family, her kids and Big Daddy, along with completing the complicated move into their new home in the hills with all its prerequisite modifications and renovations. And also, of course, tasting new varieties of tropical fruit. During the six or seven years that I have now known her, I have witnessed no symptoms of unhealthy obsessions, no negative fixations. Her Facebook account alone suffices to show how she stays happily busy supporting her kids and maintaining an active social life. She is, to be sure, a bit flamboyant and larger-than-life (her alternate online name is "sexyouijaqueen," and she fully lives up to it), but not in any way that suggests her basement is a nexus of numinous artifacts. Her semidemihemiheptapara-hyper-object project remains simply a pleasant *divertissement*: one more part of her life that makes her happy, and one which she is altogether happy to discuss.

And what about you, dear reader? What are the objects, artifacts, heirlooms, assemblages, and souvenirs that occupy space in your attics, basements, crawlspaces, garages, safe-deposit boxes, and storage units? What are the things that you rarely examine but would not part with for all the coal in Newcastle? How often do you even think of them? Do they link you to the past, to friends and family long gone? Or to the future, as you ponder the pieces you have yet to acquire? I hope the psychic weight of that package you are tracking never rises to the critical mass of my long-lost friend's racecar photos, and that any spiritually charged artifacts in your possession remain inert and inactive, that all portals remain unopened, that any haunted dolls stay in their boxes and keep their eyes shut. May you stay grounded in the here and now, in our three dimensions and material world; may your collections spark joy without carrying you off to some tesseract racetrack that breaks your spirit and your heart.

## References Cited

Benjamin, Walter. "The Work of Art in the Age of Mechanical Reproduction." *A Museum Studies Approach to Heritage*. Routledge, 2018. 226-243.

Gell, Alfred. *Art and Agency: An Anthropological Theory*. Clarendon Press, 1998.

Merrill, James. *The Changing Light at Sandover*. Knopf, 2011.

Morton, Timothy. *Hyperobjects: Philosophy and Ecology after the End of the World*. University of Minnesota Press, 2013.

The Museum of Talking Boards. https://www.museumoftalkingboards.com/index.html. accessed Sept. 1, 2024.

The Mysterious Planchette. https://www.mysteriousplanchette.com/. accessed Sept. 1, 2024.

Newell, Sasha. "The Matter of the Unfetish: Hoarding and the Spirit of Possessions." *HAU: Journal of Ethnographic Theory* 4.3 (2014): 185–213.

"The Time of Clutter: Anti-Kairos and Storage Space in North American Domestic Life." *Anthropological Quarterly* 96.2 (2023): 229–254.

Hammer, Langdon. "Object Lesson: Poetry via Ouija" *Yale Alumni Magazine* Jan/Feb 2012 https://www.yalealumnimagazine.com/articles/3363-object-lesson, accessed Sept. 12, 2024.

Thompson, Stith. *Motif-Index of Folk-Literature*. Indiana University Press, 1955.

---

World Fantasy Award winner **Scott Nicolay** is an archaeologist, author, translator, and caver, whose primary research focuses on the prehistoric use of caves. His most recent story collection, *And at My Back I Always Hear*, was nominated for a Shirley Jackson Award. In addition to translating the major works of the Belgian fantasist Jean Ray, he is currently working on a volume of "nonfiction Weird Tales," of which his contribution here is one.

**Allison Whittenberg**

# *Swedge*

travel one hundred miles, calling
the 99th, half way
understand one thing:
I am no longer
misinformed

as the dogs
yelp at nothing
the arrow of time flies
swift, straight
there is luck in the leftovers
a mingle of delights to merge with the hardships

every sheet of paper
has two sides

my difficulty has made me a jewel

# After Shagging

you are silent
I wait
ice crunches
jaybirds fly
years pass

I wait
you are silent
time versus language
the abyss neath solid ground
years pass

years pass
how do you feel?
how do I feel?
how does it feel?
as years pass

---

Born in Pennsylvania and educated in New York and Wisconsin, **Allison Whittenberg** is an award-winning novelist and playwright. Her poetry has appeared in *Columbia Review, Feminist Studies, J Journal,* and *New Orleans Review.* Whittenberg is a six-time Pushcart Prize nominee. *Driving with a*

*Poetic License* and *They Were Horrible Cooks* are her collections of poetry.

**Steve Tomich**

# *The New Regime*

Dateline: Washington D.C.

With the new conservative majority firmly in place at all levels of the federal government, sweeping changes are being implemented that will impact every American citizen and dramatically affect behavior in both the public and private domain. Much attention has been focused on the executive branch of government, with the creation of the new titles of Emperor and Chief Inquisitor replacing the previous and now-quaint-sounding offices of President and Vice President. But as is shown by the detention of the cast of Sesame Street and the no-knock raids of elementary school teachers in search of their "Satanic familiars," the legislative branch has also been flexing its muscles, passing dozens of new laws. The shadowy but powerful bicameral Committee on Decency has been especially active, taking its motto of "Clean It Up Or Burn It Down" very much to heart.

Acting on a tip that a series of digits typed into a calculator could spell the word "boobs" when the calculator's screen was inverted, the scandalized Committee sprang into action, launching a multi-month investigation into whether "indecency" could extend beyond speech and behavior into the realm of abstract symbols. That investigation has now culminated in the swift passage of the Safety In Numbers (SIN) Act. Unprecedented in its scope, the text of the Act describes the numerals 0 through 9, familiar to all Americans since childhood, as "indecent, suggestive, and downright salacious" and finds that these symbols are "the prime cause and the common denominator for the moral decay of our country, adding to our divisions, taking away from our shared values, multiplying our woes, and providing a constant threat to our country's security." To protect Americans from this dangerous lewdness, the Safety In Numbers Act, when it goes into effect, will ban all usage of traditional numerals in all forms of communication, education, technology, and commerce.

While the Committee is intensely secretive about its agenda and decision-making process, a recently obtained audio recording of its closed-door meetings sheds some light on the discussions that led to the passage of the SIN Act. Since the Committee does not, and is not legally required to, explain the reasons behind any of its decrees, the leaked audio provides some insight as to the deliberative process employed by the Committee in coming to their historic decision.

The haste with which the Committee crafted the new law is reflected in its defiantly inconsistent terminology. During the meetings, a staffer can be heard in the audio recording asking for clarity on whether the text of the SIN Act would be referring to "numbers, numerals, integers, digits... or what?" She was immediately excoriated as "inappropriate," "contentious," and "uppity," then fired on the spot. Since the Act itself is unclear on the subject, we will follow its lead and use those terms interchangeably in the following summary and analysis.

According to the covertly recorded audio, the Committee's consensus as to what is objectionable in our traditional 0 through 9 numbering scheme breaks down as follows:

0. Simply too suggestive, orifice-wise.

1.  Too phallic, obviously.
2.  The "bent knee" and "arched neck" profile was too evocative of oral sex, especially for several staff members of the Committee (see below).
3.  Failed on two counts, since, by rotating one's head ninety degrees, it could be perceived as "looking down a woman's blouse," while rotating in the opposite direction could cause the perception of "looking up a woman's skirt."
4.  Committee members found the "crossed legs" appearance of this numeral "too suggestive." One member went so far as to call it a "floozy."
5.  The Committee could not find anything specifically wrong with this number but were convinced it was "probably up to something."
6.  This number was found to be acceptable by itself, but, as Committee members noted that it was as likely as not to be paired with the number 9, it was rejected soundly.
7.  In one of the most dramatic parts of the audio recording, several Committee aides, both male and female, were suddenly triggered by this number. Its profile,

one said, reminded her of "what my boss's slacks looked like when he'd call me into his inner office and then lock the door." When both 7 and 2 were displayed together on a whiteboard during the meeting, another staffer fainted, causing the Committee Chair to call a recess.

8. Also from the audio recording, this number was rejected, with one male member of the Committee wistfully remarking that the number "reminds me of my teenage niece lying on the couch in a bikini top," followed by a pause and an audible sigh.

9. See #6 above.

Having banned these numerals, the SIN Act mandates the Roman numbering system as a replacement. The straight lines, the confining bottom and top caps, and the lack of a representation for zero were all hailed as "a great improvement" over the "ambiguous, sinuous, sensuous, seditious" curves of the Arabic numerals, which have been dominant in Western culture since the 15th Century. In the recording, one member can be heard praising the rigid, angular visual representation of the Roman system as "really quite butch." Still, the Committee is taking no chances, mandating that an extra space be inserted between any two Roman numerals, "lest they get too friendly," and banning the depiction of the Roman numerals for the value of thirty: "XXX," specifying that it must be written out in English.

The Committee also made sure to get ahead of any anti-Arabic inferences in their revamp of the American numbering system. In a press release posted shortly after the SIN Act's passage, the Committee members extolled such things as a suffocating, theocratic patriarchy, oil, LGBTQ+ intolerance, oil, overhyped real estate, oil, overblown sports events, an insufferable sense of entitlement, a casual acceptance of corruption, and oil as important ties between the U.S. and its select group of favored Middle Eastern conglomerates.

The audio recording also confirms that the Committee was well aware of the impact of the SIN Act on the world of digital technology, since binary code—the series of ones and zeroes that form the foundation for all software and digital devices—would also be banned. The entire Committee was troubled by the suggestiveness of so many erect "1's" and inviting "0's" placed so closely together, and in so many "abnormal" and "perverse" combinations. A simple code sequence such as "01010011", according to one Committee member, "looked like a damn orgy, pardon my French."

Going forward, the SIN Act authorizes the various digital standards bodies to write code in either Roman numerals or "plain English." During the Committee meetings, this was seen to have the dual benefit of reducing the impact of computer malware by "dirty foreigners" (though Italian coders might have a slight advantage here), while "sticking it to all those queers in Silicon Valley." Executives and senior staff at Apple, PayPal, and Microsoft were unavailable for comment.

Realizing that such a vast overhaul of the numerical underpinnings of American society would take time, the Committee built some delay into the effect of the SIN Act. The fine print indicates that the full implementation of the Act will be tied to the issuance by the U.S. Mint of the new, re-imagined American currency, which replaces the pictures of former presidents and historical figures with AI-generated images of the Emperor and his family, along with the introduction of the new $III bill.

In the meantime, having established that abstract symbols can be potential vectors for lewdness and debauchery, a new panel, the Committee On Internal Threats to the United States (COITUS) is gearing up to investigate how the letters of the alphabet might also constitute a danger to public decency. Each letter will be scrutinized individually, both upper and lower case, and any fonts deemed too provocative, androgynous, or found to be concealing impertinent tattoos will be blacklisted. Homonyms and homophones, long suspected of being "double agents" advancing their own agenda, will be prime targets of COITUS, which has also pledged to eliminate unfortunate and potentially embarrassing acronyms from American discourse.

---

**Steve Tomich** is a fairly unremarkable guy living in Berkeley, California, and way too much in his own head. Lucky to be surrounded by a loving, supportive wife and family, he is working on his skills as a full-time eccentric and a passable practitioner of aikido. In addition to a short stint editing a magazine, Steve spent many years as a TV producer and editor, slicing, dicing, and massaging other people's words and ideas on tight deadlines, and he doesn't miss it a bit.

**Heather Truett**

# *Fifteen*

He called me jailbait.

When I wore that dress,
he pictured  me against
the bricks, his hands
on my thighs, he couldn't
help himself. I pressed
against the ice of him,
he told the truth, he would
hurt me, he would not love
me, he would leave me.

I pushed till cracks spread
like his fingers, offered
everything he couldn't have.

I like to be not gotten, but desired.

I send my husband photographs
when he is away, barely any clothes,
wicked lingerie, but only when
he's absent, traveling, my gifts a cellular
mirage, tokens of that girl in me.

I feel off-limits, untouchable, alive,

fifteen.

# Horse Girl Ode and Elegy

I.

Nicole's thoroughbred, Leia, might have mastitis, needs a
    needle, large, inserted
in her nipple. Nicole says Leia may have a biopsy. She is a
    horse prone

to unique situations. I tell Nicole I'd like to see her milk her
    horse. She laughs,
moves her head, thick brown hair catches sunlight like
    mane,

and she is Epona, horse goddess, war goddess, riding,
    breeding, bleeding deity,
half-clothed on a mare's bare back. Nicole computes chem-
    istry, strings proteins, creates

battle plans and war maps of medication, targets disease
    with her biological
bow, arrow-headed vaccines and antibiotic missiles. Epona
    leads the cavalry

to battle, the farmer to a field, the dead to another place,
    cupping each soul
in the palm of her hand, whispering peace, foaling in storms,
    staring

death down with life. My friend looks at me out of both
    women's
eyes—science and mythology.


## II.

I rode an hour on the middle school route from bully
taunts to trailer home, but some days stayed with Elizabeth,
dismounted early from the humid bus and followed
my friend along a dirt road to bright barns. She groomed
a horse, offered Epona a sugar cube sacrifice, a carrot made
from all her praise. I wasn't allowed to touch

the horses, could not ride my own fantasies across
the fields, wild stallion dreams tied tight to the bench
by the ring where Elizabeth rode. Goddesses trotted, gal-
    loped,
leapt, never even looked at me. So free. The day behind
was forgotten with me there flipping pages, not reading
the paper story—living hopeless dreams instead. I wanted

so bad to be a horse girl, to tame *Black Beauty*, bond
the fire inside of me to peace and passion
and horseflesh, fleet of foot, flying mane, goddess
inside my own brain, where I was beautiful

and other kids could never matter as much as
my *Misty of Chincoteague*, but bank numbers meant
the saddle club was closed, and when Elizabeth
finished her lesson, we climbed into her mother's car,
and a gravel road led back the way we came.

## III.

Horses have the largest
eyes of any land mammal. They can see
nearly 360 degrees straight
through your bullshit, even when
it is thick, is dark, is cloaked in piety
or soaked in holy war, battle blood. Horses
like sweetness, reject sour
and bitter. Nicole shows me, now,
a photo of her thoroughbred's new
boots, pony posed with a horse's
haughty pride. All eight pounds of this
mare's pumping heart hoof beats to a love
song, only she and Nicole can sing.

## IV.

I ride with Epona when I'm sleeping. We mount strong dark
horses. We are long and lean against their grace. My body is
    held

tight, fingers woven in soot mane, hooves pounding against
    the green

of graves. I see myself dreaming from that ringside bench
  where shadows

lurked amid my fantasies. I wanted so hard and closed my
  eyes like hands
on leather reins, pretended not to see the horseless tomor-
  rows bearing down.

Now I'm a mother, and a lover, and a woman grown. I open
  my jealous
eyes and saddle fear. I break free inside this verse, mount
  confident a wild

horse. We race. We fly. We haul a battered warrior from her
  ancient grave. Epona's
hand holds a wicked truth, nurtures life, aims with needle,
  carves with knife,

smiles wide as we wave goodbye. My future gallops, goddess
tangled in its limbs, saddle falling away like memory.

---

**Heather Truett** holds an MFA from the University of Mem-
phis and is doing PhD work at FSU and is a Pushcart nominee. Her debut novel, KISS AND REPEAT, was released from
Macmillan in 2021. She has work in *Hunger Mountain*, *Sweet Lit*,
*Whale Road Review*, and others. Heather serves as an assistant
fiction editor for *the Southeast Review* and as a reader for *Bea-
ver Magazine*. Find out more at www.heathertruett.com.

# *42*

There's a little half acre deep in the piney woods of East Texas that neither man, beast, nor fowl has stepped foot, paw, or claw on in more than a god's hour. The humidity is as thick as the vegetation and neither are breathable. The woods are so quiet you can hear the sound of tree rings forming and roots pushing down into the rich black soil.

There are moths, flies, beetles, centipedes, millipedes, and ants (ants cannot be kept out of anyplace) but no mosquitoes. Mosquitoes fall dead less than three feet inside the circumference of the little half acre deep in the piney woods of East Texas.

In the center of the little half acre deep in the piney woods of East Texas sits a perfectly square log cabin. The log cabin is finely made and sturdy. The porch overhang is extra deep, extra tall, and not one floorboard creaks. On the porch there is a wooden table, four wooden chairs, and a brass spittoon. The wooden table and four chairs are expertly handmade. The chairs are comfortable and all are pleasing to the eye.

Inside the cabin in the middle of the little half acre deep in the piney woods of East Texas, a spry old man by the name of Pancake Bob scurries about making ready. Pancake Bob sweeps the dirt floor of the sturdy, perfectly square log cabin which is a bit of an exercise in futility. The front door, which is the only door, is open and through it walks a tall, thin man with no outstanding features save a pencil thin mustache. His clothes are black and for a splash of color, he wears a lavender beret rakishly tilted atop his head. The man does not appear from the tree line, walk up the path, onto the front porch, and through the front door. He simply walks through the front door.

Pancake Bob is elated when he sees the man. "Mr. B! You're early, you are always early, you're looking dapper, can I take that from you?"

The man, now standing in the middle of the one room cabin, is holding a twelve pack of Shiner Bock. Pancake Bob takes the twelve pack. "I'll put this on ice and bring you a cold one. Do you want a glass or just drink from the bottle? What am I saying! You want a glass." Heading to the kitchen area of the cabin Pancake Bob reaches up on a shelf and pulls down a Luminarc La Maison Pilsner glass. "You always prefer a glass."

Mr. B turns, walks out onto the porch and takes a seat in a chair with his back to the wall. Pancake Bob soon follows on the porch with the pilsner glass and ice cold Shiner longneck. He pops the cap off the Shiner using a bottle opener nailed by the door and pours the beer in the glass leaving a two inch head. He sets the glass and bottle on the table in front of Mr. B.

Turning, Pancake Bob bumps straight into a hooded figure carrying a scythe in one skeletal hand and a bottle of Scorpion Mezcal Anejo in the other. The specter is so tall he can barely stand straight under the porch.

"Big D! You snuck up on me, you scamp. You always sneak up on me. I know, that's what you do, sneak up on people, but one day you'll scare the bejeebers out of me. Have a seat, let me take your scythe." Pancake Bob grabs the scythe. Big D does not let go. Pancake Bob smiles sheepishly. "Come on, Big D. We've talked about this." He pulls to no avail. The tug merely rattles Big D's bones. "Remember the last time? You got mad when you didn't make that trick." Pancake Bob makes a slashing motion across his neck. "And we definitely agreed you're not to carry the scythe inside anymore after you knocked over the oil lamp and pert near burnt down the cabin." Pancake Bob laughs nervously. Big D reluctantly let go the scythe. "There's a good specter. See? No worries." Pancake Bob walks across the porch and hangs the scythe from a brass hook by the door. "I made a nice hook, right here, in easy reach and in sight."

Big D sets his mezcal on the table and takes the chair across from Mr. B.

Pancake Bob excitedly claps his hands. "I'll just pop in and get you a proper glass to sip your mezcal."

Walking into the cabin Pancake Bob is stopped dead in his tracks. "Mary," he mouths. He mouths her name because he has no breath. The sight of the woman standing before him took it away. Mary is petite with a button nose, and deep brown eyes. Her kinky curly hair is sandy blonde and shoulder length. She wears a little black dress and has a girl-next-door air about her with more than a dash of sex. Not sex appeal. Sex.

She smiles. He smiles back. She walks towards him holding a crystal tumbler. Pancake Bob eventually catches his breath. "That is just what I was coming for. Thank you, Mary." She nods, places the tumbler in his right hand, takes his left hand in hers and leads him out on the porch.

When Mary and Pancake Bob step onto the porch Big D is opening a box of dominoes and pouring them on the table. He and Mr. B turn the dominoes face down as Mary and Pancake Bob take their seats with Pancake Bob sitting to Mr. B's left. Mr. B scrambles the dominoes, then Pancake Bob, Big D, and Mary each draw seven dominoes. Mr. B takes the remaining seven.

Pancake Bob sets his dominoes on their sides and and begins to arrange them. "Oh my what a wonderful evening. I can't thank everyone enough for coming. It is such a pleasure to be in your company." Everyone else has set their dominoes but Pancake Bob is still fiddling. "The barbecue will be ready in a couple of hours. The potato salad and beans are already ready. The potato salad is chilling and the beans are warming on the stove."

Mr. B spits a wad of tobacco juice in the brass spittoon, looks at Pancake Bob, cocks his head and raises one eyebrow. Pancake Bob looks at Mr. B and flashes a sheepish grin. "I'm sorry, I do go on and on." He looks at his hand one more time. "I bid 35."

And the game is on. All through the night the four play 42. They laugh, cuss their luck, slap dominoes on the table, eat barbecue, potato salad (except for Big D who loathes potato salad), and beans, but mostly they laugh.

In the rest of the country and around the world people call the game Texas 42. In Texas, it is simply called 42. The game was invented in Texas so calling it Texas 42 would be redundant. The game was made up in Garner by two local boys who wanted to play a game of chance, but card playing of any kind was heavily frowned upon by the local Baptist church. Dominoes were deemed less sinful so the boys, William Thomas and Walter Earl, to give credit where credit is due, adapted the mechanics of a trick taking card game to dominoes. The game became quite popular in Garner. When the fathers of both William and Walter moved to Windom in Fannin County on account of work, the game took root there as well. Before long 42 had spread far and wide across the Lone Star State and eventually the world.

•

When the sun broke the horizon and rose over the sturdy, perfectly square log cabin in the middle of the little half acre in the Piney woods of East Texas the game was over. The sturdy, perfectly square log cabin disappeared without a trace. Mr. B went back to tending his business. Big D went about his rounds, Mary never existed to begin with, and Pancake Bob went back to being one of the faceless. The poorest of the poor. The Last Person.

One of the balms of the universe is the creation of the concept of The Last Person, specifically, Pancake Bob. He is the one person who has it worse than every other person on the planet.

There are a finite number of people on Earth. If there is always somebody worse off than yourself, and somebody worse off than that person, then if you follow those links of people all the way down the chain there has to be one last person. The one person who has it worse off than everybody else. The one person everyone else can look to and think, 'at least I'm better off than that poor person.'

Enter Pancake Bob. All his life he had been the last person. When it came his time to die, he discovered he was the Last Person and with his passing, a new last person would be born. He cut a deal with Big D, and the deal was approved by Mr. B, to live forever, or at least indefinitely, therefore saving anyone else from the fate of being The Last Person.

Big D and Mr. B are not easily touched nor overly sentimental, but they take pity on Pancake Bob one night every one hundred years. They all gather in the sturdy, square cabin in the middle of the little half acre in the Piney Woods of East Texas, and give Pancake Bob a respite. They enjoy good food, fine liquor, cold beer, the visage of a beautiful woman Pancake Bob once saw getting out of a Lincoln in North Dallas who plum took his breath away, and a spirited game of 42.

Sometimes they even let Pancake Bob win a hand or two.

---

**Mark A. Nobles** is a sixth-generation Texan. Born on Fort Worth's infamous Jacksboro Highway, Mark proudly claims blood and kinship with Thunder Road's gamblers, outlaws, and wastrels. He is a Pushcart nominee and his work has appeared in various publications and anthologies. He is the author of Fort Worth's Rock & Roll Roots and his historical novel, We're for Smoke was published by TCU Press. Mark lives in Fort Worth but hopes to die in the desert.

**Amanda Yskamp**

# *Hole*

What I have to say demands
fleshly witness, its beginning
with my own, its end sometime before

and after, beyond the girl who folded
a kleenex into her pocket as
she left the house that day.

Follow me to the gully
where she lies like salt
on a tide-stranded shell.

If not for horror, she would not look
out of place, days there
becoming part of the weedy

ditch. She'd drawn me to the game
like a dead-eyed wooden mallard,
like magnetic kisses lure an iron-clad

love and flecks of shavings equally.
She made me give up on what I thought
about time. Look at her, once young,

now an escapee. Something is always leaking
out the beauty hole, a whoosh of air
through a punctured lung. She'd become

a glimpse that seals vision, a hovering
zero that adds magnitude to one alone.
My looking on from no safe distance made us like

Siamese twins, joined at the instant in strange
kinship. Her ears faint blue and rimmed
in frost. Once I'd thought some things

were like stars, visible from anywhere
in the hemisphere even after completely
extinguished, and maybe that is so.

I'd see her everywhere. The whole
season summed up like that.
Who can count that high?

More than anything, it was
like a license plate whizzing by, the numbers
crucial to something hunted but missed.

# *Walking the Ward*

In the days after they cut into my heart
and the beat went all Cucamonga,
it was all I could do to push
my I.V. tree ahead of me to make the lap
around the heart attack and stroke ward.
They told me it would strengthen the healing
muscle, but overdo it, and I could burst
something, dislodge a clot, or some other
kind of fatal shit. I was wired for 3
kinds of signal, a monitor broadcasting
my stats in a neon ticker feed.

Past the sunrise mural, past the wall of "angels"
a.k.a. nurses noticed and honored with halo stickers,
past the room from which warm blankets emerged,
past other patients' rooms gaping and gasping,
from which I averted my eyes. They were older
than me. They were sicker than me.
Look at me: I was walking the ward,
pushing my tree, walking the ward, pushing
my tree, in my treaded booties, walking,
counting laps in my doubled johnnie, walking,
in my floating mind, mine forever, or for as long

as my heart fed it rich blood, my eyes and ears
and other senses fed sensations for thought
and being, walking, pushing my tree,
what's a set of numbers to a grand heart
such as mine? Breathing, walking, pushing
my tree, one bootied foot and then the next
in an integrated gait, body cooperating
with the central force, and the will
from the top of the column, drawing
from the heart to take another lap.

# *Hart Island*

In hazmat suits, they stack coffins in trenches on Hart
    Island.

With no one to afford death's formal gesture, the unclaimed
    dead—disposed of quickly—
will repose, soundless, off Long Island Sound, longer than
    their own lived history, in cloth sacks and pine boxes,
    names, if known, scrawled across the grain.

Central Park's storage can't keep up. Funeral parlors, over-
    whelmed.

Thousands lie buried on Hart Island, for those who die, in-
    digent and unclaimed, are brought by barge, laid straight
    with untold others in trenches, numbered and named, if
    known, if not, simply numbered, interred, no longer to
    cast figured shadows.

---

**Amanda Yskamp's** work has been published in such magazines as *Threepenny Review, Hayden's Ferry Review, The Geor-
gia Review, Boxcar Review, Rattapallax,* and *Caketrain.* She
lives on the 10-year flood plain of the Russian River, from
which she serves as the librarian at a local school and teaches writing from her online classroom.

J. S. Allen

# Starting Over

## The Dogs of Chaka

Uvrit could no longer pass as a boy, so when she saw the dust cloud rising over the crooked horizon, she did as her father had trained her, leaving the flock with the dogs and hurrying uphill toward her closest hiding place, a small dug-out where they stashed supplies.

Father needed her at the farm. Neither of them wanted some city busybody shipping her off to school. Or worse, some cattleboy seeking for a wife.

But she had not yet reached the shelter when two unexpected visitors arrived a moment ahead of her, politely making their presence known by lying down and thumping their tails. Uvrit stopped in her tracks. Dogs! But not any of hers. These wore vests and carried pouches. Mottled and mud-brown cousins of hers, but much better trained.

"The dogs of Chaka," she said, clasping her hands in joy. The dogs, wagging vigorously, came to her and put their wet noses against her knuckles, making her laugh. The dust cloud, some distance off, now meant something else entirely. "The Chaka are coming!"

One of the dogs barked once in affirmation. "Come on," she said, and the three of them ran together down to the farmhouse.

•

## The Monkey Balancer

Father was in a foul mood, but when he saw Uvrit with the dogs, he brightened.

"The Chaka are coming," said Uvrit, breathless.

"Well," said Father, eyes sparkling, "let's see what they've brought us." He called the dogs over and worked to untie their baggage. "These'll be our gifts."

Uvrit's gift so enthralled her that she didn't see or even contemplate Father's. Her gift was a balancing toy, a miniature circus performer with six weighted monkeys to hang from his outstretched arms. This unexpected treasure came all the way from Kortholomoth, made by a master craftsman; it said so on the little card tied to the drawstring of the soft cloth bag. (Mother had taught her to read the Laginese script.)

Nothing so clean or fine had ever existed in Uvrit's world. The toy was perfect. She balanced it on the fence post, she balanced it on the clothesline. So long as the acrobat's load was balanced, with equal numbers of monkeys on both sides, he stood fast, even against a desert breeze.

•

## Loss Management

Father broke her reverie. "Well, what about the flock then?"

"The dogs have 'em."

"Well, bring 'em in, Uvrit! We gotta make ready for the Chaka." Something in Father's voice, a quiver of nervous anticipation she'd never heard before, made her look up from her toy. He was loading the dog's pouches full of precious cherries, the last of the season. She'd had plans for those cherries, but she couldn't begrudge the Chaka their due.

Uvrit put away her acrobat and monkeys, drawing the string closed, and hurried back into the hills to find the flock.

The dust cloud had settled down. The Chaka would be making camp nearby.

She spotted them in the canyon valley below, a caravan circle at rest—wagons, horses, camels, sheep, goats, dogs, men, women, children.

More than three hard years at the farm had passed since the caravan had last come to this valley. After the well dried up last year, Mother and the little ones had to move to Othkin. Uvrit stayed behind to help with the farm, such as it was. "Managing the loss," as Father called it.

●

## Sheep Number 37

When she returned home with the flock, Cousin Yagel was there with Father, counting the sheep and goats as they came down the hill. Uvrit came last, and Yagel counted her as "sheep number 37," before embracing her with a laugh. "Can it be Cousin Uvrit? You've doubled in size!"

"So 36 sheep," said Father, "and the eight goats."

Yagel's smile faded slightly but his reassuring hand rested comfortably on the nape of Uvrit's neck. "They have the itch, you can see that," said Yagel, gesturing to a scratching ewe.

"It's not the itch," said Father, though he and Uvrit both knew otherwise.

"It's not a problem," said Yagel. "We just can't mix 'em with the flock. We'll sell 'em on the local market."

Uvrit, confused, asked, "Are we selling the flock?"

Father's mouth quivered, forming into something like a smile. He opened his mouth to speak but found himself without words.

"A hard life, scratching in the dirt," said Cousin Yagel, squeezing gently the nape of her neck.

●

## An Easy Decision

Uvrit was slow to understand.

"We're selling the farm," said Father. "We made a good run at it, Uvrit. But the soil here, it's no good."

The notion of leaving the farm had never occurred to her. "But where would we go? What would we do?"

Father took her hands in his. "You don't have to come with me. You can live in Othkin with your mother and brothers."

"Go with you—where?" She looked into Cousin Yagel's gentle smile and cried out, "Do you mean join the caravan? Is that what you mean?"

Father lifted his eyebrows.

"Yes!" cried Uvrit.

"Not forever—"

"Yes!" cried Uvrit.

•

## The First Day

Excited as she was to join the caravan, when departure time arrived, Uvrit wept, grieving for the farmhouse, the fields, even the dry well.

Father did not so much as look back. He walked with a new spring in his step, his great burden lifted. The Chaka had taken care of everything. Fetched good prices for the livestock, the farm, its improvements and implements; settled his debts; and sent money to Mother and the boys.

Father was proud of his Chaka heritage, but he'd never so much as mounted a camel. After his first day riding scout with the men, Uvrit had to help him dismount, and he could scarcely walk on his own. The drawn expressions of the other men spoke volumes. Uvrit ran tent to tent, seeking for some ointment for Father's poor thighs.

At council that night, it was decided Father should be reassigned to women's work. Cousin Yagel came to them with this news as Uvrit and Father were preparing to bed down in their new tent. "There's no shame in it," Yagel repeated, more than once.

When Yagel was gone from earshot, Father whispered from his blanket, "Thank the gods." And they both laughed, happy and weary, together.

•

## Child of the Desert

Father wan't the only man on women's duty. Any man too old, ill or lame stayed full-time with the caravan. Then there was Cousin Djeri, queer as a one-feathered arrow, as Father said, who simply didn't fit in with the men.

If the men were responsible for scouting, commerce, and security, the women were responsible for everything else: the business of living; of preparing food and medicine; fixing and mending; putting tents up and down; tending to livestock and children; divination, weaving, artisanship, and so on.

Uvrit and Father were both good workers and soon earned a respected place within the clan.

Day piled upon day as the caravan made its way northward, far beyond the reach of any road. The deep desert was home to the Chaka, where few others dared tread. On this great, wending journey north, Uvrit would experience all three great deserts of legend: Daylid, Yebic, Thaabin. Each touched her heart, each changed her.

This is to say, by the time the caravan reached its northernmost terminus outside Kortholomoth, Uvrit had become well and truly Chaka.

•

## The Vine Watcher

Father was a different story. He did not take to the travel, the heat of the desert, the camels.

One night on the Maelor Platt, he confessed to Uvrit his intention to separate from the caravan at Kortholomoth. He wanted a fresh start, to reinvent himself in a new place. Perhaps try his hand at cultivating some tree fruits.

There was no denying it. Father wanted to be a "vine watcher," Cousin Yagel's contemptuous term for someone who chose to anchor themselves to one tract of land, waiting, hoping for plants to grow and feed them. The Chaka had many jokes about such fools.

Uvrit loved her father, but this was not the life she wanted. But then, seeing her expression, Father took her hands in his and clarified: "I don't mean here, in Lagin. I want to go to the New World, Uvrit, where the land is rich, where opportunities abound."

The New World!

"I'm in," said Uvrit.

•

## True Numbers

Cousin Yagel was not surprised when Father told him of his intentions.

"This is a good thing for the Chaka," said Yagel, clasping Father's arm. "We need good people and investments in the New World. I will advocate that the Council support your enterprise."

And so they did. After a careful study of the prospects, Elder Manu declared, "The numbers are true." A common Chaka expression for a solid investment.

As before, the Chaka took care of everything, securing with favorable terms a land certificate for 90 acres of suitable property near a booming colonial city off the coast of Greatland. They needed workers and industry, and at this time the colony of Belzea was offering generous subsidies guaranteed by the Bank of Sarta, for hardy colonists willing to come live and work on the far side of the Green Sea.

●

## The Opera House

Father asked Uvrit to read and reread all the documents. They studied the maps, learned the geography of Belzea, a place neither of them had heard of until now. "We will have to brush up our Westongue," said Father, as that was the dominant language in Belzea.

The opera house at Belzea was, by all accounts, an architectural wonder. They both thought it would appeal to Mother, and said so in the letter they sent, dictated by Father, written by Uvrit. They enclosed a sketch of the opera house included as part of a "community profile" from the investor's packet. "By fall, we hope to have the house built, and then we will ask you and the boys to come to Belzea." By then, the boys would be old enough to help with clearing and planting in the spring.

●

## Kortholomoth

But first, they would need to cross the sea, an exhilarating and terrifying prospect that thrilled Uvrit each time she thought of it.

Their ship was to be the Motley Miser, captained by one Leon Leodr. It did not depart for another two weeks.

In the meantime, Uvrit and her father were free to enjoy the wonders of Kortholomoth, one of the greatest cities in the world. Wherever they went, they remained under the watchful protection of Yagel or another cousin, and more than once they found themselves glad of this security. By night, they slept with the caravan outside the city.

When the day of their departure arrived, Cousin Yagel came with them to the docks. Uvrit was unprepared for the press of the throng, the sheer confusion about where to go, the obnoxious fishy smell. Even Yagel was out of his element in this place.

Finally, it was Uvrit who sorted out the confusion and found the correct berth where the Motley Miser bobbed in wait for them.

•

## The Old Shoe

She wasn't much to look at, The Motley Miser. True to her name, she was covered in patches.

Nor did Captain Leon make a good first impression. Uvrit first mistook him for some disorderly lurk-about, a drunk perhaps, but when he spoke, saying, "Don't worry, she'll float," Uvrit looked again. His shirt was open, exposing a sunken, sallow belly; his bare feet dangled from the dock; he was definitely drunk.

Other passengers were already aboard, queueing to stow their luggage.

It was not the elegant schooner of her imagination, but with a short time Uvrit would discover some affection for the "old shoe," as Captain Leon called her. "Old shoe, tried and true," he said with a tooth-gapped grin. "Home to me, and now to you."

•

## The Sea

As it happened, Uvrit came equipped with sea legs. "You gots salt water in yer veins," said Captain Leon approvingly.

Father, on the other hand, suffered greatly during the nearly three-week voyage. He became partners in misery with a Laginese man named Ihrael. They had much in common, both being farmers starting over in Belzea. And when they compared land certificates, they discovered they were to be neighbors. Already, the two of them discussed the possibility of going in together to bid on the adjoining tract.

Uvrit was glad Father had found a friend.

•

## Fast Times

"What's Belzea like?" asked Uvrit one day.

"No idea," returned Captain Leon, surprising her. Uvrit had assumed a grizzled Sartan like Leon Leodr would have visited every sea port in his day.

"You mean you've never been there?"

"None of us has," he said with a shrug. "These new colonies, they spring up overnight."

"What an exciting time to be alive," said Uvrit. The world was changing so fast, anything was possible.

•

## Tree Crazy

The coast of Greatland crept into view the following day. They were still a long way from Belzea, but the sight of mountains made the New World far less theoretical.

"Do you smell that?" said Father, inhaling deeply. "Trees!"

His friend Ihrael laughed and said to Uvrit, "He is tree crazy."

It was true. All Father wanted to talk about, to anyone who'd listen, was trees and his budding plans of arborism.

They passed a mountain island thickly forested, and Father was spellbound. "Look at them all! Look how tall they are!" It was the most trees Uvrit had ever seen in one place, a mere appetizer for the wealth of the New World that lay ahead.

●

## The New World Ports

Their first New World port was Astina, an impressive sight gleaming white in the sun. There the Motley Miser resupplied, and a few of the passengers disembarked.

Uvrit, Father, and Ihrael had only a few hours to walk about on solid ground before Captain Leon, drunk again, called them back aboard so as to "ride the tide" back out to sea.

Late the next day they encountered their first bad weather. Uvrit, overconfident, was nearly washed overboard. Father was in a bad way.

After the storm, the Motley Miser was discovered to be slowly taking on water. "Nothing to worry about," the captain assured us. But they would have to divert to Port Nomin for repairs.

Thus the passengers found themselves ashore once more, this time for several days. Port Nomin was no Astina and certainly no Kortholomoth. A dreary place to be stranded, perhaps, but a welcome respite from the sea for Father and Ihrael.

•

## Sea Life, Land Life

Freshly patched, the "old shoe" was returned to service, and the captain came, drunk, to the dreadful inn where the passengers were all hunkered, to tell them the news. "Next stop, Belzea!"

Before they departed, Uvrit left letters for Mother and the caravan cousins, to be included in the next semiweekly parcel run to Kortholomoth.

They sailed south along the mountain coast of Greatland. Beyond Nomin, no further signs of human settlement troubled the coast. It was just rocks and seals and trees. Once Uvrit thought she saw someone, a person, perhaps, but they hid amongst the rocks, and she couldn't be sure. A barbarian, maybe, or a grithi? She found either notion thrilling.

"These are new waters for the old shoe," remarked Captain Leon, gazing with appreciation at the mighty cliffs. "We're making good time, and it shouldn't be but a few days more to Belzea."

The captain, Uvrit observed, only drank when he was on land. When she asked him about this, he looked at her a long time before answering, "Life at sea's easy, lil nugget; life on land, well—that's where I need the help, see?"

•

## Arrival

Belzea itself was situated on what was essentially an island, semi-detached from the mainland. As Uvrit had read, depending on sea conditions, it was sometimes possible to make the crossing on foot at low tide.

The bay could only be entered from the south. As the crew brought the ship about, all the passengers crowded on deck to catch their first sight of the colony.

The bay, red with lichen, was home to a cloud of unpleasant biting flies. A tangle of mangroves dominated the shore, and farther inland, tall magnificent trees stood sentry. A small stretch of beach offered the only interruption to the mangroves.

Swatting at the flies, Father asked, "Where is the city?"

The captain called for his navigator. There was a brief argument over the map.

•

## The Welcoming Committee

Some of the passengers, mostly women, fled belowdeck to escape the biting flies.

The remaining expectant passengers looked to the captain. He raised his hands apologetically. "It seems there may have been some confusion as to the location of the colony."

"No confusion," insisted the navigator. "This is the place."

There was no denying the geography: the semi-connected island, the south-facing bay. There was even an inlet where the stream emptied into the bay, just as it was shown on the map they'd received.

This was Belzea. But there was no opera house. No dock. No governor's mansion overlooking the bay. Only flies and mud to greet them.

·

## The Mistake

"It's some kind of mistake," said Captain Leon. "Either something happened to the colony, or there never was a colony."

"What do you mean there never was a colony?" demanded an angry passenger. Uvrit moved closer to Father, in case of trouble.

"Look," said Leon, pointing to the mangrove forest. "Do you see a colony?"

"They've brought us here to kill us," someone whispered, too loudly.

"No, no," said Leon, rubbing the bridge of his nose. "Look, folks, we can't stay here. Let's get back out to sea and away from these biting flies, at least."

"Absolutely not," said Father, startling Uvrit.

Leon, exasperated, spread his arms. "What, sir, do you want from me?"

"Do your job," insisted Father. "We paid our fare. Take us ashore."

●

## Home, Regardless

"Father, are you sure?" whispered Uvrit.

"Sir," said Captain Leon. "You would be going to your death. I can't allow that."

"Are we prisoners, then?" Turning to the other passengers, Father said, "This is our land. We paid for our place here. It is our right. Who is with me?"

Swatting at the flies, the others avoided looking at them. Only Ihrael, with some hesitation, raised his hand.

"Give it up, sir," said Leon gently. "There's nothing to be gained from going in them wilds there. We'll return to Nomin, regroup—"

"No," insisted Father. "We are here. We are staying."

●

## Commitment

Uvrit had stuck with Father through everything. She wasn't going to abandon him now.

As the captain gave the reluctant order to ready a rowboat, Uvrit took Father's hand. He was too angry, too proud, to look at her, but she could tell he appreciated her support. "We are Chaka," he whispered fiercely. "We will not die here. We will live, we will thrive."

"What about me?" whispered Ihrael.

"Listen, my friend," said Father as the remaining passengers moved belowdeck. "These fools may do as they like. I will have what was promised. Whatever deceit has occurred here is another's dishonor, not ours. I hope my tribe seeks retribution against those who cheated them; but as for me, my land is here, I am here. I will work the land, I will make it ready. Come with me, if you will, and we shall both benefit."

Impressed with Father's speech, Ihrael's doubts were calmed. "You can be an honorary Chaka, too," whispered Uvrit with a smile.

•

## Good Luck

"You sure about this, lil girl?" asked Captain Leon before letting her on the rowboat.

"I'm sure, Captain. Thank you for everything." As she stepped into the rowboat, she asked, "You'll get this sorted out, won't you?"

"I expect so. Just don't go dying on me. I'll see what I can do to have someone check on you in a few weeks."

Two crewmen rowed them through the eerie red water, their oars catching on water weeds. Father and Ihrael clutched their documents and what few supplies they had. Turtles surfaced left and right, witnessing their passage.

They made for the small beach, unloaded their things.

"Well," said the older of the crewmen, "good luck."

•

## The Argument

Hardly had the Motley Miser disappeared from the harbor before Father and Ihrael began to fight.

Uvrit wasn't sure how it started. She'd been busy surveying their immediate surroundings, trying to understand this alien new place. The mangrove forest was like nothing she'd ever seen, an impenetrable landscape, no place for a human being.

When she turned around, the two fools were nearly at blows, and she had to come between them.

"You may die if you wish," Ihrael spat. "I will not enter that snake-infested swamp. I will be setting up camp here on the beach."

"Do as you like," said Father, throwing up his hands. "But as for me, I am going to find my land."

•

## Lot 97

In fact, it would take them several days to find the 90-acre lot promised to Father. It lay beyond the mangrove swamp, on higher ground.

On the map and land certificate, this plot of land was identified as Lot 97. It featured three ponds and a spring, and a long, gentle south-facing slope suitable for agriculture.

Several existing stands of wild fruit trees were noted to be already present.

The ponds and spring were real, but the fruit trees a fiction.

Father and his cousins had been drawn to this lot, not only for its water resources, but also for its high vantage. The northern extreme of the property commanded a view over the harbor. "Knowledge is power," the cousins had said. Wherever they went, the Chaka liked to keep eyes on the movement of trade.

Uvrit stood with Father atop the slope, when he declared, "This is where we shall build the house."

•

## Cornerstones

They camped there on the hill. Father got so far as laying out rocks where he intended to build the foundation, before he fell ill.

His fever quickly became serious.

Uvrit left him lying in the spring to try and cool his fever. "Stay here," she said. "I'm going to get Ihrael." Father was too weak to protest.

Uvrit ran down the slope, falling in her haste and bloodying her thigh. She rose quickly and limped on as fast as she could, heedless of her pain.

The mangrove swamp held more than a foot of rising tide water, imperiling her crossing, but urgency drove her on, her progress desperately slow and halting. When finally she emerged on the beach, she was completely covered in mud.

She hadn't seen Ihrael since the argument. It was clear he had not been idle. A nearly finished lean-to stood at the edge of the beach, and rocks had been arranged as makeshift furniture and working surfaces.

But Ihrael was not around. She'd been calling to him for some time, even while entangled in the mangrove, but no answer came.

•

## Silent Beach

Uvrit searched the beach, calling Ihrael's name. In the lean-to, she found the last of Ihrael's hard bread sitting out, partially gnawed, new tendrils of mold growing.

A troubling silence enveloped the scene.

Down near the rising water line, she saw something on the beach. Only when she was nearly upon it did she recognize what she was seeing.

A foot. A severed human foot. Ihrael's foot, ant-covered.

Uvrit stood a long time, trying to understand. "Ihrael?" Where was the rest of him? She looked around, calling his name. Then, slowly, it occurred to her: Whatever killed Ihrael might still be around. And with this thought, she fell silent, covering her mouth with her hand.

•

## The Worst Day

As the worst day of Uvrit's life drew to its close, she found herself the sole inhabitant of Belzea.

Father and Ihrael had been fools, she admitted to herself as the sun sank. *I was one, too, to follow them.* Now they were gone, the time for foolishness was past. Uvrit was in charge now, and she was no fool.

Uvrit moved camp that same night to a defensive position, a cliffside niche—not a cave, exactly, but a place sheltered from the wind and sun, where she was not exposed. A natural cistern held water here.

In the morning, she set to work making spears. She wasn't sure what manner of beast had killed Ihrael, but she wanted to be ready.

After her third spear, Uvrit began to feel dizzy. Touching her forehead, she found it blazing hot to the touch.

●

## The Sheep of Greatland

For days Uvrit lay in her cliffside hiding spot, growing weaker.

She lay in delirium, re-experiencing the deserts of Lagin, the streets of Kortholomoth, sailing the Green Sea.

It would have been an easy thing to die. But she remembered the words of her father: "We are Chaka."

Uvrit woke from her delirium, crawled to the water and drank.

Below her grazed a family of great-horned sheep, thrice the size of any sheep she'd ever seen, their breath showing in the crisp morning air. Uvrit watched, astounded. Her fever had broken.

●

## Visitors

Six weeks later, Uvrit was collecting mushrooms on the slopes when she saw, dreamlike, a great three-masted ship sail into the bay.

Hesitating, she tied up her bundle of mushrooms. She moved to an overlook for a better view. Captain Leon had said he'd try to send someone to check on them.

But the ship in the bay was huge, its deck teeming with folk, including children. Its flag, Laginese.

A colony ship.

●

## Directions to the Colony

Uvrit went to the beach to meet the landing party, who had gathered at the ruins of Ihrael's lean-to. They drew their weapons when they saw her.

"I am just a girl, alone here. Have no fear. Why have you come?"

Hearing her Laginese speech put the men at ease. "Can you tell us please, where is the colony of Belzea?"

Uvrit looked at them, aghast. "Did you not receive word? It's a farce. There is no Belzea. You've been swindled."

"I told you," said one of the men to the other.

•

## The Miser's Fate

"But surely Captain Leon returned and warned you?"

Their blank looks told her otherwise. She tried again: "Captain Leon Leodr of the Motley Miser, out of Kortholomoth? I landed here with him many weeks ago."

The men looked at each other. "The Motley Miser, you said? Yeah, I heard about that. You were one of those?"

"Then why did you come?" Uvrit asked, exasperated. Then, seeing their expressions, she cocked her head in confusion. "Wait—what happened to the Motley Miser?"

"They all perished, miss. Sorry to say."

"What! What happened?"

"They caught the fever, miss. Port Nomin wouldn't allow 'em to dock, in case of contagion. They had to anchor in the bay and wait it out. Only none of 'em survived."

•

## The Source

Uvrit sat on Ihrael's stone table, stunned. The captain and all the rest, too? What would have happened to her if she'd stayed on that ship? Perhaps Father wasn't such a fool after all.

"You should get out of here," said Uvrit. "Quickly, before the same fate befalls you. It's this sickly place, it must be, the source of this fever."

"Surely you're coming with us?"

"No," said Uvrit.

"But why? Who are you? What is your name?"

When she told them, another man spoke up for the first time. "Did you say Uvrit? Miss—we have a letter for you."

•

## The Letter

Uvrit made them retrieve the letter from the ship. She was afraid if she were to go aboard, she'd be in their power, and they might not let her go.

No sooner was the envelope in her hand than it was open, the single page unfolded. It was from Mother.

She wouldn't be joining them in Belzea, it said. The boys didn't even remember Father, and besides, she didn't want them to grow up Chaka. They're better off in the city, she said. She'd met someone new, and as a matter of fact, they were expecting a child. He was a good provider, she said in the letter, and they shouldn't worry. She hoped Father understood, and that he was able to find what he was looking for in the New World.

The two crewmen who'd rowed the letter to her looked at Uvrit expectantly. She was too upset to speak. She waved them away, managing to say, "I'm still not going with you. Now get out of here!"

And she turned and ran away, dropping the letter on the beach. All her grief came out then. For hours she wept until, mercifully, sleep took her.

•

## The Blanket

Three weeks later, Uvrit was again on the slopes, hunting for rabbits, when she saw a small sailboat pulled up on the beach below.

With a start, she realized someone had slipped into the bay without her noticing. And they had already landed.

She hurried down. Friend or foe, she wanted to know what she was dealing with. If she approached through the swamp, she could probably avoid detection.

But no one was at the beach. Cautiously, she looked around. The sailboat was small, with room for only a few. Inside the boat, draped across the bench, she saw something that took her breath away—a blanket. What made this blanket so remarkable was that it was unmistakably one crafted by a grandmother of Chaka.

Behind her, at the edge of the beach, Cousin Yagel emerged from the mangrove.

•

## The Chaka Way

"Little sheep?"

Uvrit ran to him. She fell into his arms, crying. Yagel held her for a long time while she cried.

It wasn't necessary for her to explain about Father.

"Come," said Yagel at length. "Let's go home. The grandmothers have been missing you."

Uvrit sniffled and looked at the tiny sailboat. "Where's your crew?"

Cousin Yagel laughed. "Just you and me, kid. The time has come for you to learn to sail the Chaka way."

---

J.S. Allen, Ph.D., is a neurodivergent author in Albuquerque, New Mexico. His debut novel *A Bad Place Best Forgotten* is an adventure story set in a rich fantasy world. Interconnected short stories set in the same world have appeared in past volumes of the Spoon Knife Anthology. By day, Dr. Allen works as a data scientist for non-profit organizations.

# Epilogue

I learned about erasure poems from slp and Aubry Threlkeld's excellent piece "Reinscribing Madness through Poetry: Irrationality and Interdependence in the Wor(l)d," published in *a Mad turn: anti-methods of Mad studies*, edited by phil smith (2024). Erasure poems are a form of found poetry in which an original text is transformed by redaction: The poet deletes from the original text to create something new.

I thought it would be fun to try an erasure poem made from the text of this book itself. This poem was created by excising one line from each contributor, placed in order of appearance in the book. The resulting Frankenstein narrative is almost comprehensible, touching on some of the common themes of the collection.

—J.S. Allen

## 9

A thin, dangling shred of hope.
She remembers all her long lost summers
embers of some dormant forest fire perpetually smoldering

"What was I supposed to be?"
somewhere else, things could at least theoretically be better.

my marriage, my labor and delivery, my assault,
Calm isn't everything when your legs are spread

Days stack up.
Her entire life had been in this trap
fingers that grapple with letting go
a series of movements for the children
like a stifled laugh in an inappropriate moment

Music to me
sleeping under the bushes with feral dogs
the quizzical stares of strangers
the tip of someone's finger

Occurrences preserved, catalogued, sorted.
Admissibility of evidence
shouting from the moon
What the person on the other end of the phone said

red-handed
funded by our government at no charge to you.
they could never bind my feet
They don't have any bones.

Her ex-husband, the topologist, said there was no difference
after sunset
was in no way going to allow something like that in the
   house.
as years pass

Safety In Numbers
from bully taunts to trailer home
and not one floorboard creaks
numbered and named
a respected place within the clan